Darryl,

Everyone in [illegible]

should write a book.

great storytellers

Dan

NEVER SAFE

NEVER SAFE

Charles Girsky

www.ivyhousebooks.com

This is a work of fiction. Names, characters, places, and incidents are either a product of the author's imagination, or are used fictitiously. Any resemblance to actual events or persons, living or dead, is entirely coincidental.

PUBLISHED BY IVY HOUSE PUBLISHING GROUP
5122 Bur Oak Circle, Raleigh, NC 27612
United States of America
919-782-0281
www.ivyhousebooks.com

ISBN: 1-57197-419-9
Library of Congress Control Number: 2004101678

Printed in the United States of America

To my wife, Lois, my best friend and love of my life, without whose constant support I would never have finished.

To Debbie and Kelly, who have been there from the beginning.

To Bonnie, Stephen, Marc and Tami, my number one fans from the day they were born.

To Andrew, Seth, Brett, Hayley, Jenna, Josh, Aaron and Sara, my eight grandchildren who are on line right behind their parents.

Prologue

"Can you believe they left their door unlocked?"

"They were probably in a hurry to get away for the weekend."

"It's only Thursday night. I wonder where their heads are?"

"Did you log it in?"

"Yeah. You know, working for Besafe can be a royal pain in the butt sometimes. I used to work for All Alarm and we never had to fill out this much paperwork."

Carl Rojas, a five-year veteran of Besafe, smiled. "You didn't earn as much money, either."

Hank Preston nodded. "You're right about that. The money's a lot better and the people seem friendlier. When I checked in last Thursday morning after my first week on the job, the guy that runs this company stopped me in the hall and asked me how everything was going."

"Aaron?"

"Yeah, him."

"I bet he even knew your name."

"He called me Hank." After a few seconds, he continued, "Does he do that to every new guy?"

"I'm not sure. A few years ago, his wife died and he kind of checked out for a while, but now he's got himself a girlfriend and he's better than ever."

Hank looked at his watch. "We're going to be late for the check-in at our next stop."

A few miles away, two men sat in a car with the motor idling. One of the men, known only as Dennis to the people who worked for him, sat listening to the driver, Paul Kiesler, grumble with annoyance.

"Where the hell is that security car?"

Dennis smiled. "They're usually here by two thirty. Maybe they changed the schedule."

"The truck with the door opener is due to arrive any second. What should we do?"

"Don't worry about it. It only takes fifteen seconds to break in the door and another minute and a half to clean out the place. If they show up at the wrong time, we'll just have to improvise," Dennis replied.

Paul said, "I heard there are over three million dollars worth of semi-conductors inside for the taking."

"There may be more than that."

Headlights appeared from behind the black Chevrolet, which sat outside of an electronic parts distributor in Newbury Park.

"Dennis, here comes the truck."

Dennis looked up at the rear view mirror. The Dodgers baseball cap covering his blond hair shaded his eyes, making them look like sparkling black diamonds. He took a pistol out of the glove compartment and opened the car door. The interior light came on and illuminated his black slacks, black golf shirt, and black tennis shoes. Paul wore tan slacks and a pale yellow shirt with the name Sunrise Gym written across the back and his name stitched over the left breast.

A filthy, dark green garbage truck pulled into the alley behind the parts distributor. Three men jumped down as Dennis gave hand signals corresponding to the direction of the forks hanging over the front of the truck. When they were lined up to his liking, Dennis pointed at the door and brought his arm down. The door came off its hinges in less than ten seconds. The three men ran into the building, heading straight to a locked fenced area. Using wire cutters it took them less than thirty more seconds to enter the caged area. Each man grabbed a box and started running to the back door. This trip, as laid out in a very precise plan, would be taken six times, and they would then leave with eighteen boxes of integrated circuits worth almost five million dollars.

Chapter 1

"Sergeant, an alarm has been activated at Active Components. Should I notify the police?"

"Yes, and make sure you tell them which alarm."

"It's the rear door."

Sergeant Michael Harran picked up the microphone that allowed him to reach all patrol cars at the same time. He yelled to his coordinator.

"Do we have any cars in the vicinity?"

Shelly Barnes, looking at the GPS system that tracked every car on patrol, answered quickly, "Car twenty-three should be on their way to that location now. They called in and reported being held up at their last stop because of an open door."

Michael Harran was a twenty-year veteran of the San Francisco Police Department and a five-year employee of Besafe Securities. He was a trusted employee who didn't panic easily, but he had a bad feeling about this situation. Over the years Michael spent in San Francisco Police Department, he had learned to trust his instincts.

"Who's in car twenty-three?" he bellowed over the noise of ringing phones and people talking.

"Carl Rojas is driving and the new guy, Hank Preston, is shotgun."

From another desk, someone yelled, "The police ETA is three minutes."

Michael spoke into the microphone, "Car twenty-three, be

advised there may be a robbery in progress at Active Components. Approach with caution." He hesitated a second and then continued, "The police have been notified, ETA is now two minutes, forty-five seconds." He looked at Shelly Barnes and asked, "Are there any other cars available?"

The question was asked of his coordinator and anyone else listening on the Besafe frequency.

"This is car sixteen. We're in Agoura Hills about five or six minutes from that location and heading in that direction."

Michael looked at the active duty roster board. Two experienced were in car sixteen.

"Make it two or three. Car twenty-three, where are you now?"

"We're less than two blocks away."

Michael recognized Carl's voice. "Carl, don't get heroic, the police will be there in . . ." he looked at his watch, "less than two minutes. Keep talking to me."

"Don't worry, Amigo. I have two kids at home. It's quiet out front. We're driving into the alley in back."

The radio went quiet. Michael could picture the scene. "Carl, talk to me," he whispered, afraid to raise his voice.

Carl and Hank never saw Dennis as their car glided into the alley. Dressed in black and standing flattened against the building, Dennis was almost invisible. The two security men exited their vehicle and cautiously worked their way toward the back. Hearing a noise, they drew their weapons simultaneously. They had been trained never to charge in on a hold up in progress, but to wait until they were sure no innocent people could get hurt. They were also trained to stop any vehicles trying to leave the premises.

Paul Kiesler stepped out of the building with his gun pointed at Carl and Hank. Carl Rojas fell to the ground. He yelled for the man with the gun to stand still. Hank just stood there frozen, pointing his pistol at the man with the yellow shirt. Neither of them saw Dennis emerge from the shadows and open fire.

As two bullets entered Hank's back, he discharged his pistol into the ground. The bullet ricocheted, hitting Paul in the thigh. Blood immediately stained his tan slacks. Carl turned and fired off a round at the man who had shot Hank, but missed completely as three bullets entered his body.

The police arrived one minute and twenty seconds later to find both men lying on the ground. One was dead and the other looked critical. They radioed for backup and requested an ambulance. It was this call that alerted the staff at Besafe.

Michael's first call was to Aaron Carlyle, the president of Besafe. His next two were to Tom and Scott, both vice presidents who had started the company with Aaron twelve years earlier. The message was the same.

"There's been a break-in at Active Components. We've lost one of our men and the other is in serious condition. Car sixteen is less than two minutes from the scene and I'm leaving now. I'll keep in touch."

Chapter 2

Michael Harran arrived in front of Active Components fifteen minutes after the initial alarm sounded. His eyes roamed over the scene. The only thing he was sure of was the pandemonium. He finally spotted the men from car sixteen.

"What's the situation?" he asked.

"We can't get near the place. The regulars have it closed down tight."

Michael looked around. "Is there anyone we know here?"

"No one I know of any importance. I've shared a cup or two of coffee with some of the foot soldiers, but no one higher than that."

Michael took a deep breath. He stood well over six feet tall and his skin was almost as black as his hair. He walked to the police tape and stepped over it without losing stride. The uniformed policeman standing guard started to say something, but thought better of it.

"Who's in charge here?" Michael asked the dozen or so officers standing in a circle. His voice had a hint of authority and the men standing around quickly deferred to the officer with three stripes on his jacket.

"Who wants to know?" asked the sergeant.

Flashing his badge, Michael replied, "Me. My name is Michael Harran, and I'm the sergeant in charge of the two men that got shot."

"Lieutenant Sizemore is in charge of the investigation. He's the guy walking around with the unlit cigar in his mouth."

"Thanks. Where have you moved my men?"

"The one that didn't make it is still on the ground in the alley. The other one is on the way to the hospital. I gotta tell ya, he didn't look good."

Michael nodded and walked up the alley. He hesitated a second before he knelt and pulled back the blanket covering the body.

"What the hell do you think you're doing?" Michael turned and looked up at a man with an unlit cigar sticking out of his mouth. He stood about five foot nine and had jet-black hair that set off his angular Asian features.

Michael didn't totally ignore him, but he didn't answer either. He took another look at the man on the ground, laid the blanket gently back over him, and stood.

"I was looking at the body of one of the men that worked for me. My name is Michael Harran. I'm the duty officer from Besafe."

"I don't give a shit if your name is Saint Michael. You don't come messing up a crime scene on me."

"How's my other man?" Michael asked in a monotone voice.

"Why don't you just step back behind the tape with the other looky-loos and when I have time, I'll come talk to you."

"Why don't you get off that horse you rode in here on and smarten up? In an hour, you'll be looking for all the help you can get, even from people like me."

"Me, look for your help? Not likely. You rent-a-cops think you're hot shit. Well, let me tell you something . . ."

"Hold on, Lieutenant Sizemore." Both Michael and Lieutenant Sizemore turned to find Captain Barry Sands looking straight at them.

"What's the problem, Captain?" Sizemore asked in a suddenly polite, respectful tone.

"I just spoke with Mr. Carlyle, the president of Besafe. I've had some prior dealings with him. Until you hear otherwise, from me, include his representative here in any and all aspects of the case." He turned and walked toward the back of the building without saying another word.

Rubbing his eyes, Sizemore turned to Michael. "Jesus. I've been working for him for over a year, and this is the first time he's come out at this time of night to check up on what's happening. This Carlyle fellow must have some heavy clout."

Michael shook his head. "It's more than that. Word is, they go back ten or twelve years. Your captain even married one of the women from Besafe. Mr. Carlyle was his best man at the wedding."

Sizemore scowled. "It figures that the first time I catch a homicide, it has shadows."

Michael looked at him. "I can't believe this is the first robbery homicide you've been involved in."

Sizemore stood a little straighter. "No, it's not. It's just that I was the first officer on the scene, so I get to run the investigation."

"How old are you?" asked Michael.

"Why? Sizemore responded with a touch of hostility in his voice.

"Let's start again. My name is Michael Harran. I spent twenty years with the San Francisco Police Department. The last five were in robbery homicide. I'm forty-five years old, married with two kids. One is a senior at UCLA and the other is a sophomore at Berkeley. I've paid my dues and I promise not to get in your way."

"Why did you want to know how old I was?"

Michael smiled. "Once I knew that, the next question was going to be whether you're married. My wife is a matchmaker deluxe."

Sizemore smiled and held out his hand. "Sometimes I can be a real shit. My first name is Cassius. I'm twenty-eight, not married, and I graduated from USC five years ago."

"Five years and a lieutenant? You must have done some good things in your young life."

"I've been lucky. Being in the right place at the right time certainly helps."

"Are you two finished with this mutual admiration society bullshit?" Captain Sands had walked up behind them as they were talking. "How about walking me through the crime scene and let's see if we can figure out what happened."

Sizemore started talking as they walked through the door that had been ripped off its hinges. "It looks like they used some sort of battering ram to knock the door off of the frame. Since we were here so soon after it happened, I sent out a call to all cars to look for a van or truck big enough to hold some type of battering ram."

"Any response to your alert?" Captain Sands asked the lieutenant.

"Not so far."

"What happened next?"

"It looks like they went inside the warehouse area, cut this fence, and left with something. We don't know what they took yet."

Michael interrupted, "We've put a call into the owner. He wasn't home, but we contacted number two on the list." Michael looked at his notes and continued, "A Mr. Owen. He should be here within the next thirty minutes. He lives in Reseda."

"Have we gotten anything from the security guard who was transported to the hospital?" the captain asked.

"I had one of our men go with the ambulance, but I haven't heard anything."

Captain Sands turned to Michael. "What's his name?"

"Rojas. Carl Rojas. He's been with us for a little over five years."

"What's the name of the guy that didn't make it?" he lowered his voice as he asked the question.

"Hank Preston. He's been with us four weeks. This is only his second week in a car. He used to be at All Alarm, but we still required him go through the two-week training."

One of the uniformed police approached. "Captain, there's a Mr. Carlyle out front looking for you. He says he's with Besafe."

"Bring him back," the captain replied.

"I'm already here."

Everyone turned at the same time.

Cassius Sizemore looked closely at this unshaven man. He had a look about him that made you want to be his friend rather than an enemy. Aaron Carlyle stood a little over six feet tall. He had a full head of uncombed hair and a well-muscled body under a light green golf shirt.

He held out his hand and said, "Barry."

As they shook hands, it was obvious that they were friends.

Both Michael and Cassius acknowledged Aaron's presence with a respectful nodding of their heads.

Aaron looked at Michael, nodded in return, and then held out his hand to Lieutenant Sizemore.

"I don't think we've met. My name is Aaron Carlyle."

The Lieutenant stammered as he forced the words out of his mouth. "My pleasure, Sir. My name is Lieutenant Cassius Sizemore."

"Lieutenant, can you tell me what happened?" Aaron asked.

"I was just briefing the captain. It looks like your men interrupted a robbery in progress. Both of your men fired one round each. Rojas was hit three times, twice in the back, and Preston was hit twice in the back. They probably passed the shooter as they entered, and he got them from behind. We don't know what, if anything, was taken yet, but all indications are that something inside of a caged area was removed."

"Thank you." Aaron's eyes kept going back to the body on the ground. "How long do we have to keep him there?"

"Not much longer. We're expecting the coroner any second. We're not allowed to remove the body until he says it's okay."

Michael started walking up the alley with a flashlight pointed at the ground.

"Let's get some light over here," he called out.

Captain Sands, Aaron, and Lieutenant Sizemore walked over to where Michael was pointing.

"This looks like blood, and it's too far away to be Preston's."

"You could be right, Lieutenant Sizemore." He turned to the police officers gathered nearby.

"Samuels! Rope this area off and get one of the lab people over here. I want to know what this is, and I want to know now." He turned to Michael and said, "Thanks. I almost missed this. It could be our first break." He hesitated and then added, "If your wife knows any nice Vietnamese girls, tell her to keep me in mind."

Chapter 3

"I'll have another cup of coffee, please."

"That's your fourth cup," Aaron said to Barry as they sat in a Denny's all-night restaurant.

"You don't tell Carole, and I'll keep my mouth shut to Karen."

"I haven't even called Karen yet." Aaron looked at his watch. "It's four fifty. She'll be getting up in about ten minutes. I'll call her then."

"How are you two doing?" Barry asked Aaron.

"I think great. We get together almost every weekend and once in a while during the week. We talk about getting married, but there doesn't seem to be a pressing need to get it done in a hurry."

"How's her business?" Barry asked.

"You would know better than me. Doesn't she handle your account?"

A smile crossed Barry's face. "Yes, she does. She's taken the original money we invested and turned it into almost three-quarters of a million dollars in less than three years."

Before Aaron could answer, Barry nodded toward the door. "Here comes Scott."

Scott slid into the booth next to Barry and called to the waitress, "Coffee please." His unshaven face and his red eyes only added to the sense of tension filling his voice. "He's been under the knife for almost two hours. The last report we had said it's still fifty-fifty. Have you guys heard anything from the crime lab yet?"

The waitress quietly approached, filled the cup in front of Scott, and poured more for Barry.

Barry looked at his watch. "Being Captain is a pain in the butt. When I tell them I need something done in a hurry, you'd think they'd do it. This waiting is for the birds."

A cell phone rang. All three men reached for their phones before they realized it was Aaron's that was ringing.

"This is Aaron."

"Aaron, its Karen. I just saw the news on the television. Do I know the men?"

"You may have met one of them at the company picnic. His name is Carl Rojas."

Karen was quiet for a second. "I remember. Nice wife and two kids in college."

Aaron thought, *Of course Karen would remember.* He replied, "The one who died has only been with us four weeks. You couldn't have met him yet."

"Have they caught the shooters?"

"Not yet, but they will. I'm here with Barry and Scott now. We've never lost a man before."

"I'll be up there late this afternoon. You'll want to visit their wives, and I can go with you."

"Thanks. You know where the extra key is hidden if I'm not home."

As Karen broke the connection, Aaron looked at Barry and said, "We will catch those sons of bitches."

"Aaron, let us do our job. We'll catch them. Just don't get in the way."

Scott looked into the eyes of his friend and partner and thought, *These crooks have started up with the wrong guy.*

The clock on the wall looked as worn out as the four men in the conference room felt.

Aaron started the meeting by tapping a pencil on the table. "Michael, bring us up to date on what you've found out so far."

"Let me start by saying that I'm trying to stay close to the lieutenant running the investigation."

"What do we know about him?" interrupted Tom Greenberg.

"Not much. I've fed most of the basics to my friends in San Francisco. They're running him through the computers as we speak. My first impression is that he is bright, hard working, and honest. We'll know more this afternoon."

"What else do we know?" asked Scott Miller, the other vice president of Besafe.

Michael stood and went to the chalkboard where key elements of the investigation were scrawled in yellow chalk.

"We think that one of our men wounded one of the crooks. The blood that was found not far from Preston's body was a different type." He put a check mark next to the word blood. "The police had an all points bulletin on the air within five minutes of their arrival, and still couldn't locate the truck that broke down the door." He put a check mark next to the word door, and added a question mark.

"What's the question mark for?" Aaron asked.

"I had a thought that maybe the truck was parked in one of the buildings nearby."

"Good thought." Aaron turned to Scott. "We should find out how many of the buildings we patrol, and maybe we should call Min and find out how many of the buildings his cleaning service takes care of."

They looked at the board. There was one more word scrawled in chalk at the bottom—semiconductors.

Aaron motioned with his head for Michael to proceed.

"They got away with over four million dollars of parts that are easily sold on the gray market. The owners are screaming. Their insurance doesn't cover all of their loss."

Aaron turned toward Tom. "You understand all the numbers. See if you can find out how much they're covered for and how bad the hurt is. While you're talking to people, see if you can get some idea of how these parts would get sold and who would buy them. I've heard of the gray market, but I didn't think they were moving stolen goods, just surplus parts." He turned to Michael. "This is a police matter and will be handled by them. Barry Sands is a friend of mine whom I trust explicitly. Saying all that, we will find the people that did this and make sure they are punished. I would like you to be our point man." When no one said anything, he continued. "You have worked for us on other cases where you weren't required to break the law, but you may have had to bend it a little. If you feel uncomfortable, just say no."

Michael looked down at the table. "Mr. Carlyle, I understand what has to be done. I will find these people. How they get punished is for someone else. There's just one thing I require."

"That is?"

"A promotion. It will give me a little more clout when dealing with outsiders."

"With a raise in pay?" Scott asked.

"That part isn't necessary," Michael stated. "Carl is a friend of mine, I just want to get it done."

"Sorry, Michael. I wasn't asking you. I was asking Aaron," Scott replied.

"The title demands a raise in pay. Make it fair." Aaron spoke to the room. "I want daily briefings. Whatever assets are required to do this put them in place. Let's all get back to work. Before I forget, Tom, you better tell Emily to put on a happy face. If I was a betting man I would bet the line of people going to Human Resources today will be long."

The four men rose and each headed off to his own world. As hard as they might try to pretend otherwise, today would be different than other days. Today, they had lost one of their own.

Chapter 4

Aaron sat at his desk and stared blindly out the window. He wondered if one of the cars in the parking lot belonged to Mike Preston, and wrote a note to remind him to find out. The sun seemed to be casting more shadows today than normal, or maybe it was his imagination. He was glad Karen was coming up from San Diego. He didn't want to be alone. The intercom buzzed and his new secretary's voice came through.

"A Mr. Tuloc from the janitorial service is on the phone. I told him you were busy, but he insists on talking to you."

"Please put him through." *Aaron thought to himself, I wonder what this is about. I haven't talked to Tuloc in over three months, and he hasn't called me here since he left.*

The phone rang and Aaron pushed the hands-free button.

"Tuloc, how are you? More important, how are Sookie and the baby?"

"Mr. Carlyle, they are fine. Thank you for taking my call. We have heard of your misfortune and were wondering if there might be some way we can offer our help?"

The "we" of course was Min, Tuloc's "uncle" and grandfather in-law. When Aaron and his friends were forced to walk out of Vietnam, Min and Giac, generals in the South Vietnamese Army, were their guides. Giac, the senior of the two men, settled in Colorado; Min settled in Southern California. When Giac died, Min took over the running of both families. Tuloc, who was Giac's youngest son, ended up marrying Soo Kim, Min's grand-daughter. Over the years, Min had become one of Aaron's closest friends. Nine years before, at Aaron's suggestion, aside from the gas stations and God knows what else he already had in place, Min started a building maintenance service. Aaron tried to place them with as many of Besafe's customers as possible. Min guaranteed there would be nothing missing from any desks, supply cabinets, or warehouses, and Aaron trusted Min fully.

"Thank you for your concern, but I think we have it under control."

"My grandfather thought you might say that, so he has suggested that I pose this question to you." There was a slight hesitation before he started again. "If there were other security services like your own, would you share information? If the answer is yes, we would suggest that you set up a meeting, first with Interstate Security and then with All Alarm. If the answer is no, we wonder if you would think it a betrayal of trust if you brought Miss Williams to dinner tonight and business . . ." His voice stopped and Aaron realized Tuloc had put his hand over the receiver. "I am sorry, other people's business would be discussed."

Aaron scratched the back of his head before replying. "You pose an interesting question. We never share information because of the competitive nature of our business, but that doesn't mean we couldn't. The more interesting question is how you knew Karen would be up here tonight?"

Again the phone was quiet. "We guessed that she would be joining you because of what happened last night."

Aaron grinned. "Tuloc, you are getting more like him every day." Aaron knew Tuloc was smiling on the other end of the phone.

"Not quite. I would have anticipated your question if I was more like him."

"Tell you what," Aaron replied. "Let's reverse it. Why don't you come to my place for dinner? I will get some steaks, Karen will make a salad, and you will explain how you knew Karen was coming up. During dessert, we can discuss my competitors and why you think information has to be shared."

"Please hold on while I check. Never mind, of course I accept.

Soo Kim would love to see Karen. If it is okay with you, we will arrive at seven o'clock tonight. There will be four of us, plus the baby."

"Make it six thirty. It will give us a little more time to talk."

After he hung up, Aaron called in Tom and Scott and briefed them on his conversation with Tuloc. "Are either of you free for dinner tonight?"

"I can't," Tom answered. "I'm having dinner with the insurance investigator."

"See if you can find out if there have been any other robberies similar to this one in the area. Min must know something."

"I can make it," said Scott. "Constance called a half hour ago and wants to go out for Chinese, but this sounds a hundred percent better."

"That'll make eight of us. I wonder who the fourth person is?" Aaron mused.

"Mr. Carlyle, may I speak to you please?"

Aaron looked up. "Sure, come on in Michael. Something happening?"

"Maybe. Those integrated circuits that were stolen last night weren't all ordinary parts."

"What does that mean?"

"Almost a quarter of them were made as specials for a customer in Woodland Hills."

"Which customer?" Scott asked.

"The company's name is Providence. They manufacture a board that's put in your computer. It has an imbedded circuit that doesn't allow anyone but you to use your credit card when buying online."

"I thought a lot of companies have that technology."

"They do, Mr. Carlyle, but . . ."

Aaron interrupted, "Michael, we just promoted you. How about calling me Aaron?"

Michael looked like he was thinking it over and finally said, "Okay."

"But what?" Tom questioned. He was getting antsy.

"A lot of companies are talking about having the technology

and some of them do, but unless Providence gets those parts, they're out of business."

"What do you mean out of business?"

"Lieutenant Sizemore tells me they are screaming worse than the guy who owns Active Components. It seems that he invoiced the parts last night, but they missed the delivery truck. By invoicing them, he's covered by insurance as a lost in transit item, with a hundred-dollar deductible. Providence, if they don't have the parts to ship by the end of the month, loses their contract. That means over one million dollars worth of parts goes into an eight-and-a-half-million-dollar shipment. Without this shipment, they can close their doors."

"Can't Active Components get any more?" Aaron asked.

"It's my understanding that it takes ten to twelve weeks to have them made."

Aaron turned to Tom. "While you're at dinner with the insurance agent, find out how that works. See if you can also find out at what time last night he invoiced the parts. Also find out, if you can, if this company Providence has any recourse."

Aaron looked at his watch. "Has anyone heard from the hospital?"

Chapter 5

Aaron left the office early and went to look in on Carl Rojas. He stood in front of the community hospital. Stopped by an invisible hand on his chest, Aaron felt a wave of sadness engulf him. It was only three years ago that Marcia, his wife, died here, as he sat holding her hand. Thanks to Karen, who over the past two years had helped him enormously to get on with his life, he usually didn't get this type of reaction. The only other time he remembered going back to this hospital was to visit Emily, the Human Resources director of his company, when she was admitted after her car was forced off the road.

He started to smile as he remembered Emily, lying in bed and telling him she wanted a detailed description of his first date with Karen. She had known that night was going to be the first date he had in over a year. He took the elevator to the second floor and found Emily, Michael, and Carl's wife sitting in the waiting room.

Emily stood. "Aaron, he should be taken to UCLA Medical Center." She was whispering. "But they're not going to transfer him."

"Why?"

"He's not responding, and the doctor told me he was afraid he might not be strong enough to make the two-hour trip."

"Where's the doctor?"

"He went to get a cup of coffee," she answered sarcastically.

Aaron walked over to the nurse's station and said. "Pardon me.

Can you tell me where I can find Mr. Rojas's doctor or the person in charge of the hospital?"

"I'm not sure the administrator is still in the building. Why don't you wait for the doctor to return and maybe he can help you?"

Before Aaron could answer, Karen came walking out of the elevator. She waved at Aaron and walked over to Carl's wife. She put her arms around her and whispered into her ear. Aaron felt a lump in his throat thought, *Men aren't supposed to cry.*

Karen came over and kissed his cheek. "Having a problem?" she asked.

The nurse Aaron had spoken to said, "I don't think so. Your husband asked for the person in charge, and I told him I'm not sure he's still here."

Karen faced Aaron and mouthed the word, "Why?"

"They told Emily they wanted to transfer him to UCLA, but they're not sure he'll survive the trip down."

She touched his stubbled cheek gently. "What were you going to do, take him yourself?"

Aaron shook his head. "No. I was going to arrange for a helicopter."

Karen turned back to the nurse. "Listen carefully. You find that person now or be prepared to become part of the biggest lawsuit this hospital has ever seen. My fiancé is not a reasonable person when things don't go his way."

The nurse's lips tightened and her eyes became little slits as she stonily stared at Karen. "I'll get the doctor."

"Maybe you didn't understand me. If he's not the person to get it done, don't bother."

Two other nurses had appeared out of nowhere, but they were keeping their distance. Karen turned to them and raised her voice,

"If either of you is in charge, I suggest you do something. If you're not, I want your names and hospital I.D. numbers. You will be witnesses and maybe even co-defendants when this hospital gets sued."

They looked at each other and finally one of them picked up the phone.

"Please find Dr. Robert McKee immediately."

"Doctor McKee, we have a little problem in ICU. I think it's a relative of one of your patients. He's demanding a helicopter to transport the patient to UCLA. The patient's name is Rojas . . . yes, that's the one. I'll let you speak to him." She handed Aaron the phone.

He held it away from his ear as the doctor started talking.

"I don't know who you think you are, but Mr. Rojas is my patient. I will decide the best course of action and right now I want you out of the hospital. I don't know if you noticed, but there is an armed policeman standing outside the door. You either leave this instant or I'll have you arrested."

Aaron looked at Karen, and then at Michael and the policeman he was standing next to. Michael gave him a thumbs up signal and smiled.

"Listen to me, McKee. As of this minute, Mr. Rojas is no longer your patient. I am taking charge of his welfare. All I want from you or this hospital is a doctor up here in a hurry. When that helicopter lands here in ten or fifteen minutes, I want him ready for transport."

"It takes hours to arrange these things. You just don't barge into a hospital and start pushing your way around. There are rules and procedures. By the way, what is your name?"

The doctor's voice had started becoming a little more conciliatory; he was beginning to re-think his position.

"Come on up and find out," Aaron replied as he hung up the phone.

Less than a minute later, Dr. McKee came out of the elevator. He glanced at the nurse's station where the head nurse nodded her head in Aaron's direction.

"I'm Doctor McKee. You are?"

"My name is Aaron Carlyle. I'm the president of Besafe Security and Carl Rojas works for me. Can you please brief me on his condition?"

"I usually only talk to the family or the police in these type of situations." Looking at Carl's wife sitting right there, he continued, "We had to perform emergency surgery. We removed two bullet fragments, but one is still lodged in his chest near the aorta. We need a bypass machine to safely remove it."

"Where is the closest hospital with that type of equipment?" Aaron asked

"For an operation that delicate, probably UCLA," the doctor replied.

"So let's get him transferred," Aaron replied calmly, but with conviction.

"I wouldn't feel safe in transferring him in anything less than a Medivac helicopter. His blood pressure has been falling and any trip over an hour could . . ." He stopped and looked at Carl's wife. "Let's just say this could be very dangerous."

"Call the helicopter. If it's a question of money, I'll guarantee the payment."

"It's not the money. There are only two, and twenty minutes ago, one was in Pasadena and the other in Orange County. Now Mr. Carlyle, if you'll let me get on with the job of saving his life."

"Karen, let me borrow your cell phone," Aaron said.

Aaron dialed Barry's private number as everyone in the vicinity watched.

"Hi, Barry. This is Aaron. I need some help. Can you get me one of your Medivac helicopters to transport Carl Rojas to UCLA? They aren't sure he'll make it in an ambulance and we're running out of time. If it's a problem, charge my company."

While he held on for Barry's reply, Aaron looked up and saw three hospital security guards standing nearby. He waved at them. They were all employees of Besafe who held the contract for security at the hospital.

"Aaron?" It was Barry back on the line.

"The chopper will be landing in less than three minutes. My office is notifying UCLA to expect them. I can't afford to lose the one witness we have to the robbery and murder. By the way, we just received a call from the hospital that someone was creating a ruckus. Could that by any chance be you?"

"Me?" Aaron smiled. "You know I wouldn't do anything like that. Thanks for the help."

"The helicopter will be landing in less than three minutes, let's get a move on," Aaron yelled to everyone in listening distance.

All of a sudden, the nurses and two doctors started moving.

He turned to Karen. "I forgot to tell you. Guess who's coming to dinner?

Chapter 6

After seeing that Carl and his wife were airborne, Aaron followed Karen to his house. As they entered, Karen looked at the clock on the wall and said, "Okay master chef, put your ass in gear and get the charcoals going. I'm going to change my clothes and start the salad. Are you sure he didn't give you any idea on who the extra person was?"

"He just said there would be four of them. The thing that's driving me crazy is how he knew you were on your way up from San Diego."

"Nothing Min says or does surprises me anymore, and I guess Tuloc is very much like him," Karen said over her shoulder as she left the kitchen to get dressed.

Upon returning to the kitchen, Karen continued talking without missing a beat. "He's been training him for a long time," she said as Aaron moved closer and reached for her.

"I'm starting to think you're just a sex starved overgrown kid." She laughed and blew him a kiss. "I'm just starved. Start the grill, this fooling around can wait until they're gone."

She kissed the tip of his nose and walked to the dining room, just as there was a knock on the front door. She turned in mid stride and said, "I'll get it."

"It must be Scott and Constance." Aaron grumbled. "Min won't arrive until six thirty on the button."

From the other room, Karen's voiced trembled, "Aaron."

"Who is it?" He was now shouting. When she didn't answer, he turned and came face to face with an Asian woman holding a gun.

"Are you Aaron Carlyle, president of Besafe?"

Aaron stood quietly willing Karen not to do anything crazy. "Yes I am," he finally replied, stepping between Karen and the woman. "Who are you, and why are you holding that gun?" He closed the front door.

The woman looked at the gun as if she was surprised it was in her hand. "My name is Lan Burnett, and here, take this thing." She handed him the pistol with shaking hands.

There was another knock on the door and Aaron asked, "Are you alone?"

"Yes I am."

"Karen, keep Miss . . . it is Miss, isn't it?"

"No, it's Mrs."

"Keep Mrs. Burnett company while I see who's at the door."

Checking to make sure the safety was on, Aaron tucked the gun in his waist. This time it was Scott and Constance. Aaron held his finger to his lips and quickly explained what had just happened. As he finished, two black Lincoln Continentals pulled into the driveway.

"Scott, take Constance inside and get acquainted. Let me explain to Min what's going on."

Tuloc was the first one out of the car on the right. He held the door for Soo Kim as she handed him the baby. The rear door of the other car opened and Min stepped out, waved at Aaron, and turned and offered his hand to another passenger. Both Tuloc and Soo Kim were watching as Aaron's mouth fell open in surprise. The woman hanging on the end of Min's arm was more than beautiful. He recognized her immediately. It was Mai Ling, Sookie's older sister. He hadn't seen her in over two years. She was living in San Francisco and Min referred to her as his niece instead of his granddaughter to keep her safe.

"Aaron, I would like to re-introduce you to Mai Ling. I think you may have met briefly some time in the past."

"Yes we did, and it is my pleasure to welcome you to my home. The door is open. Why don't you all just go on in?" Aaron hung back. “Min, Tuloc, we have a little problem. I think I’d better explain before you enter.” He again explained the situation. Min stuck his head back inside the car and spoke to the driver in Vietnamese. Two more black Lincolns pulled up in front of the house.

“Min! This is starting to look like a Lincoln dealership. There’s only one woman inside.”

“I understand. My nephews and nieces will ensure there are no more outside.”

Aaron shook his head as they walked into the house. “They have a name for this—they call it paranoia.”

“In my country, they call it staying alive.”

If there was any danger it wasn’t evident inside. Everyone was cooing over the baby, and Karen’s face was glowing as she called over to Aaron. “Have you said hello to little Aaron yet?”

He smiled. It still blew his mind that they named the baby after him.

He pecked Soo Kim on the cheek and turned to Mai Ling. “Are you on vacation?”

“No, I’ve decided to come home and live with my family.”

“How nice for both of you,” Karen replied, looking from Mai Ling to Min.

After five minutes of saying hello and looking at the baby, the entire room went quiet. Everyone kept looking at Mrs. Burnett who still sat at the dining room table with her head buried in her hands.

Sensing the gazes, she glanced up and said, “This isn’t turning out like I wanted.”

Aaron took out the gun and handed it to Scott and sat down across from her. “What were you trying to accomplish coming in here with a gun?”

“I wanted to hire you.”

“Hire me for what?” he asked incredulously. Holding up his hand he said, “Let’s start at the beginning.”

She looked around the room. “I had hoped this would be confidential.”

“It’s a little late for that, but I’ll tell you what.” He turned to Karen. “Why don’t you start the salad and maybe Tuloc can put up the grill. Scott and Min will come with me and listen to Mrs. Burnett's story."

She nodded and turned to Tuloc. "I hope you're good at cooking."

Aaron was watching Min, who hadn't taken his eyes off Mrs. Burnett.

When everyone but Scott, Min, and Aaron had left the room, Min said something in Vietnamese. Mrs. Burnett smiled and said in English, "I have not spoken my native tongue in over thirty years. I still understand some of the words, but my parents spoke only English at home."

"Your parents are?" Min asked.

"My biological parents were Viad and Serlyn Tran. They were killed in an explosion when I was eight. I was put in an orphanage run by the French for two years until an American couple adopted me. John and Carole Lott had no children of their own and they made sure I was given the best education and family life available. It was at Clemson that I met my husband, William Burnett. He died three years ago—one day after our son's fifth birthday. I took over running the company my husband founded, Providence."

Aaron looked at Scott, who was examining the pistol. He nodded and asked Mrs. Burnett to continue.

"The company has been in the design stage for the last year, designing an imbedded chip that can stop anyone from using someone else's credit card to make purchases online."

"It is my understanding that there are other companies working on the same type of chips." Min surprised Aaron by making the comment. It showed knowledge of something Aaron didn't believe Min had, but he decided with Min, nothing should surprise him.

"Yes there are, but we think we have at least an eighteen-month head start on the rest of them."

"And the reason you wanted to hire Besafe?" Aaron kept trying to get her back on track.

"The police told me that it was your men that discovered the robbers, and I was hoping that you were going to investigate. By hiring you, I could accomplish what I want."

"And the reason for the gun?"

Her face paled. “I think I am being followed. When my husband was alive, he kept this in the house for protection. I brought it with me just in case.” She smiled apologetically. “It was never meant to scare you.”

“Would you have used it?” Min asked.

“I don’t know. I’ve never used a gun in my life.”

“I believe that,” Scott said. “There are no bullets in it.”

“What would you expect us to find in this investigation?” Aaron asked.

“The parts. If I don’t get them back by next week, I could be out of business.”

“How so? You can always get more parts.” Min was starting to get more involved in the conversation.

“I have mortgaged everything I have to get this shipment out the door. We have an order that, if not delivered by a week from next Friday, puts my company into a default condition.”

“Which means?” again Min was asking questions.

“Which means that the price of the units goes down by five percent every five days. In fifty days, or less than two months, I have to deliver the parts at a fifty percent discount. But that’s not the worst part. I expected to deliver the order this week. I would be able to get funds equal to seventy percent of the invoice, or a little over five and a half million dollars. Without that money, I can’t make payroll, or pay my suppliers. I will effectively be out of business inside of thirty days.”

“Mrs. Burnett, I’ve got a little background in this type of stuff, and I would think if your product is that good, your patent would be worth more than that.” Scott was doing some quick calculations as he spoke. “If your suppliers would wait a little longer for their payment, maybe you could sweeten the wait with an extra one or two percent.”

Before Mrs. Burnett could answer, there was a knock on the front door. Everyone turned and watched Karen look out the window and then open the door. She nodded her head and looked back at Min in the dining room.

“Min, one of your nephews would like to talk to you.”

Chapter 7

Min returned in less than a minute. "Aaron, do you think we might ask Mrs. Burnett to join us?"

With a look of surprise, Aaron replied, "Of course I can. Mrs. Burnett, I'm sorry for my lack of manners. Would you like to join us for dinner?"

She looked at Min before answering him. "I am afraid that I have already intruded on a family dinner. Please excuse my lack of manners, but I must go." She didn't move to leave, and Aaron guessed she had nowhere to go. She was out of options.

"Mrs. Burnett, where is your son?" The question from Min surprised everyone, especially Mrs. Burnett.

She looked around the room with panic in her eyes. "He's waiting for me in the car. Why are you asking?"

"One of my nephew's saw a boy of about eight sitting in a car and they thought he might belong to you. I am sure that Aaron's invitation included your son. Why don't you bring him in and we can all have something to eat. I think you will find my granddaughter's husband, Tuloc, a very good cook."

Flustered, she nodded her head. Min's invitation left very little room for her to say no.

"Mr. Min, My original goal was to hire a private detective to help me. I must continue my search. Your offer to feed my son and me, while very thoughtful, is only prolonging my search."

"I think your search is over. Join us for . . ." He searched for the word. "I think you would call it barbecue. After dinner, we will discuss it further."

His smile flustered her even more. Over the years, Aaron had seen Min be very charming, but somehow today, Min turned up the wattage.

"I'll get my son and bring him in, as long as you think it's okay." She was now facing Aaron. He had the feeling that she somehow was afraid to look directly at Min.

"We would love to have both of you join us for dinner." Aaron smiled as he spoke. This was a very strange day.

Her eyes moved from Aaron back to Min with obvious relief. She went to the front door, turned and smiled, her first genuine smile since her arrival. "I'll be right back."

As the door closed, Aaron looked at Min. "What's this all about?"

"My nephew has told me that she is being followed. Her car is under the watchful eyes of two men. They do not seem to have a car with them, so we are assuming that there is at least one other person who is in contact by phone."

Scott rose and went to the window. "I see Mrs. Burnett with her son, but no one else."

"If my nephews say they are there, they are there."

"Min, that reminds me, how did you know Karen was coming up today?"

His teeth became visible in all their glory. "Sometimes things just happen. Soo Kim called Karen to ask if she was coming up tomorrow. She wanted her to stop on the way so she could introduce her to Mai Ling. Her mother answered and told her she had already left for your place. The rest was easy."

"Was this why you wanted to get together?" Aaron persisted.

"No. It was because of the break in and some other strange happenings . . ."

He stopped as the front door opened. Mrs. Burnett entered holding the hand of her son.

"We will finish this conversation later. Now's the time to enjoy ourselves."

What started out a little strange turned into a wonderful time for everyone. Karen kept brushing into Aaron, smiling and apologizing; Mai Ling found an instant admirer in William, Mrs. Burnett's son; and Mrs. Burnett found an admirer in Min.

When the last dish was cleaned and put away, Min suggested that they go into the dining room to discuss the problem. It was almost like everyone was choosing sides. Scott sat next to Aaron with Karen and Constance on their flanks. Min and Tuloc sat across from them with Soo Kim and Mai Ling sitting along side of them. Mrs. Burnett sat at the head of the table with William, baby-sitting in front of the television.

The dining room had a Danish designed wood top table that seated twelve comfortably, with high back chairs with blue velvet box seats. There was a picture window that ran the length of the room overlooking the swimming pool in the back yard. The lighting was recessed and the controls allowed the room to be dimmed or brightened, depending upon the mood of the people.

Aaron turned the lights up as bright as they would go.

Min began speaking. "Mrs. Burnett's company is in trouble. She's here to hire a private detective to help her retrieve the semiconductor chips that were stolen from Active Components. I believe that Besafe should take on Mrs. Burnett and her company as clients."

"Min, you understand that we are not a private detective agency. We're a security guard service." Aaron leaned forward as he spoke.

"That is what you call it. You investigate when someone steals or breaks into firms that hire you. You are licensed to carry guns for no other reason than for protection. How much different are you from a detective agency?"

Scott answered, "When someone becomes a private detective, he takes an oath to uphold the law. Our men don't have to take that oath. They only have to follow the rules as set up by us."

"Obeying those rules is similar to taking an oath. Again, we are talking words," Min stated.

"Min, what do you think would change if we were a detective agency?" Aaron asked.

Min nodded at Tuloc.

"What you would be able to do is investigate and stop crime before it happens."

Aaron focused on Tuloc. "Isn't that what we are doing now?"

"No. What you are doing is trying to deter crime. You put in cameras, you visit during the night, and you run background checks on new employees. There are things going on, much like what has happened to Mrs. Burnett, that the people that run the companies don't come to you for help."

"And where would you fit in?" Aaron asked, suspecting that Min and Tuloc had discussed this scenario at great length.

"My wife's grandfather would be willing to invest in such an enterprise."

Aaron could feel Karen's hand tighten behind him. Scott stood and walked into the kitchen. Aaron could hear him pouring water in a glass.

"It would seem to me that this should be discussed in a different venue, not at a family get together, with strangers present," Aaron finally responded.

"It is important that we talk now." Again, Tuloc spoke for Min.

This had to be the strangest conversation Aaron ever had with them. Min always did his own talking. Something was definitely wrong.

"I would never dishonor Min by talking business in this manner." Aaron looked directly at Tuloc as he again responded.

"It is not dishonorable to talk as friends. I have only worked for my esteemed grandfather-in-law for two years, but in that time, I have found out you are friends."

Aaron was now positive something was wrong. Tuloc had worked for Besafe for three years prior to his going to work for Min. He knew their friendship went back many years. Before he could figure out what they were up to, Soo Kim started talking.

"Tuloc, you are shaming all of us. We must leave."

"Wife of mine, you will not disagree with your husband in public."

Soo Kim bowed her head, but now Karen jumped in.

"Listen Tuloc, husband of my friend, what she doesn't need is a lesson on manners from someone that obviously has forgotten his."

Everyone in the room was now on edge. Aaron rose and addressed Min.

"Old friend, I think it is time you took your great grandson home. It is past his bedtime."

Min stood and without acknowledging the confrontation that had just transpired, looked at Mrs. Burnett. "It was very nice meeting you. I am sure that we will meet again soon. It is time for us to leave."

"Grandfather, I wish to stay and visit with Mr. Carlyle. It has been over two years since we last met. I want to get to know Karen; Sookie says she is so nice. Please let me stay."

Min looked around the room and in mock exasperation said, "Children have no respect for their elders' wishes. I will see Mrs. Burnett home and then I will return for you. That should give you about one hour."

Karen looked at Aaron who shrugged his shoulders. The events of the evening made almost no sense at all. It was like seeing a play where everyone had lines to say. Min, Tuloc, and the girls were all talking like they had rehearsed their speeches.

"Tuloc, take two of the cars and make sure Soo Kim and little Aaron get home safely. I will follow in about an hour after Mai Ling has finished her visit."

Sookie kissed Aaron on the cheek and handed him the baby. "Hold him next to you so that he may learn your smell. It is said each person has a different odor that children can distinguish forever."

The baby gurgled and smiled as Aaron held him out at arm length. After hugging him close for a moment, Aaron looked at Karen and handed her the baby.

"Might as well let him know that there's two of us," he said with a huge smile on his face.

Chapter 8

As the last of the four cars pulled away, Mai Ling put her hand on Aaron's arm.

"Grandfather will return shortly. He wishes to speak to you and Mr. Greenberg privately. He could not do that with Mrs. Burnett present."

"I knew this whole thing was crazy. Can you tell me what's wrong?" Aaron asked.

"He will explain. Please let me use this time to get to know Karen."

Aaron looked over her head at Karen who nodded before she said, "I think that's a great idea. Come sit with me by the pool. It's cool and private. The men won't disturb us there." She turned to Scott's wife and said, "Constance, why don't you take Mai Ling to the back while I get something for us to drink?"

With the women gone, Scott sat down across from Aaron and shook his head in bewilderment. "What the hell do you think is going on?"

Aaron shook his head. "I don't know. I can't buy their story of how they knew Karen was on her way up here, and I don't understand the part about the detective agency and Min investing money."

Scott contemplated for a second as his fingers rubbed his brow. "You know it's not such a bad idea about us setting up a detective agency. With the training we give our people and the background that most of them have, we probably have the nucleus of a pretty good cadre."

Aaron looked at him. "Does it make sense from a financial point of view?"

"I don't know. Maybe tomorrow, you, Tom, and me can sit down and work through it. It might make sense, but that still doesn't answer what Min has in mind."

From where Aaron was sitting, he could see through the window as one of the black Lincolns pulled into the driveway. "I think we're about to find out. Min's back."

As Min walked in, he said, "I am sorry for the display of bad manners shown earlier."

He followed Aaron into the dining area where Scott was nursing a bottle of beer.

"Would you like a brew?" Aaron asked, his lack of formality was a sign he was pissed.

"No, nothing for me. Thank you."

With Scott at one end of the table and Aaron at the other, Min was forced to sit between them. They knew from past experience that this would cause him to be uncomfortable. He would not be able to look at both of them as he talked.

"You have now apologized, but you haven't told us why you and Tuloc went through that charade. How about starting there?" Aaron asked.

Min stood and walked slowly to the center of the table where they had the bottles of beer in a tub with ice. He picked up a bottle, and after taking off the cap, drained it in what looked like one gulp. He was showing Aaron and Scott that he was accepting the rebuke, and leaving it behind them.

He began, "The break-in at Providence is one of seven that has occurred within the past three months. It is only the first that is protected by your service. When I had Tuloc call you, it was to discuss these robberies."

They waited in silence for him to continue.

"The newspapers say the thefts are being done by a Vietnamese gang. It is my belief that the people being robbed can't tell the difference between Chinese, Japanese, or Vietnamese." He again hesitated. "I am again straying from my thoughts. I do this a lot lately." He looked sheepishly around the table. "The police have started investigating my company and the people that work for my company. We have already lost three customers and I have a feeling we are about to lose more."

"Why do you think that?" Scott inquired.

"Executives from Interstate Security and All Alarm have both visited. They are saying that my people have access and knowledge of the plants that have had thefts."

"All eight robberies were at plants serviced by your company?" Scott asked incredulously.

"Yes," Min whispered.

"So what was that act you put on earlier all about?" Aaron asked.

"We have been doing some investigating on our own. Providence is the second company that has been hurt because of failure to deliver parts."

"What do you mean hurt?" Scott interrupted.

"The other company, Western Amplifier, had to sell out at half of its worth rather than lose everything. When I realized who Mrs. Burnett was, I wanted it to look like we were not in agreement on certain things. Everyone knows we are friends. We cannot hide that, but just in case she or her company does get compromised, I did not want too much information available. I also thought that we could use her to find out who is behind these robberies."

Aaron smiled and thought, *Lan Burnett, though dressed like an American woman, was in every sense of the word, Asian.* "I also think that you believe Mrs. Burnett is very pretty and very charming."

Min looked at Mai Ling and Karen. They had entered the room after the discussion started. His eyes took on a vacant, lonely look. Aside from Mai Ling's Asian features, the two women could have been sisters. They both had dark hair, lean hard bodies, and perfect white teeth that showed when they smiled.

"That also." Min continued, "Her name means orchid. It is a good name."

"What is it you would like us to do?" Aaron questioned.

"I want you to investigate the robberies. I would be your client."

"Why us? There are a lot of qualified detective agencies around." Aaron asked the question even though he knew the answer.

"If you found something inside my company, you would advise me prior to the police."

"If we were a licensed company, I'm not so sure we could . . ."

"I also want you to add Mai Ling to your company."

Min, for the first time that Aaron could remember, looked old. He ran his fingers through his graying hair and his eyes had a tinge of red spider tracks that gave the impression of sleepless nights.

"As what?" Scott asked.

"As an investigator. She has had experience, which you are aware of, and I would be able to get needed information quickly."

Mai Ling stood quietly next to Karen. Her expression revealed nothing—neither surprise nor knowledge of this request.

Aaron rose from the table. "Min, Scott and I will have to talk to Tom. I can tell you now that Scott believes we should look into becoming a detective agency. As far as having Mai Ling join our staff, I would like to talk to her alone."

"You would not hire her as a favor to me?"

"Hire her, yes. Have her work as an investigator so that you could get timely information, no. If she comes to work for Besafe, she reports to whomever she works."

"Would you take my word?" Mai Ling asked quietly. "My grandfather has a saying, 'promises are made to be kept.'"

Aaron looked at Scott, who nodded his head slightly.

"Yes I would," Aaron replied.

"You have it," she answered. "When can I start?"

"Monday morning," Scott replied. "What time can you be at our office?"

"I can be there by six thirty. Whom should I ask for?"

"Emily is in charge of Human Resources, but she doesn't arrive until about eight o'clock."

"I will be there by seven thirty. When Miss Emily arrives, I will be ready."

Aaron listened to her voice, but he never took his eyes off Min. Min was watching Mai Ling with a stoic face, but his eyes couldn't hide the pride.

"Min, we will contact you Monday afternoon with our decision on the detective agency. Will you be seeing or talking to Mrs. Burnett before then?"

Scott looked up. Aaron's question had surprised him. It also surprised Min.

"Why are you asking that?" Min questioned.

"You mentioned earlier that she was being tailed. I just had a feeling that you would follow up on that," Aaron replied as he looked at the floor.

"She was followed by a car with two men. The car was parked at the bottom of your hill. My nephews took the license plate number down, and I will see if we can find out whom it belongs to. There was also a sign on the side."

"If the car was at the bottom of the hill, how did you know it was following her?" Scott questioned.

"Two Asian men sitting in a parked car in this neighborhood with an Interstate Security sticker on their car is what made us think she was being followed."

"Interstate Security? Why would they be following her? I guess you know whom the car belongs to," Scott replied quickly.

"Following her or guarding her? I'm not sure which. She said followed." Min looked at his watch. "It's time for us to leave, Mai Ling."

"Thank you Mr. Carlyle and Mr. Miller. I think you will find that I will be a good person to have working for you."

She walked out after giving Karen a hug. Min shook everyone's hands and bowed for both Karen and Constance. When the door closed, Scott said, "I'll give Tom a call and brief him on what happened here. Suppose we meet tomorrow at nine o'clock and go over everything."

Aaron looked at Karen. Tomorrow was supposed to be for the two of them.

Before he could say anything, Karen spoke, "Aaron, that would work great. If you could give me a desk in your office with access to a computer, I could catch up on some work that I missed today. I could be finished by noon and maybe get a chance to kick your butt on the golf course."

"You can try." Aaron turned to Scott. "See you at nine o'clock tomorrow."

Aaron walked both Scott and Constance to the door and then went looking for Karen. She had just finished putting the dishes in the dishwasher.

"Do you have any idea what's going on?" he asked.

"Only that she had a boyfriend who died in some kind of accident, and she felt a need to return to the fold, so to speak. She also wants to be somewhat independent from Min or the family. I'm not sure which."

"She certainly is a beautiful lady," Aaron commented as he turned out the lights.

"You noticed that." Karen punched him lightly in the ribs as she put on her pout face.

"Hey, I didn't mention her great shape, did I?" Aaron joked.

"You noticed that also?"

"What I noticed is that she didn't hold a candle to you," he said, taking Karen's hand as they went to bed.

Chapter 9

They rose at five o'clock and went for a four-mile run. Living on the top of a hill made the last half-mile more of a walk. As they started up the hill on the way home, they passed an empty car with Interstate Security license plates. It was parked next to an empty lot and Aaron stopped to take a look.

"What's the matter?" Karen asked.

"I'm just surprised this car is still standing here empty," he answered.

"Do you think this is the same car that Min's nephews saw yesterday?"

"Probably."

"Do you think Min had anything to do with the two men not being here?"

Karen is very perceptive, Aaron mused. He replied, "I doubt it."

"Liar, liar, pants on fire." She laughed, watching his face.

"When I get to the office, I'll call Interstate and tell them about the car. I'll call it a professional courtesy."

"If they were really following Lan, they should have called in their position."

Aaron looked at Karen and asked, "Is that a question or a statement?"

"I think it's both," she responded. "What would your men have done?"

"First of all, we're not a detective agency." He looked back at the parked car. "Second, if they were following her and didn't call in, we would have sent out another car to take a look."

They were almost to the top when Karen said, "There are two other possibilities."

He smiled and asked, "Yes?"

"One, something is wrong with their car and they had to leave it to be picked up this morning. Or, they are investigating or watching someone else's home and happen to be inside right now."

He continued walking.

"Well, what do you think of my deductions?" she asked.

"You could be right, but just to be on the safe side, I'll call Interstate and let them decide," Aaron replied.

The phone was ringing as they entered the house, but stopped before either could answer it.

"See if they left a message. I told my mother she could reach me here if she had a problem," Karen called from the bedroom.

Aaron pushed the play button.

"This is Dennis Canon. I'm the president of Interstate Security. I know this is going to sound strange, but we lost one of our cars last night and I thought you might know where it is. Please call me when you return. My private number is 805-555-2223."

"Talk about coincidences," Karen said as she began tugging off her running shorts and top.

Aaron's eyes had a gleam to them. "It's more than that. He didn't say they lost any men, just a car. He also knew that I wasn't home and since he thinks I know where it is, he must know approximately where he lost it and hasn't sent anyone to look around."

"What are you going to do?"

"First, you and I are going to take a shower," he said with a smile on his face.

"Together?"

"I certainly hope so." He shucked off his shorts.

"And then what?" Karen asked.

"Call Dennis Canon back."

"Don't you think you should do that first?"

"Not after you've agreed to take a shower with me."

She smiled. “You know you have a warped sense of priorities.” She turned and ran to the bathroom.

He smiled and said, “There’s nothing wrong with yours.”

Chapter 10

Arriving at the office, Aaron was surprised at how many people were at work on Saturday. He knew that their patrols ran around the clock, but this many people was unusual. He found Tom and Scott in the conference room with the morning papers, a pot of coffee, and what looked like at least a dozen bagels with cream cheese.

"I'll be with you guys in a sec. Let me find some place for Karen to work."

"She can use my office," Tom replied. "My laptop has the most memory and fastest response time."

Karen stuck her head in the door and said, "Good morning, and thanks. I promise not to disturb any of your papers."

She was dressed in white slacks with a blue golf shirt, which set off her dark flowing hair.

As Karen and Aaron left, Tom turned to Scott and said, "I'll bet you ten bucks she kicks his butt this afternoon on the course."

Tom smiled. "Aaron's been taking lessons, but the way she looks . . . I think I'll save my money."

"Save your money how?" Aaron asked as he re-entered the room.

"Scott thinks Karen is going to kick your butt this afternoon and I was thinking of taking some of his money, but I decided to let it go."

"Coward!" Aaron replied. "Before we start, what's the latest report on Carl?"

"I spoke to Michael last night and again this morning. You probably saved Carl's life with the move to UCLA." When Aaron didn't respond, Scott continued, "Michael is waiting at the hospital. Carl hasn't said anything yet, but the doctors think he should be able to at least answer questions sometime today."

"We should have one of our men sitting outside his door, just in case he saw something that the crooks don't want him to tell us," Aaron said as he made himself a note.

"Will do," said Scott.

Scott shuffled some papers in front of him. "I briefed Tom on our meeting with Min and Tuloc, and my thoughts on the idea. Let me summarize and then we can kick it around." He rose and went to the chalkboard where he put down numbers one through five. He spoke as he wrote. "One, our cost would be minimal due to our present hiring policies. Two, it would allow us to get closer to our accounts. Three, we would be able to branch out into markets that we are not presently in. Four, our invoicing would rise. And five, our stock will hopefully go up."

Tom stood and poured himself a cup of coffee. "As far as our hiring policies, you must mean that we screen the people we hire thoroughly?"

"That and we hire retired police," replied Scott.

Aaron jumped in, "By getting closer to our accounts, you mean what?"

"Tuloc was right yesterday. We do try to prevent crime. We sell a guard service to check people coming in and going out. We install monitors and we patrol the building at night and weekends. If a crime occurs, we obviously don't investigate. We leave that to the police. If we were a detective agency, we would also be able to help the executives with personal problems."

"Which I guess is the new markets we could get into?" Aaron asked.

"It's more than just that, but yes, that would be one of the new markets."

Tom said, "I understand the last two, but let me ask you a question. Wouldn't we be better off forming a new company, just in case it didn't work?"

"We should form a new company anyway. We would then have two divisions reporting back to us as a sort-of corporate staff. Our stockholders wouldn't get hurt and we could fund it out of ongoing operations." Scott sat back down and shrugged his shoulders.

"Who would be our competition?" Tom asked.

"A host of one man offices, a couple of larger firms, and some firms the same size as us. In fact, Interstate Security would be a competitor."

"That reminds me," interrupted Aaron. "I got a phone call from Dennis Canon, the president of Interstate. It seems he lost a car and called me to ask if I knew where it was."

"Why would he think you knew?" asked Tom.

"The funny thing is, I did know. I saw it this morning when Karen and I went out for a run. It was at the bottom of my hill. And it was empty."

"Is that the car that Min's nephews saw yesterday?" asked Scott.

"Karen thought the same thing. I would think so, but I'm not sure. It's just odd."

The three men spent about another hour going over how they could implement this new venture without actually deciding if they should proceed.

Finally, Tom said to the other two, "We're going to have to decide if we should proceed."

"I'm comfortable with what we are doing now," admitted Aaron. "I'm not sure starting something new is the right thing to do."

Before anyone else could speak, there was a knock on the door and Karen walked in.

"I don't know what this means yet, but I thought I should show this to you. While I was working inside, I pulled up ISSC, which is the symbol for Interstate Securities. Aside from the security company, they own a cleaning service company called Interstate Cleaning, three small electronic assembly companies, two game manufactures, five liquor stores, something called Sunrise Gym, and a small casino in Nevada just past the state line."

"Do they say how big any of the operations are?" asked Aaron.

"Not that I could tell, but overall, they do about four hundred million, and their stock in the past year has gone from a little over thirty dollars a share to over one hundred as of today."

"Have we run into them as competition at any of our accounts?" Aaron turned and asked Tom and Scott.

"I haven't seen them," Scott said.

Tom shook his head no.

There was another knock on the door and one of the secretaries stuck her head in.

"Michael's on line three. I wouldn't have interrupted, but he said it was important."

"Thanks," Aaron replied as he pushed the blinking light on the phone.

"Michael, its Aaron. Go ahead."

"He's awake, or he was five minutes ago. He saw one of the shooters."

"That means there's at least two?" Aaron asked.

"There was one of them who stepped out of the shadows in front of them, and another that fired from behind. It was the one behind that did the damage. Carl thinks the one in front was wounded."

"Well at least we know the blood came from one of the bad guys," said Scott.

"We know more than that," Michael responded. "The man in front was wearing tan slacks and a yellow shirt with the name Sunrise Gym across the back. The name Paul was on the front."

"How did Carl see all of that in the few seconds he had?" asked Scott and Tom almost simultaneously.

"Carl said that when he stepped out in front of them, he saw the name Paul. When Hank was shot from behind, he fired off a round and the man in front spun around. That's when he saw Sunrise Gym."

"Have the police taken a statement yet?" asked Aaron

"No. They were on a break when he came to."

"Get back in there and tell him not to talk to the police. We will have round the clock people down there in about thirty minutes. Stay with him until they arrive and then come on back. We have to talk." As Aaron finished, he turned to Karen. "Sorry about the golf. I owe you."

"I guess you think that it's too much of a coincidence that Sunrise Gym turns up in a conversation twice inside of five minutes," Karen asked sarcastically.

Chapter 11

Aaron looked at Karen and said, "One of the things we've learned over the years is that a coincidence is nothing but the rate of occurrence when something is going bad. Coincidences never seem to be good things."

"What are you going to do now?" she asked.

"First thing is to get some guards over to the hospital," Aaron replied as he looked at Tom.

"I'll have three men round the clock." Tom thought for a second and then said, "I think I better change that to two men during daylight hours and three men at night."

"Why?" asked Karen.

"Until we tell Barry, we don't want to make it look like a mob scene," Tom answered.

"You're not going to tell Barry?" Karen asked with a funny look on her face.

"I'll tell him soon enough, but not through official channels. I want Michael to be able to give something to Sizemore. Sort of like a quid pro quo," Aaron explained.

"Barry's not going to be happy," Karen said as she ran her fingers absently through her hair.

"I think he'll understand. Worst case, I'll tell him it's a payback for letting him be a hero by saving Carl's life." Aaron's tone told Karen that the discussion was over.

"Scott, contact our lawyers and have them file a new company name."

"What should we call it?" Scott asked. "Any ideas?" He looked at his two friends who just shrugged.

"Have any thoughts?" Aaron asked Karen.

"A couple. The name should be something with easy letters to remember. If you spin it off and take it public, something like Besafe would be great."

"Why couldn't we keep the name and just change it to Besafe Detective Agency, a division of Besafe Security?" Scott asked.

Aaron looked at Tom and then looked back to Scott. "Sounds like a plan, let's go with it."

They waited while Tom made some notes and then Aaron continued, "We have three things left to decide." He walked to the white board and wrote as quickly as he spoke.

"What do we tell Min? What do we do with Dennis Canon and Interstate? Who heads it up for us?" He threw the magic marker back in the tray.

"Any thoughts?" Scott asked.

"Yes," Said Tom. "Do you think Tuloc wants to come back and head it up?"

"That would certainly answer their behavior last night," Scott added.

"I don't think so," Aaron interjected. "Min's business is getting bigger and bigger every day. He needs Tuloc to help run it." He hesitated a second and then continued, "But, I wouldn't put it past the crafty bastard to find a place for Mai Ling."

"I forgot about her," said Tom. "Scott tells me she starts work on Monday. Have we figured out what to do with her yet?"

"May I interrupt?" asked Karen.

"Sure," said Tom.

"When you decide who runs the detective agency, why don't you put Mai Ling as his administrative assistant. That would solve what you do with her at Besafe, keep Min very happy, and from what I saw yesterday, give you a very smart, tough, and loyal employee." She looked around the room to see what everyone thought.

"You said as his administrative assistant. Was that generic or did you have someone in mind?" Aaron smiled as he asked.

"You all know who should have the job," Karen responded.

"She's right," agreed Tom.

"Is it unanimous?" asked Aaron.

Everyone nodded in approval.

"When he gets back from the hospital, we'll tell him. After that, I'll call Min and tell him. We'll let Michael tell Sizemore, which will filter to Barry."

"That leaves only Dennis Canon to deal with," Tom responded.

"One more thing has been added," Aaron said. "We also now have to find this Paul Character."

They were quiet, thinking of what course of action to take when one of the secretaries stuck her head in the door and said, "Sorry to intrude, but your phone is on do not disturb. I've got Michael Harran on the phone and he says it's urgent."

"Put him through," replied Aaron

The phone rang and Aaron pushed the speaker.

"What's going on Michael?" Scott asked.

"I've got four of the Interstate Security people standing outside of the door demanding to see Carl."

"Demanding?" Aaron looked around the room.

"Well, let's put it this way. They've got the regulars scared stiff. They're threatening to sue everyone they talk to. They say they are investigating the theft of parts from one of their clients and unless they get instant access to Carl, they're going to sue the hospital, the police department, and Besafe for denying access to a material witness."

"What have you told them?" Aaron asked urgently.

"Excuse my French, but I told them I would shoot the first mother fucker that sticks his head through the door."

Aaron couldn't stop the grin that spread across his face. Tom and Scott were also smiling.

"Anyone there?" Michael asked.

"We're here," Aaron responded. "I'm trying to explain to Karen what you said. Meanwhile keep them out of the room until one of us arrives. I'm going to call Barry and make sure his men back us up."

"Will do, boss. And don't worry. I won't shoot them . . . unless I have to."

Chapter 12

The disconnecting click of the phone galvanized the three partners. Scott had the duty officer send four cars with two men each to UCLA Medical Center. Their job was to do whatever was necessary to keep outsiders away from Carl, and to take further instructions from Michael, who was already at the hospital. Tom went to his office to call the corporate lawyers, and Aaron put in his first call to Captain Barry Sands.

"Sands here."

Aaron could tell by the sound of his voice that he was not having a good day. "Barry, its Aaron."

"I figured you'd be calling. Doesn't anyone understand that today is my day off?"

Aaron smiled. "Tell Carole I owe you dinner, or if you want, we can go to breakfast tomorrow. Karen's here."

"You ain't getting off that easy. Now tell me why you called," Barry responded with a touch more warmth.

"If you knew I was going to call, you must already know why. Who called you first, your men or Dennis Canon from Interstate?"

After a slight hesitation, Barry answered, "Both. And the hospital. My man is scared shitless that he's going to be sued. The hospital doesn't want any trouble, and this guy Dennis Canon is screaming that Carl is getting special treatment. Remember, my man is there as a courtesy. The hospital is in L.A. territory."

"What did you tell them?" Aaron paced around the office.

"I told my man to stay put and not to let anyone in until Sizemore gets there."

"What did you tell the hospital? Aaron prodded. Getting a story from Barry was like pulling teeth.

"Basically the same thing, except to remind them that the patient had private security guards that I had no control over."

"And what did you tell Dennis Canon?" Aaron asked the question quietly, which immediately told Barry something was wrong.

"Is there something you and I should be talking about?" Barry asked.

"You didn't answer the question."

"Neither did you . . . I told him he had no jurisdiction, and if he had a problem, he should take it to Lieutenant Sizemore."

When Aaron didn't comment, Barry went on, "Maybe we should do breakfast tomorrow. I'll have Carole put out a big pot of coffee and you and Karen can come by around ten o'clock."

"I've got a better idea. Let's do breakfast at my house. Why don't you invite Sizemore and I'll invite Michael and his wife. We've got some things we would like to go over with you both. Make it around nine thirty and I'll make sure we get those donuts you like."

"I'm on a diet," Barry replied, and then conceded, "but I like your idea better."

Aaron heard Barry's muffled voice call out to Carole. "Hey honey, Aaron wants us to come to his house for breakfast. I told him I was on a diet and he said he'd cook accordingly." Aaron couldn't hear her reply, but Barry came back on and said. "She'd love to. See you tomorrow."

Aaron hung up and reflected on what Barry had just told him. Dennis Canon was becoming a pain in the butt. He started putting notes on a pad in front of him, and after writing five lines, he called Min. As always, the phone was answered on the first ring.

"Who is calling please?" It sounded like Mai Ling, but Aaron didn't want to guess wrong.

"This is Aaron Carlyle. Could I speak to Min, please?"

"One second, Mr. Carlyle. I will see if he is available."

In less time than it took for her to say hold on, Min was on the phone.

"Aaron, I thought you were playing golf with Karen today."

"We were supposed to, but I had to come in to the office," Aaron replied.

"Is there a problem?" Min inquired.

"There could be. I think you and I should get together as soon as possible to discuss some things."

"What type of things?" Min asked.

"We've been friends too long to start being cute. Let's put our cards on the table and come up with a plan. We can do it over the phone, or we can sit down in person. Your choice."

There was a silence on Min's side of the conversation, which was finally broken by Min saying, "Aaron, I did not mean to be . . . cute. You are of course right. We have been friends for too long not to discuss openly any questions or problems we may have. Are you and Karen free for dinner tonight?"

It was now Aaron's turn to be quiet. He had hoped to spend some time with Karen. He sighed inwardly. "We were planning on having dinner at my club, but this meeting is a priority. How about joining us around seven o'clock?"

"I thought we might want it a little more private than that."

"I'll request a private table in the corner," Aaron promised.

"I will be bringing Tuloc. Will you have anyone else besides Karen?"

"Maybe one other person, but I haven't asked him yet so I can't be sure."

"Do I know the other person?" Min asked.

"I think so," replied Aaron, "but you'll have to wait for dinner for his name."

"What was it you said about being cute?" Min asked

Aaron laughed. "But I am. You can ask Tuloc what that means. See you tonight."

Aaron's phone rang as soon as he hung up. Wearily, he picked up the receiver.

"Aaron, this is Emily."

In all the years that Emily had worked for Besafe, both as a secretary and as the Human Resources director, she never just said hello. It was almost like she was afraid he would forget who she was.

"Hi, Em," he replied. "How can I help you?"

"I have two men from Interstate Security sitting in my office demanding that I give them Carl Rojas's home address."

"What?"

"I have two men from . . ."

"I heard you. Where are you?" Aaron was already standing.

"I asked Ann to sit at my desk and I'm using the phone at the switchboard."

"I'm on my way down. Call Scott and Tom and tell them I may need some backup."

Karen walked in as he strode across the room. "Ready for some lunch?" she asked, and then looked at him more closely.

"Maybe in a couple of minutes. I have a little problem that needs fixing first."

"Anything I can help with?" Karen asked as she looked at his eyes, which had gone steel gray.

"I don't think so. It's just down the hall."

"Mind if I join you?" she asked, already following him out the door.

"I don't mind. Just make sure you stand out of the way."

In the hall, Karen saw Tom and Scott walking ahead of them. Tom was sticking a pistol in his jacket.

"Aaron!" she exclaimed. When he didn't answer, she called his name again. "Aaron!"

Aaron turned and without breaking stride said, "I told you to stay out of the way!"

"Be careful," she whispered.

Aaron swallowed. With a cocky grin, he headed towards Emily's office with Tom and Scott. "Aren't I always?" he winked.

Chapter 13

"Can we help you?" Tom asked as he and Scott entered Emily's office and looked at the two men lounging casually in two armchairs. One of them must have weighed over two hundred and fifty pounds. He was in a suit that looked like he had slept in it. The other man was smaller. He had the look of a scrounger, someone that you would find in alleys looking through garbage cans.

"Only if you have the authority to give us Carl Rojas's address," the scrounger replied.

"And you are?" Scott asked pleasantly.

"We work for Interstate Security. Your Mr. Rojas could be a material witness in a robbery that took place two nights ago and we're trying to contact his family to advise them of his rights."

"Which are?" Scott continued.

"What do you mean which are?" the larger of the two men asked.

"You said you wanted to tell his family his rights. Explain them to me and I'll see that they get passed on." Scott again did the speaking for the group.

The two men looked at each other and a smile appeared on the face of the smaller man.

He stood and looked at Scott. "Listen, pal. We're here to get information, not give out information. If you got the juice, just tell the lady to give out the address and we'll be on our way"

At this point, Aaron, who had been standing back by the door, entered the conversation. "And your name is?"

"What's the difference what my name is? Let's just say its enough that I work for Interstate, and if you don't give us the address, you may be in violation of the law, which forbids the withholding of pertinent information from an investigating person."

"And the person that's investigating is?" Aaron now started to smile.

"Are you deaf or something? What do you need my name for?"

"When you get thrown out on your ass, I would like the correct spelling for our daily log."

"Who's going to do the throwing?" asked the bigger man as he hooked his thumbs into his belt.

Both Tom and Scott took their pistols out of their pockets.

"We are," they said in unison.

Aaron walked over to the two men and removed pistols from their pockets.

"Let me give you some advice. If you ever walk in here with weapons again, you'll find yourself in jail faster than you can say Interstate."

"I don't know who you guys are, but our boss will double your salaries to come to work for Interstate."

"And your boss is?" asked Aaron.

"Our immediate boss is Paul Kiesler."

Aaron turned towards Emily. "Please get Paul Kiesler on the phone please."

Emily picked up the business card she had on her desk and started dialing.

"Hold it!" the scrounger shouted.

Emily stopped.

"Paul's not in. He's on vacation. He'll be back in about a week or so."

"Who gave you your instructions?"

"I don't know."

"You don't know? Emily, call the police. I've had enough of these two clowns."

They both looked at Aaron.

The smaller of the two held up his hand. "Hold on a second. We didn't do anything wrong. We're just here to get some information, not to start a ruckus. You don't have to call the cops."

"Who's going to call the police?"

Everyone turned as Lieutenant Sizemore walked into the office. He looked at Tom and Scott with the guns in their hands, and then looked at Aaron.

"Captain Sands suggested I stop by. Are these two men the reason?"

"No," said Aaron. "We wouldn't bother Captain Sands with such an inconsequential matter. He must have something else in mind."

"Who are these two?" inquired the Lieutenant.

Both men from Interstate became very nervous.

"They never got around to telling us their names. They say they're from Interstate Security and need to find Carl Rojas's address to explain his rights to his family."

Sizemore looked at Aaron, and then at the two men.

"What do you think his rights are?" Sizemore asked.

The two men were beginning to squirm in their seats. The larger of the two started to rise.

"No one said you could stand," barked Scott as he motioned for the man to sit back down.

"You have no right to hold us here," he responded as he sat back down.

"Just to make sure we understand each other, my name is Lieutenant Sizemore of the Ventura County Police. When I ask you a question, I expect an answer." When he was sure they understood, he continued, "What rights were you going to explain to Mr. Rojas's family?"

"We were instructed to tell them that he had to divulge any information in regard to a robbery the other night."

"Or?" Sizemore asked.

"Or, I don't know," replied the smaller man.

Sizemore turned back to Aaron. "You were right not to bother the captain with these two idiots. He would probably still be laughing." Turning back to the two men, he said, "Empty your pockets, produce some identification, and when we confirm who you are, get the hell out of here."

Aaron, with a smile on his face, said, "Let our men finish this up. Come on inside and join us for a cup of coffee."

Over coffee, Aaron found out more about Cassius Sizemore.

"The man I've called my father for almost as long as I can remember was among the first troops stationed in Vietnam. He met and fell in love with my mother. As I heard the story, she cut a deal with him." His face had a smile that covered his discomfort. "She would live with him, and marry him if he wanted, but he had to promise to bring me to the states. During their second year together, thirty days before he was scheduled to come home, some infiltrators killed her. He brought me up as if I was his own. I couldn't have asked for or wanted a better dad. He took an early retirement from Hughes Aerospace and is living in Hawaii. He calls every weekend. He wants to become a father-in-law. He says no man is complete without a woman."

"Do you have a girlfriend?" Asked Aaron.

"Is your wife a matchmaker also?"

Aaron laughed. "Who else's wife is a matchmaker?"

"When I met Michael Harran, he said his wife was a matchmaker."

"Sorry, I didn't want to mislead you, but I'm not married . . . yet."

"Does that mean you're getting close?" Sizemore asked.

Aaron didn't answer. He just sat there staring at the door. He rose and said, "Very close. Stay where you are. I'll be right back."

Aaron walked out of the conference room, leaving Lieutenant Sizemore with Scott and Tom. As he walked to Tom's office, he saw Michael enter and stopped.

"How's everything at the hospital?" Aaron asked.

"Under control. I hear you had a visit from Interstate here at the office."

"Yeah, we did. Sizemore is in the conference room with Tom and Scott. Why don't you join them? I'll be right in."

Aaron walked into Tom's office.

Karen looked up from the computer she was working on. "Hi," she said.

"Hi yourself." After a slight hesitation, he continued, "I need a favor."

"Sure, what do you need?" She put down her pencil and leaned back.

"Why don't you wait to hear the question before you say yes?"

Karen had a puzzled look on her face. "Okay, what's the favor?"

"Will you marry me?"

"Will I marry you?"

"Is that a yes?" Aaron asked. When Karen didn't answer, he continued. "I have people waiting for me in the conference room."

Chapter 14

Aaron strode back into the conference room. As soon as he entered, his friends knew there was something wrong.

"Aaron, everything all right? asked Scott.

"Sure. It's just sometimes I'm as dumb as rocks," Aaron muttered.

"Anything we can help you with? questioned Tom.

"No, I don't think so. Let's finish this up." Aaron looked back into the hall. "Where were at?" he asked the group sitting around the table.

His two friends looked at each other.

Finally, Tom spoke. "You wanted to have a meeting with Michael."

Aaron nodded his head. He spoke softly, "Lieutenant Sizemore, would you like to come to breakfast tomorrow morning? Captain Sands and his wife will be there, and maybe some other people."

Lieutenant Sizemore could feel the tension in the room. "What time?" he asked.

"About nine thirty. Here's my address." Aaron scribbled on the back of a business card.

"I'll see you then." Sizemore rose from the table and walked out the door without anyone else saying a word.

"Scott, why don't you outline our plans for Michael?" Aaron said as he walked over and looked out the window.

Scott started and Tom filled in some of the details. As they talked, they continued to glance at Aaron. The meeting didn't take long. Michael was thrilled with the promotion, but he also seemed to wonder what was bothering Aaron.

As they went through the details, there were three knocks on the door and Karen entered. She glanced around the table and then at Aaron standing by the window.

"Am I interrupting?" she asked, approaching the table.

"No, come on in." Scott looked from Karen to Aaron.

"Something wrong?" asked Tom, walking to the door and looking out into the hall, expecting to see something that would explain his friend's behavior

"Your friend didn't tell you?" Karen's voice rose as she gestured toward Aaron.

"Tell us what?" Scott asked.

"He asked me to marry him!"

"He asked you to marry him?" Scott shot a glance at Aaron. "What did you say?"

Aaron finally turned around. "She just stared at me. She said nothing."

Scott and Tom started laughing. Michael was too confused to do anything but stare.

Karen turned red. "Why are you two laughing?"

"It's a long story," said Tom, remembering when Aaron proposed to Marcia.

"Or maybe not so long," added Scott. "But it's definitely something Aaron would do. Let me call my wife and we'll all go out for dinner and explain." He looked at Tom who nodded his head in agreement.

"Hold on guys. I just told Min to meet Karen and me at the club for dinner."

"How about tomorrow morning at your place?" Tom suggested. "You've already got Sizemore, Barry, and Michael coming for breakfast. Just add us and our wives."

"Ask Min and Tuloc also," added Scott. "They're part of the family. We'll have a celebration."

"Doesn't anyone want to hear my answer first?" Karen waved her arms at the group.

"Not until tomorrow," replied Scott. "Right after we tell you why we were laughing."

"You can tell me," Aaron said as he walked toward her.

Karen looked around the room and started smiling. She shook her head slowly and put her hand against his chest, "I don't think so. I would like to know what is so funny before I give you my answer."

Aaron turned toward his friends. "What is so funny?" Everyone started laughing again.

Chapter 15

"I still don't know why you won't give me your answer," Aaron said for the tenth time as he maneuvered the car up the driveway of the country club.

"Obviously, there is a very funny story attached to your proposal, and I'd like to hear it."

"But I don't know what it is, and what difference would it make?"

Karen turned serious. "Aaron, you know that I enjoy being with you. You must know that I love you. What I don't understand is this sudden urge to make an honest woman out of me. If it's because of something someone said, or out of some misguided sense of, of a man thing, we don't have to get married."

Aaron sighed. "We can discuss it later. Now let's concentrate on tonight. A couple of things have been bothering me."

"Aside from my not giving you an answer?"

"Yes. Aside from your not giving me an answer." Aaron parked, turned off the car, and sat in the dark with his window partially open. "How did Min know you were on your way up to see me on Friday morning? What's his interest in All Alarm and Interstate? And what's Interstate's possible involvement in what's going on? Finally, what is the deal with Mrs. Burnett and Providence?"

"I can understand your interest in Interstate and this guy Denis Canon, but why Mrs. Burnett and Providence?"

Before Aaron could answer, he was startled by a knock on his window. He turned to see a smiling face he had never seen before.

"Mr. Carlyle, let me introduce myself. My name is Denis Canon."

With an alarm going off in his head, Aaron tried to open the door, but with the president of Interstate Security leaning against it, found it impossible.

"No need to get out," Denis Canon said. "I can tell you what I need from here. I want access to Carl Rojas. I want your friend Min to stay out of my business, and stay the hell away from Mrs. Burnett. I am going to hold you responsible if I don't get what I want." When Aaron didn't respond, he continued, "Your lady friend lives a long way from here and she could have an accident going back and forth. You need a friend that could help her out if one occurred. Do you understand me?"

Aaron noticed a second man approaching Karen's side of the car.

"I understand that if you don't back away from my car, I will put a bullet through your head."

"Mr. Carlyle. Such anger. I was told you were a reasonable person. I haven't asked for anything unreasonable. I need access to Carl Rojas to help with my company's investigation. Your friend Min is just a pain in the ass getting involved in things he would be better off ignoring and . . ." Before he could finish, the man on Karen's side of the car let out a gasp and fell to the floor. Canon turned and came face to face with Tuloc, who was holding a pistol pointed at his nose.

"Who the hell are you?" he shouted.

"Let's just say I am a friend of Mr. Carlyle. Back away from the door or I will take great pleasure in putting a bullet in your head," Tuloc warned.

Canon was scared. Aaron shoved on the door, which now swung open as the president of Interstate Security backed away.

"Stay put," Aaron said to Karen as he left the car. When he stood eye to eye with Canon, he continued, "You were telling me about Ms. Williams needing a friend."

"I don't think you understand," Canon backpedaled. "I'm trying to catch a thief and a killer. I need help."

Aaron's eyes had turned cold. He stood at least three inches taller than Canon and outweighed him by ten or fifteen pounds.

"I don't think you understand. If you ever send any of your men to . . ." Aaron hesitated a second, "help Miss Williams, I will personally make sure that your insurance company goes bankrupt trying to pay your doctor and hospital charges. Now let me go over some other things that I think you have to understand."

Before he could say anything else, a police car came into the parking lot, stopping with its headlights pointing directly at Aaron and Dennis Canon.

"Is there a problem?" asked one of the policemen in the car.

"No," replied Aaron. "I was just explaining to Mr. Canon some of the club rules."

"What happened to that guy on the floor?" The cop continued shining his flashlight on the man on the ground.

"He tripped," replied Tuloc.

"Why don't you help him up?" the officer asked.

"That was part of the rules I was explaining to Mr. Canon as you drove up," Aaron answered.

"Do you people have identification?" the policeman asked as he got out of the car. "I don't need yours, Mr. Carlyle."

"I do," said Canon as he walked away from Aaron.

Tuloc reached into his pocket and withdrew his wallet.

The policeman looked at each of the wallets he was given, handed them back, and said, "Why don't you finish this some other time?"

Aaron nodded and Canon said, "With pleasure." He walked into the darkness.

"What about this guy?" the cop called after Canon.

"When he wakes up, he'll find his way home," Canon yelled back as he disappeared from view.

"Your friend is a really nice guy," the officer said to Aaron sarcastically.

"Really nice," Aaron muttered.

Chapter 16

"Tuloc, I get the distinct impression that you are looking over me like a guardian angel." Aaron raised his glass in Tuloc's direction.

"There is no need to watch over you, but I do seem to be in the right place at the right time," Tuloc answered with a smile on his face.

Aaron surveyed the rest of the table, with a feeling that everything was as it should be now that friends surrounded him. Directly to Tuloc's right sat Min with Mai Ling on his right. Karen sat between Mai Ling and Aaron with Michael's wife on his right and Michael next to Soo Kim. After the obligatory hellos, the conversation shifted quickly to Denis Canon and his antics. Aaron got the impression that Tuloc and Min were holding back information, but couldn't figure out why until halfway through dinner.

Min asked, "Does Mr. Harran have a different status inside Besafe than he did last week?"

"I'm glad you brought that up," Aaron replied. "Michael is now a vice president of Besafe. He is, in fact, running our new operation, Besafe Detective Agency. The first person on his payroll, aside from himself, is going to be Mai Ling."

Aaron watched as Tuloc's eyes went briefly to Mai Ling and then back to the people around the table. The boy still had a lot to learn. Min never would have done that.

"I am sure you won't have a problem with that, Mai Ling,"

Aaron continued. "Michael is one of our best men and richly deserves the promotion. When Karen suggested you as his administrative assistant, everyone was in agreement."

Min leaned over and whispered, "When I suggested Mai Ling's coming to work for Besafe, I did not expect it to be in this type of capacity."

"Is there a problem with Mai Ling working for me?" Michael asked.

"I have no problem with you. In fact, I very much believe that you are the right person for this task. However, I think there may be danger, and this is why I hesitate."

"In what way is there danger?" Aaron asked.

Min looked around the room before he explained. "When you start this new enterprise you will find Denis Canon a formidable foe. Some of the things he or his company have done border very closely on illegal."

"Such as?" Michael prodded.

"He started with a security service much like Besafe, but he quickly branched off into other ventures. He is somehow attached to a small gambling casino just across the border in Nevada, and his company owns a gym where the members are not like people that go to gyms in your neighborhood."

"His company is openly traded on the NASDAQ," Karen interjected.

"That is true. They are also into manufacturing, but every plant they have bought was purchased at distressed prices. The plants are broken into and parts are stolen, which causes the companies great hardship."

"Doesn't insurance cover the losses?" Aaron asked.

Min nodded at Tuloc who continued, "In most cases, the company gets paid from the insurance company, but only for the loss of components, not for the loss of time. His company has approached us with an offer to buy us out. When we turned them down, some of our men were hurt in unrelated accidents. Others were offered jobs at considerably higher wages than we were paying, and some of our customers have cancelled. We do not have problems at companies that you service, but at companies serviced by Interstate there are all types of little things that go wrong. The people at All Alarm were made an offer three weeks ago. When they said no, the vice president's car was run off the road. The president's two children disappeared for about four hours one afternoon. When they were found, they told the police three men took them to a movie. We have doubled the security on our people, but unless we find out what Interstate is really after, we are in trouble."

"And what is it that bothers you about Mai Ling working for Michael?" Aaron asked, looking directly at Min.

"I thought she would work inside your security company. This detective agency, if it is headed where I think, could put her in the line of fire. There is already no love lost between Interstate and us and after tonight, it will be worse."

"Old friend, you must know I will not allow this man or his company to hurt or even threaten any of us. Besafe has many assets of its own that are already in place, and we are prepared to add to them if necessary."

The table went quiet, each person thinking what this meant to them personally. Karen broke the mood. "Before I forget, you are all invited to Aaron's tomorrow morning at nine thirty. We're having a party."

"What is the party for?" Sookie asked.

Karen looked at Aaron. "Would you like to tell them?"

"It's just a get together." When no one said a word, Aaron continued, "I asked Karen to marry me, and she won't answer until she finds out why Tom and Scott think it's so funny."

Sookie started to let out a giggle, but her upbringing made her cover her mouth with both hands. Both Mai Ling and Michael's wife turned to look at Karen with big smiles on their faces.

"Who will be there tomorrow?" Min asked.

"Hopefully all of you—Tom, Scott, their families, Barry, and Lieutenant Sizemore."

"Who is Lieutenant Sizemore?" Tuloc asked.

"He's in charge of the investigation into the robbery at Active Components. His full name is Cassius Sizemore, and I am cultivating him for the future," Michael responded.

"If he is as good as you are, we will be lucky," Min commented. Turning toward Karen, Min continued, “Can we have advance information on your answer?”

Michael realized from Min’s response that he thought Sizemore was black. He decided not to say anything and let it be a surprise.

“I don’t think so. I’ve told Aaron in the past that marriage wasn’t the most important thing in my life, but saying that, I think he certainly is cute and I think it could be fun.” She hesitated before continuing, “I’ll wait until tomorrow.”

Before anyone else could comment, an Asian man entered and whispered in Min’s ear. Min stood, a scowl appearing on his face.

“We must be going. There has been a break-in at Providence. One of our men was hurt.”

“Badly?” asked Michael.

“I am not sure. We will see you tomorrow at nine thirty. I can’t wait to hear your answer.” Min turned and quickly left the dining room.

“Michael, you have your work cut out for you. See you both tomorrow.” Aaron rose and holding Karen’s arm, said to her, “We have some things to discuss.”

Chapter 17

"We'll have to get up early and get some food. How many people do you think are coming?" Karen asked as she put on her seat belt.

"You know this is ridiculous. Why can't you give me your answer tonight?"

"And spoil everyone's fun?"

"Karen, I probably did this wrong, but I love you. We've been together for over two years, and I want to spend the rest of my life with you. Please say yes."

Karen sat there for a few seconds and then asked, "Can I borrow your phone? I want to see if my mother is home."

Aaron handed her the phone as he started the car.

"Mom, it's Karen. I'm glad you're home. Yes I'm fine, and Aaron is fine. The reason I called is that Aaron has asked me to marry him." Karen held the phone away from her ear.

"I hope you said yes!" her mother yelled.

"Mom, yelling won't help me hear you any better, and no, I didn't say yes."

"What's the matter with you?" Her mother's voice rose another notch. "You're a perfect couple, and you know he loves you."

"I wanted to make sure it was okay with you," Karen said simply into the phone. Her mother went silent.

"Mom, are you there?"

"Yes I'm here, and yes it's okay with me."

They could both hear her mother crying. Aaron took back the phone.

"Mrs. Williams, we're having a party tomorrow morning at my house. We'd love to have you join us."

"What time?"

"Nine thirty."

"I'll be there. Tell me the truth. Has she said yes yet?"

"No, not yet, but I think she's close."

"Good night, Aaron, and thank you. You've made me very happy." With that, she broke the connection.

"Well, does that mean yes?" Aaron looked at Karen.

With tears rolling down her face Karen said, "Of course it means yes. I love you, you big goof."

The words were no sooner out of her mouth when the windshield exploded. Aaron saw two men with automatic rifles standing about twenty yards away. He jammed his foot down on the gas pedal, which aimed the lunging car directly at the men. They continued to shoot at Aaron's car, but now their shots were going high as they ran out of the way. One of them must have hit a tire because Aaron felt the car pull to the left, putting Karen directly in line with the guns. With all his strength, Aaron jerked the car. The front bumper slammed into one of the men before it smashed into a parked car. The air bags ignited, blocking Aaron's view, also giving him cover from the man with the gun. Aaron grabbed his pistol from under the front seat and rolled out into the parking lot. The only thing he could see was a car speeding towards the exit, which was gone before he had a chance to open fire. He turned back to the car and ran around to Karen's side. He opened the door and found her lying against the opened air bag, bleeding from her head and chest.

"Karen! Karen! Talk to me."

"It hurts . . . please." She gasped for air, not being able to move, pinned by the seat belt and air bag.

A crowd had begun to assemble and one of the men came forward.

"I'm a doctor. The police and ambulance are on the way. Let me get close to her."

Aaron stepped aside for the doctor as a woman pushed through the crowd.

"Cary, I've got your bag. Please let me through!" she yelled at the people. "I'm his wife."

Aaron's mouth was dry. Blood was running down the right side of his face. One of the women in the crowd whispered to the people standing next to her, "Look at his eyes."

Another women hearing her said, "They're a funny color of gray. I wonder if he's okay?"

The people started to move back as the first police cars arrived. The first officers to arrive were the ones Aaron had met earlier.

"Mr. Carlyle, what happened?"

"Where the hell is the ambulance?" Aaron shouted.

"It's less than a minute away. Are you okay?"

"I'm fine. It's my fiancée who's been shot. Contact Captain Sands and Lieutenant Sizemore. Tell them what's happened and we're headed to . . . Doctor, where are we headed?"

"The Regional Medical Center. I'm calling for a full team to be ready. She's in bad shape."

Aaron gritted his teeth. "Does anyone have a cell phone?"

One of the people came forward and handed Aaron their phone.

Aaron dialed and after two rings, the phone was answered by Constance, Scott's wife.

"Constance, it's Aaron. Tell Scott . . ." He tried to calm himself, not wanting to yell at one of his closest friend's wife. Finally he continued, "Constance, there's been an accident. Please let me talk to Scott."

He heard her shout, "Scott, pick up the phone. Aaron's had an accident!"

"Aaron, what's wrong?"

"Karen's been shot! It wasn't a robbery attempt. I think they were after me." He took a deep breath and continued, "If they were, you and Tom might be on the list. I'll fill you in later, but you better get word to Min. Dennis Canon stopped by tonight and made some innocuous threats against Min and us, and he got roughed up by Tuloc." He looked behind him and saw them loading Karen into the ambulance. "I've got to go. I'll keep in touch."

Chapter 18

Scott looked at his watch. It was eight thirty on Sunday morning. He couldn't remember a night as long as the one he had just endured. After Aaron's call, he and Tom had mobilized every Besafe security person they could find. Michael Harran was placed in charge of security for their families and Lieutenant Sizemore had augmented their men with four of his own to watch over Karen at the hospital. Michael would only allow them to stand guard around the perimeter. He had placed his most trusted people up close.

They had started off with everyone working out of the office, but had gravitated to Aaron's home when they couldn't find Karen's mother. Aaron had called her from the hospital to tell her what had happened. When the phone went unanswered, he dispatched one of the local Besafe cars to her home. They had also decided that if whoever was responsible for the shooting had anything to say, they would probably call Aaron's home.

Tom walked in eating a banana. "I just heard from Aaron. Karen's been moved into intensive care. The doctors said that the bullets missed her vital organs, but she's still listed as critical. It'll probably take another day or so to really find out how she's doing."

"What's Aaron doing?" asked Scott.

"He's on his way home. Min called and told him he still expects to be here by nine thirty. His man died in the robbery."

"Who died?" They both turned as Barry entered the room.

"That's some security you guys have. I could have shot both of you," he continued before they answered.

"Not likely, Captain. We had you under surveillance the minute your car started up the hill."

Michael Harran appeared behind Captain Sands. Before anyone could speak, Michael held up his hand and pulled his cell phone from his belt clip. "This is Michael."

"We have a single woman starting up the hill in a new blue Chrysler. Her plates do not match any on our list."

"I'll watch her. If I need any help, I'll call. Stay alert!"

The four men walked to the living room window and looked out through the blinds. The blue Chrysler pulled into Aaron's driveway.

"Oh shit!" exclaimed Scott as they watched Karen's mother get out of the car.

"She doesn't know?" Barry asked.

"No. We've had men stationed at her house, but no one knew where to find her. Some of us were getting concerned."

"Who gets to give her the news?" Michael asked the group of men looking out the window.

"I'll do it," Tom said as he walked toward the front door and waited. He stood behind it until he heard the bell ring. Upon opening the door, he smiled and said, "Hi, Dorothy. I thought you were going to arrive about nine thirty."

Dorothy Williams entered the room and looked around. "Where is everyone?" "Don't tell me she said no and everyone went home!"

"Where have you been? Aaron has been trying to reach you. We sent one of our cars to your home and they said you weren't there."

"When I heard from Karen last night, I was so excited that I packed my clothes and came on up. I stayed at the . . ." She stopped and again looked around the room. "Where are Aaron and Karen, and why was he trying to reach me?"

"There was an accident last night. Karen's in the hospital."

"In the hospital? Oh my God." She spun around and ran toward the door. "Where is she?"

Tom took her gently by the shoulder and guided her to the closest chair. "Dorothy, wait. Aaron's on his way home. You need to stay here."

She closed her eyes for a few seconds and then looked up at Tom. “What happened?”

“When Aaron and Karen left the club last night, we think there was an attempted robbery. Something went wrong and the robbers opened fire. Aaron drove the car into one of them, but they both got away. Karen is in intensive care and the latest prognosis is that she will be fine. The last time I was in contact with the hospital was fifteen minutes ago. Aaron is headed home and we have a team of people standing by to assist in any way they can. I wish I could tell you more, but that’s all I know. After you talk with Aaron, I’ll have one of our men drive you over.” Tom delivered the message in rapid fire, not letting Dorothy get a word in.

“Can I have something to drink?”

“Of course. What would you like?”

“Get me a scotch, and then sit down and tell me the story again.” She looked at her watch. “How long before Aaron gets here?” As Tom started to answer, she held up her hand. “The scotch first.”

Scott, followed by Barry and Michael, walked in with the drink.

“Good morning, Mrs. Williams. We were sitting in the other room. I think you know Barry. Let me introduce you to Michael Harran. Michael is in charge of our new investigative division, as well as the security of our people.”

She took the glass and emptied half of it in one swallow. “Why do your people need security?”

Michael again held up his hand. “I’m vibrating.” He took the phone out of his pocket and said, “Michael here!”

“Mr. Carlyle is on his way up the street.”

“Thanks!”

Two minutes later, Aaron walked into the house. Looking around, he walked straight over to Dorothy. “Dorothy, I’m glad you’re here. I was starting to worry.”

“Why were you worried about me?” She glanced at Michael. “Don’t tell me I need protection, too.”

Aaron answered, “The story for public consumption is that it was an attempted robbery. Internally, we have reason to believe that

I was the target, and we're doing everything we can to make sure that no one else gets hurt."

"Has anyone else besides Karen, and I guess by the looks of you, gotten hurt?"

"We're not sure." Aaron held his palms face up. "One of Min's people was killed yesterday during a robbery. We don't know if they're connected."

"And Karen told me the reason she came up a day early was because one of your people was killed and another hurt on Wednesday." She paused. "Now tell me about my daughter and how you're going to ensure she doesn't get hurt again."

"Dorothy, Karen is in intensive care. We have four men guarding her, and so does Captain Sands.

As Dorothy let this sink in, the phone rang. Aaron pushed the speaker. "This is Aaron."

"Aaron, this is Dennis Canon. I know we didn't get off to a good start, but I just heard about the robbery attempt last night. Maybe I can redeem myself."

Everyone in the room froze. It was like they were all holding their breath.

"How would you do that?" Aaron replied.

"One of my cars found a man they thought was the victim of a hit and run. They reported it to the police, but after thinking it over, I had a feeling it might be the person involved in the robbery attempt."

"What made you think that?"

"The police said that he was devoid of anything that could identify him. Maybe he's not the one you're looking for, but it was just a thought."

"What police station did you call it into?"

"Actually, it was the Highway Patrol in Malibu."

Aaron took a deep breath before he answered. "Thanks for the information. I'll get back to you."

"Aaron, I told you that we could be friends. I have a pretty large force of men at my disposal. If there's something I can do to help, just give me a call."

"You will definitely be hearing from me."

Pushing the disconnect button, Aaron turned to Barry and asked, “Will you have any problem checking this out?”

“None at all. I’ll use the extension in the kitchen.”

“What do you think?” asked Scott.

“I think I’m going to make life miserable for that son of a bitch.”

Chapter 19

Min sat in front of Aaron's forty-eight-inch television, watching a documentary on the leopards of Africa. He hadn't said much to anyone since his arrival two hours prior. Everyone passing him could tell that while his eyes were firmly fixed in the direction of the television, he missed nothing going on around him. Mai Ling had left with Michael Harran to fill out paperwork for her new position with Besafe, and while Min knew and liked Captain Sands, he did not feel comfortable talking to him. Scott and Tom were constantly on the phone and Aaron had taken Karen's mother to the hospital, staying to hear the doctor's latest report on Karen's condition. He and Min had spent less than twenty minutes together discussing the events of the night before, and Min had promised to remain until Aaron's return.

Min's eyes moved as he heard Scott tell Captain Sands that Aaron was on his way home with Lieutenant Sizemore. He wished that Mai Ling would return quickly. He did not know this Cassius Sizemore and didn't want to discuss some of the things that needed doing in front of a stranger. It was bad enough that Aaron included Captain Sands in their important conversations, but now there would be another stranger, with the name of Cassius, for him to deal with. He heard the strange ringing of a phone that was not being answered and watched as Tom walked across the room in his direction.

"Min! Your phone is ringing." Tom smiled as he spoke.

Reaching into his pocket, Min pulled the phone out and looked at the instrument. "I always have a problem knowing that it's mine." He held it to his ear and said, "This is Min."

"Grandfather, it is me." He smiled upon recognizing Mai Ling's voice.

"When are you returning?" he asked.

"We are on our way now. Do I detect something in your voice that tells me that you missed me?"

"I hardly knew you were gone, except there is no one here to bring me hot tea." He listened closely; there was no sound on the other end. "Mai Ling!" he shouted impatiently.

"I am here, Grandfather, and I will be there in less than ten minutes."

He heard the dial tone and closed the phone just as Aaron walked in. His eyes grew wider as he watched the man behind Aaron enter the room and walk over to Captain Sands. This man was not black, but Asian. He reached out to Tom, who was still standing beside him.

"Who is that man?" he asked Tom, pointing a finger at the man who had entered with Aaron.

"That's Lieutenant Sizemore."

"I was told his name was Cassius Sizemore. He doesn't look like a Cassius."

Tom smiled. "What does a Cassius look like?"

Before Min could answer, Michael Harran walked in with Mai Ling. Min watched as Aaron introduced Mai Ling and felt a tear start to form as she smiled and shook his hand.

"They make a very good looking couple, don't they?" Tom asked.

Min turned and asked, "Is he married?"

"I understand that his mother made a deal with a soldier that she would live with him if he would take them back to the United States when the war was over. However, Cassius's mother died and the soldier kept his promise. He adopted Cassius and brought him back to the states. Cassius went through college and doesn't have a girlfriend."

"I wonder why he doesn't have one?" Min asked.

"Michael Harran is trying to fix him up. Maybe by this time next month, he will. Michael's wife is pretty good at that."

Min stood there shaking his head. "I would like to meet this young man. He has the look of an interesting person."

I bet he does, Tom thought. *And standing next to Mai Ling, they have the look of an interesting couple.*

Min walked over to Aaron. "How is Karen?" he asked, pointedly ignoring Mai Ling and Cassius Sizemore.

"Karen regained conscious for a short time. She didn't say anything, but the doctor says that it's a good sign." Aaron continued, "Min, I would like you to meet Lieutenant Cassius Sizemore. He's in charge of investigating the shooting and break-in at Active Components."

"You are the one they refer to as Cassius?" Min asked politely.

"That's me," Sizemore said as he held out his hand.

Min turned without shaking his hand and said to Mai Ling, "I am glad you have returned. I would like a cup of tea."

Mai Ling's eyes had fire coming out of them. Her grandfather had just insulted the police officer that she needed to make friends with in her new position. "Lieutenant Sizemore, maybe you would like a cup of tea or something else to drink."

"A cup of tea would be fine, but I have another request."

"Which is?" She replied.

"How about calling me Cassius?"

She smiled and held out her hand. "How about showing me the kitchen. I don't know my way around this big house."

They walked down the hallway toward the kitchen. Aaron turned to Min and said, "She must have forgotten she was here a couple of days ago."

"Youngsters have a way of forgetting things," Min replied as he stared at their backs as they walked down the hall.

"You once told me that your people had written the original Romeo and Juliet. I think maybe that time you told me the truth." Aaron smiled for the first time in two days.

Chapter 20

"We've got our first break," Michael reported to Aaron regarding the progress of his men. "I had two men join the Sunrise Gym. They reported back that all employees wear yellow shirts with their name stitched on the front. They haven't found one named Paul yet, but it has only been two days." Michael listened to Aaron and then continued, "I'm having Mai Ling fill out the forms. There's a forty-eight-hour waiting period for her permit, and I'm expecting her to have her license by Wednesday or Thursday at the latest."

"Michael, bear with me," Aaron asked quietly. "When we're finished with this, you will be running the detective agency portion of Besafe and I'll be leaving you alone. This thing with Karen and Dennis Canon has me by the shorts. My gut tells me what the answer is, but I can't for the life of me figure out the why and the how."

"Run your thoughts by me. Maybe they'll help point me in the right direction." Michael picked up a pencil and waited for Aaron to respond.

"First, Active Components gets broken into. Two of our men get shot, one fatally. Secondly, it turns out that some of the parts that were stolen were specials for a company called Providence. Not having those parts might cause Providence to go out of business. When Min decides to personally get involved and help the owner, another building that he services is broken into and one of his men is killed. While all of this is going on, Dennis Canon, the president of Interstate, comes calling and tells me to tell Min to stay out of his affairs. It also turns out that the man who shot Carl Rojas was wearing an instructors shirt from Sunrise Gym, which Interstate also owns."

Michael looked again at his notes. "You know, Boss, there is a thread that runs through this maze."

"Which is?"

"Interstate. One of the things we know is that they've been buying out companies in the high tech arena that have fallen on hard times because of losses caused by . . . I'm not sure why."

Aaron didn't answer immediately. "Let's suppose," he started, "Interstate is causing the losses, and then buying the firms as they get close to going out of business." He paused. "No, that wouldn't work. They would need people to run the companies."

"Unless," Michael continued the thought process, "they kept the original management in place and just added the companies to their public company to raise the price of their stock."

"I wish I had Karen to talk to. She could probably figure this out in a second."

"How is she doing?"

"She rested comfortably through the night. She hasn't regained consciousness yet, but the doctor thinks it could be soon."

There was a silence that both men understood, broken by Michael. "Boss, I have to go. I might be able to put some wheels in motion that will give us some answers. I'll keep in touch."

Michael picked up the phone and dialed Mai Ling. She had given him her grandfather's number. She expected to get her own apartment closer to the Besafe office later in the week. Someone that almost sounded like Mai Ling answered the phone.

"Who is calling Min?" the voice asked.

"My name is Michael Harran. I am looking for Mai Ling."

"Please do not hang up. I will see if she is available."

After a brief delay, Mai Ling answered. "Michael, how may I help you?"

"I wondered if your grandfather has a phone number for Mrs. Burnett. She's the woman that owns Providence."

"I don't have to ask my grandfather. She is here."

"She's there! What's she doing there?"

"My grandfather invited her for dinner." She lowered her voice, "I think he is infatuated by her." Raising her voice to a normal level, she continued. "Is there something I can ask her for you?"

"I was wondering if anyone has made an offer to purchase Providence from her?"

"That is the same question that Cassius asked me to ask her."

"Cassius?"

"You know, Lieutenant Sizemore."

"Don't tell me he's there also."

"No, he's not. I think my grandfather doesn't like him, or maybe he's just being careful. He had a problem with someone from Vietnam a few years ago and he has asked me not to have any dealings with him outside of business until he can investigate his background."

"I have the impression that you'll do what you want, regardless of what your grandfather thinks or says."

"I don't know how you can say that. I will honor my grandfather's wishes. This just happens to be business."

"Did you get an answer?"

"Yes I did. She received an offer last Tuesday afternoon. She said it was insultingly low and she turned it down."

"Did she tell you who made the offer?"

"It was made by a lawyer who wouldn't tell her the name of the buyer. His name was Elliot Bronte, and his office is in Long Beach."

"Have you given this information to Sizemore?"

"No. I hoped to do that tonight."

"I hate to spoil your fun, but don't tell him until I give you the okay."

"Why not?"

"Because I'm your boss and I'm telling you not to."

"I assume there is a reason."

"Yes there is, but for right now, just leave it as I'm the one giving orders and you're the one taking them."

Mai Ling's voice became cool when she spoke. "Are you telling me that I can't talk to him?"

"Quite the contrary. I want you to be friends. I just want to limit the information he has . . . for a little while."

"I'm not sure I'm going to like working for you, but I will do what you asked. Is there anything else you want me to do, or not to do?"

"No, that's it. See you in the morning."

Michael held the phone away from his ear as Mai Ling slammed down the receiver. Just before he hung up on his end, he heard another click. Someone had listened in on his conversation.

Michael ran directly to the front desk. "How many people are in the building right now?" he yelled.

The startled duty officer looked at a piece of paper on his desk and answered, "You, me, and three others."

"Where are they?" Michael asked breathlessly.

"The men from car eleven just walked down to get some coffee, and Annie, my replacement, went to the bathroom."

"There's no one else in the building?"

"Not unless they snuck past me when I was on the phone."

"Get the three of them up here now and then call for any cars in the area. I want this place searched from top to bottom."

The duty officer turned to the switchboard and started broadcasting.

"All cars, ten-twelve, I repeat ten-twelve."

Michael internally translated the duty officer's words. He had asked them to stand by.

"All cars, this is a ten-eighteen. I need the ten-twenty of any car within two miles of Besafe. Repeat, I need the ten-twenty of any car within two miles of Besafe."

Michael couldn't hear their replies because the duty officer had earphones on, but he could tell from his actions that he was receiving calls and directing the closest cars to return to the office. The instructions were simple. Ten-eighteen told the men it was urgent and ten-twenty asked them where they were.

"Four cars were close and will be here within two or three minutes. I'm letting the rest of the cars continue on their rounds."

"As soon as they arrive, we'll start searching the building. Get me Aaron, Tom, and Scott. I'll bring them up to date on what I'm doing."

Mai Ling passed her grandfather's study on her way to rejoin the others. Min was sitting at his desk with a strange smile on his face.

"Grandfather, you are not with your guests. Is anything wrong?"

"No, nothing is wrong. In fact, everything is fine. I just had to make a phone call."

She held out her hand. "Come join the party."

"In a minute. You go ahead."

Mai Ling left the study and thought, He didn't even ask me what Michael wanted. Maybe he is changing.

Min sat at the desk staring at the phone. He smiled as he contemplated. *My plan is working, Michael Harran is helping, and he doesn't even know it.*

Chapter 21

"Mom, what are you doing here?"

Dorothy Williams was sitting in an oversized club chair with her eyes closed. She pictured Karen coming down the steps of the courthouse where she had just gotten married against her father's wishes. Karen was wearing a white dress with blue polka dots, and was carrying a wide brim white hat.

"Is Aaron alright?"

She's forgotten her father's name, Dorothy thought as she fought to open her eyes.

"Mom, wake up!"

As her eyes opened, she felt disorientated. Something was wrong. What was she doing in a hospital room?

"Mom, how long have I been here?"

"Karen? Karen, you're awake! I was dreaming that . . ." She stopped and looked around. "You're awake."

"Mom, how is Aaron? Please talk to me."

Dorothy rose from the chair and went to her daughter's side. As she pressed the nurse's call button, she touched Karen's face with her fingertips. Tears rolled down her face as the nurse answered her call.

"May I help you?"

"Karen's awake. My daughter is talking to me. Please get the doctor."

Dorothy could hear the nurses running down the hall. Their soft-soled shoes did nothing to disguise their haste.

"Please step back," a nurse said as she entered.

Dorothy looked around the room. Three of the Besafe men had entered and were looking over the nurse's shoulder as she felt Karen's wrist and looked at her eyes.

The second nurse entered. "I called the attending. He'll be right here."

The fourth Besafe man entered. "I called Michael. He's contacting Mr. Carlyle. Remember, only authorized people get in here. No strangers of any kind, even if they say they're doctors." The men exited the room to start setting up the screening procedures outside the door.

"Aaron!"

Aaron held the phone away from his ear as he looked at his watch. It was three fifteen in the morning. He'd been in bed almost five hours.

"Aaron, it's Michael. Karen's awake!"

Aaron slid his feet off the bed. "Thank God. What did the doctor say?"

"I haven't heard yet. One of the men on duty called. They are setting up a screening zone outside of the room. I'm on my way to help them. I would expect more than a few people going in and out, and we want to control who they are."

"I'll be there in about twenty minutes. And Michael, thanks for the call."

There was nothing for Michael to say. He hung up the phone.

Aaron pulled into the parking lot and ran to the lobby. Taking the stairs two at a time, he could hear the commotion before he reached the third floor. Michael and his security team were refusing entry to anyone not on their list.

"Problem Michael?"

"No problem, Mr. Carlyle. The doctor is inside with two nurses and Mrs. Williams. When the doctor gives us the okay, we'll let some of these other people in."

Aaron moved in close. "Any of them look like a problem?"

"I don't think so. In most cases, the hospital just never gave us their names. Some of the others are on staff and just want to see what's going on."

"I'll be inside if you need me." Aaron walked into the room touching Michael on the shoulder as he passed.

"At least a couple of days." Aaron heard the doctor say to Karen.

"But I feel fine now!" Karen replied. As she turned to her mother for help, she noticed Aaron standing by the door.

"Aaron, tell them I can go home today."

Karen's mother turned and rushed over to hug Aaron. "She's been stubborn since she was a baby." She smiled, the tears in her eyes shimmering.

Aaron went to the bedside and said, "We're getting married the first weekend you're out of here. I would suggest you get all the rest you can, while you can."

"Subtle, Aaron." Karen grinned, looking around the room.

"I try." Aaron reached over to brush a hair from her face.

"Are you all right?" Karen asked as she reached for his hand. "You look like you were in a fight." She winced in pain.

"Stay still," Aaron said as he grabbed for her hand. "I'm fine. Just a little scratched up from the accident."

Karen took a deep breath and asked, "How bad is it?"

"Now that you're talking, not bad at all. We may have to push the wedding out a few weeks, but that's mostly because the doctor is a pain in the butt."

"I take exception to that, but now that I'm here, how about giving my patient a chance to rest, and give me a chance to look at her up close."

Aaron turned and smiled as the doctor moved closer to the bed.

"I would have been here sooner, but getting into this room is a problem." He leaned over Karen, shined a little penlight into her eye, and continued, "I must insist that everyone leave now. After she gets some sleep, you can see her again."

Aaron leaned over to kiss her good-bye and all of a sudden, felt self-conscious. He squeezed her hand.

Karen looked around the room and mouthed the words, "You are a big goof, and I love you."

Aaron's heart hammered and his throat felt tight. He managed to nod his head before he left.

Chapter 22

"This is a strange place for us to meet." Aaron looked around the empty warehouse. The windows that were near the top of the twenty-four-foot ceilings were dirty, filtering the light from the outside. There was no furniture save for the six folding chairs that formed a semi-circle almost in the exact center of the building. Aaron could tell that his friends, Scott and Tom, were uneasy by the way they kept shifting their positions. Min and Tuloc sat opposite them, but there were six of Min's "nephews" standing by the exits.

"It is a building where we do not fear talking with friends." Min explained as he waved his hand.

"I saw a sign outside that the building is for sale. What's the asking price?" Scott asked.

"The owner is asking almost thirty percent more than it is worth," Tuloc responded.

"Probably won't sell then," Scott answered.

"And we won't be bothered by people wanting to look around." Tuloc smiled as he answered Scott's comment.

"Why are we here?" Aaron looked at Min. "I think we could've made sure that one of our offices was secure."

"Secure from ears, but not from eyes." He nodded to Tuloc who walked to a door that Aaron guessed led to a bathroom. Tuloc opened it up and held it for Mrs. Burnett.

Aaron, Tom, and Scott stood as she approached. Min, after watching the three of them rise, stood and held out his hand.

"Mrs. Burnett has agreed to join us at my request." He led her to the empty chair and waited while she sat down.

Aaron watched as she crossed only her feet and sat with her hands in her lap. Regal was the only word floating through his mind.

"I'm glad to see you again, Mrs. Burnett. How is your business doing?"

"Her business is not well, which is why I have asked you to attend this meeting. With the loss of the components that were being made for her company, she is in danger of going bankrupt. I have had Tuloc go over her books and have decided to become a partner in her company."

"Is this a celebration of some kind?" Aaron asked, looking around the warehouse.

Min nodded at Tuloc who took over the conversation. "Because of the circumstances surrounding the theft, my father-in-law thought you three might wish to participate."

"If it's money he needs," Aaron paused and then continued, "I would of course lend it. I'm not speaking for my friends—just for myself."

"I think you miss the point. My father-in-law doesn't need any money. He is doing this as a sign of respect. The people that made the insultingly low offer for Providence also own Interstate. We have not yet figured out where your friend Mr. Dennis Canon sits within that corporation, but we hope to accomplish that in the very near future."

"What is your plan?" Aaron looked at Min as he asked the question.

"It is my desire to make these people start dealing with someone other than Lan."

Aaron knew immediately that by using her Vietnamese name, Min was declaring a closer relationship than that of a buyer or even of a friend.

"Whom would that person be?" Aaron asked quietly.

"I was hoping it could be Tom. He has the accounting background and the temperament to deal with these people. It would also leave you and I free to do whatever has to be done."

"What about me?" asked Scott.

"It was my thought that you would be needed to supervise the people that were protecting our families and our business."

"What about Michael?" Scott continued.

"Michael would be required to continue to ferret out the people that broke in to Active and shot your man, and to find the two men that hurt Karen."

Min watched Aaron look at his two friends. He marveled at the way the three of them were able to communicate without saying words. He first noticed it in the jungle of Vietnam and over the years, they had sharpened this skill, which made it very tough to read their faces.

"Aside from getting the men responsible, what is our overall goal?"

Min wondered how they decided that Tom should lead the questioning.

"When I started my thoughts, I was hoping that we would be investing in Providence and as stockholders, we would make money."

"You know, of course, that they are not a public company."

"I know that, but they can become public, can't they?"

At this point, Aaron entered the conversation. "What is it that Mrs. Burnett wants?"

"What I want is for my son, William, to be taken care of, and the business my husband started to be successful."

"You mentioned nothing about yourself."

"I . . ." she stammered. "I am only concerned about my son."

Aaron had shifted his eyes from Mrs. Burnett to Min. In the brief second that she had faltered, he saw the concern in Min's face. He was positive something was going on between them.

"How much money is required, and how much of the company will it buy?" Scott now asked the questions.

Min realized that they were trying to keep him off balance with questions coming from every direction. He held up his hand. "Please, let Tuloc answer all your questions. The reason for this meeting is to decide if you are with me in this business proposition.

If the answer is yes, details can be worked out. If the answer is no, other arrangements must be made."

Aaron stared at the ceiling before answering. "We have been together in too many different situations to even think about letting you go into this without us, but there is something that we must know."

"That is?" Tuloc asked.

Aaron sighed loudly. "Is there a special arrangement between Min and Mrs. Burnett?"

Tuloc looked at Min and then back to Aaron. "None that would make a difference in this arrangement."

Aaron stared at Min and then shifted his gaze toward Mrs. Burnett. "Lan, I hate putting you in this spot, but we must be fully open with each other if this is going to work."

"There is nothing between Min and myself. Saying that, I must continue with what I feel. When I look at Min, I see someone that I find very attractive, and very interesting. I believe that when he looks at me, he feels the same way. It is our custom not to say such things out loud, but I feel I must, especially to friends." She faced Min and then looked down at her shoes. "I hope you don't find me forward, but I felt that I had to speak."

"I am glad you did. There is no reason to hide our feelings from friends." Min glanced at Aaron. "Does this change your thinking?"

"It only reinforces it. For money, we wouldn't be interested. For revenge, we would take a different path, but for love, we will overcome everything," Aaron said laughing.

"Then maybe we should ask their help with Mai Ling and Cassius?" Lan Burnett spoke in a low voice.

"What's with Cassius and Mai Ling?" Scott asked.

"Nothing. Nothing!" shouted Min

Tom started laughing. "Min, you old rascal, I can't believe you're going to pull it off."

"Pull what off? What are you guys talking about?" Scott looked from Min to Tom and back again.

"It is a private matter that need not be discussed here." Min's voice left no room for argument.

Aaron looked at his friends before he spoke. "We are in agreement. We will start an investment group with Tom as the head. The first investment will be in Providence, and Tom will become vice chairman of the board of directors. He will also become the spokesperson for Providence in any and all negotiations regarding the sale of the company." He turned and looked at Min. "Have I left anything out?"

"Only the sum of money that will be required from this investment group."

"Whatever Tom thinks is the right amount, we will agree with."

Min smiled and held out his hand. "Now that we have finished with why I have asked you to meet here, shall we discuss this different path you are planning for Dennis Canon and Interstate?"

Chapter 23

"Can I speak to Dennis Canon? Tell him Aaron Carlyle's on the phone." Aaron waited to be connected. Two weeks had passed since his meeting with Min and now was the time to start putting their plans into action.

"Aaron. What's up?"

"I think I owe you one. Your call regarding the person that shot my fiancée turned out to be correct. You were asking to be able to meet with Carl Rojas, our man that was critically wounded in the robbery."

"Yes, I was. We think he might have seen something that could help us in our investigation," Canon answered slowly

"The police and my men have asked him numerous questions, but he doesn't remember seeing anyone or anything. He does remember hearing what sounded like a big truck, but no one has been able to figure out how that ties in." Aaron paused before he continued. "The doctors have decided that he can have visitors for short periods of time. If you want, you can have two of your people interview him tomorrow. We'd like to have the police or one of our men in the room just in case you jog his memory."

"Great! Only I would like just my men. We find that too many people in the room can inhibit open conversation."

"Which of your men will be there? We'll have to advise the police and get their permission. This is a murder investigation."

"Actually, only one of my men. The other is a woman who we

contract from a behavioral institute. We find that she, shall I say, gets along better with people we interview."

"Their names are?"

"Jerry Whitney and Kebra Metcalf."

"What's the name of that institute?"

"California Institute of Behavioral Science. They're headquartered somewhere in the San Fernando Valley."

"Okay. Tell your people to arrive around ten at the UCLA Medical Center. I'll be there to make sure everything goes as planned."

Before more words could be exchanged, Aaron hung up the phone. He turned to Michael. "Make sure our men use the plastic kind of listening devices, just in case they scan the room. I want to be sure we can pick up every word that's said."

"We'll attach it to Mai Ling, and have her enter the room last, just in case they have a scanner."

The phone in the conference room rang. Michael, who was sitting closest, picked it up. "Michael here."

"Michael, this is Carole at the switchboard. I have a Mr. Canon for Aaron." Aaron took the receiver and said to Carole, "Put him through."

"Aaron, it's Dennis Canon again."

"Did we forget something?"

"You hung up before I could ask what the hell is going on with Tom Greenberg?"

"Nothing that I know of. Has something happened that I don't know about?"

"My friends tell me that Tom Greenberg has become a major stockholder in Providence. He sits on their board and is responsible for negotiating any offers they get for the sale of the company."

"Tom discussed that with both Scott and myself. It looks like a very good business opportunity. Why are you concerned?"

"Why am I concerned? I told you that night in the parking lot to stay out of things that didn't concern you!" Canon's voice was at least two octaves higher.

Aaron smiled and his eyes gleamed. "You told me to tell Min

he was a pain in the ass. I already knew that, but I told him anyway. This deal with Providence was just too good for Tom to pass up. Is there something you want me to tell Tom?"

There was silence on Canon's end of the phone. Aaron placed his hand over the mouthpiece of the phone and said to his friends, "He either died or is taking instructions from someone."

"Carlyle, listen to me. You tell Greenberg that tomorrow he's going to get a call from a lawyer friend of mine. He would be wise to listen to what he has to say."

"Tomorrow's not a good time. Tom took his family on a mini vacation."

Canon was now screaming into the phone. "You get in touch with that son of a bitch and tell him people who screw around with me end up in a world of hurt."

"I'll pass on your message, but before I forget, do you still live at 22610 Jack Rabbit Circle? I'm making out my Christmas card list and want to make sure yours arrives okay."

"Is that some kind of threat?"

Aaron laughed. "A threat? Why would you think that? Aren't we cooperating with each other? If you want, I can cancel the meeting for tomorrow and then I don't give a shit what you call it."

Again, there was silence on the other end of the phone. "Don't cancel the meeting. It's important that we find out if Rojas knows anything."

"Fine. Tell your people I'll see them tomorrow." Aaron hung up the phone and said to Scott, "Make sure we have someone covering Tom's house while he's on vacation."

"I'll make sure that it's covered. Now can we talk about your plans for this afternoon?"

Aaron looked at Scott and then at Michael. "I know you guys aren't happy with what I'm doing, but we have two men there, and I'm sure you've already given them instructions to watch over me."

Scott motioned to Michael. "You talk to him."

Michael took a deep breath. "Boss, we've only had our people there for a little over two weeks. They haven't seen anything one named Paul. At least give us another week. That's not the nicest gym in the whole world."

"I thought you told me it was state of the art equipment? I've gained a few pounds while Karen has been in San Diego. I can use the workout."

Chapter 24

Aaron walked around the gym. It had taken about thirty minutes to fill out the forms and become a member. He hadn't used his own name and was a little worried just in case he ran into someone he knew. He had declined the special they offered of sessions with a trainer. He didn't want to get hooked up with a single instructor. He wanting to talk to as many people as possible."

"Sir!"

Aaron turned. A six-foot-three hard body wearing a yellow shirt with Tommy stitched on the front was calling him.

"Yes?" Aaron responded.

"My name is Tommy. I see that you just joined the gym and I wondered if you needed any help understanding the equipment. Sometimes it can be tricky."

"Thanks, but not today. I'd like to just get the feel of the place."

"That's okay. Just remember anyone with a yellow shirt will be willing to help you out."

"I'll remember. Do you work every day?"

"I only work three or four days a week."

"Everyone in yellow work the same days?"

"No, most of the crew works eight hours a day, five days a week. I'm going to college and need the time to study."

Aaron nodded his head. "A friend told me to ask for Paul if I wanted help."

"Your friend must be a woman."

"She is. Does Paul only train women?"

"No. Once in a while he'll take on a male client, but he specializes in females."

"Is he around today?"

"I haven't seen him in about three weeks. He must be on vacation."

Aaron started walking. "If I need some help, I'll look for you."

"Any time," Tommy replied.

Aaron stopped at the row of treadmills. To make it look convincing, he would have to do something on one of the machines.

"Did you sign up for a trainer?"

Aaron turned and found himself staring at a woman in a gray body suit with blue eyes and blonde hair that hung just below her shoulders. She had a towel draped around her neck and the movement of her lithe body, as she pedaled the stationary bike, made him think of the women dancers in "West Side Story."

"Pardon me?" he stammered.

"I asked if you signed up with a trainer. I saw you talking to Tommy and wondered if he was successful."

"Do you work for the gym?" Aaron tried not to stare.

"No. I do some work for them from time to time, but I'm not an employee." She stopped pedaling and dismounted from the machine. She glanced down at herself and asked, "Is something wrong? You keep staring at me like my sweat suit is ripped."

Aaron looked down at his feet. "No, it's nothing like that. You just remind me of someone."

She smiled. "Really. Who?"

"One of the dancers from 'West Side Story'."

She nodded. "You're quick. Most men would have said their wives or someone they knew in school. Are you married?"

The question almost threw Aaron off balance. "No. My wife died about three years ago."

"Sorry to hear that. I gather she didn't look like me."

"No, she didn't. In fact, she was nothing like you."

She stood openly appraising Aaron. He felt like a walking dessert tray the way she stared. "Why don't you buy me a smoothie at the juice bar after I shower and change into something more comfortable. I'll only take about fifteen or twenty minutes."

When Aaron didn't answer, she continued, "That is unless you're not up to women with blonde hair." She hesitated a second. "If you don't feel comfortable, just forget it. My name is Kebra. You can say hello if we run into each other again." She started to walk away.

"What flavor smoothie?" Aaron asked before she had taken three steps.

"Pick one. Maybe I'm a little like your wife," She tossed the words over her shoulder, never losing a step and never looking back.

Chapter 25

Aaron checked his watch as he left the locker room. It had taken him only ten minutes to change. He had contemplated taking a long shower and not arriving at the juice bar until what he hoped would be long after Kebra had left for home, but then decided to get there early. She obviously was a regular and might be able to give him some information about the infamous missing Paul.

"I like a man who's on time."

Aaron turned. Kebra stood there in a long flowing light gray skirt, with a dark blue silk shirt tied at the waist. The only thing that might have made the change more comfortable was that she obviously wasn't wearing a bra. Aaron's eyes finally drifted up to her lips, which were shining with gloss, and smiling over perfect white teeth.

"Like what you see . . . so far?"

"Um, yes." He smiled awkwardly. "I didn't get a chance to order the smoothie yet."

"That's okay. I decided I'd rather have something with a little kick to it. You do drink, don't you?"

"Not heavily, but I do know how."

"Good. There's a hotel about a half-mile from here. We can get something to drink there and then maybe dinner or something else."

"You mean the Hyatt?"

"You've been there before?" she asked with a smile on her face.

Aaron thought back to his first date with Karen. "I've been there, but not for a while."

"Shall we go together, or do you want to follow me?" she asked brazenly.

"I'll follow you," Aaron replied, and tried not to smile when a slight frown crossed her brow.

"Something wrong?" he asked.

"Nope, I just thought . . . never mind. See you at the Hyatt."

On the way to the hotel, Aaron called his office. "Michael, take down this license number. As soon as you have a make on it, call my cell. Just give me the name. I may have someone with me."

"Need any help?"

Aaron smiled. "No, I can handle this." As he disconnected, he said, "I think."

He followed the red Corvette into the Hyatt parking lot. He parked on the street and watched as she threw the keys to the valet at the front door and turned to see where he was. As she disappeared through the lobby doors, Aaron's phone rang.

"Yeah, Michael."

"How'd you know it was me?"

"Lucky guess. Did you find out who owns the car?"

"You're not going to believe this one, but it's registered to the California Behavioral Institute. We got a little lucky on the next bit of information. It seems the driver of the car got a ticket two weeks ago."

"Probably Kebra Metcalf."

"How the hell did you know that?" Michael sputtered into the phone.

"I'll tell you tomorrow."

"Over here." Aaron heard her before his eyes could adjust in the darkened area of the Hyatt lounge. "I thought for a second you were going to stand me up," she said as he sat in the chair across from her.

"I wouldn't do a thing like that," Aaron replied.

Aaron noticed candles flickering on every other table in the lounge except for the one she was seated at.

"The candle seems to have gone out," he commented.

"I thought it might be cozier this way."

"Are you sure you're not afraid to be seen with me?"

"Why would I be afraid?" she asked as she waved for service.

"Maybe you're married."

"Would it bother you if I were?" she asked, turning her face toward the approaching waiter.

"Not if it doesn't bother you."

After ordering drinks, she turned to Aaron and asked, "What do your friends call you?"

Aaron drew circles on the tabletop with the moisture from his water glass. "First let me ask you a question. Is Kebra your real name?"

"Why would you ask that?"

"If Kebra isn't your real name, then my name is Scott."

"If Kebra is my real name?"

"Then I would have to use another name."

Kebra took a sip of her drink, smiled, and asked, "What kind of car do you drive?"

"A BMW 750 I. Why?"

"I just wanted to see if you were going to be worth the effort."

"Let's see," replied Aaron. "I'm president of a successful public company involved in selling security. I'm not married. I own a home that is over five thousand square feet. I have a checking account with more than five figures and a stock portfolio worth more than seven figures." He paused and then added, "And that's all the truth. What about you? Are you worth the effort?"

"I own a small home in Holmby Hills. I'm not hurting for money, but can always use more. I'm an executive at the California Behavioral Institute, presently under contract to a large conglomerate, and I could always use a good stock tip."

Aaron realized that when he said security company, she misunderstood and thought he meant securities, as in stocks and bonds. He didn't bother to clarify her mistake.

"The only free advice I give is to buy low and sell high. Tell me, what does this California Behavioral Institute do?"

"We interview people to see if they're telling the truth. We help companies plan their futures by delving into the backgrounds of people that work for or own companies that they are looking to buy out."

Aaron finished his drink as she continued, "I'm over twenty-seven, and I'm tired of talking. I have a room on the fourth floor of this hotel. Here's a key. Give me ten minutes and come on up. I want to freshen up."

"I don't know if that's such a good idea. We've just met."

She stood and stretched her arms above her head. "I could use a massage or some other type of exercise. You have ten minutes to decide. Leave the key at the front desk if you make the wrong decision." She walked away and over her shoulder called back to him, "Leave a big tip. They know me here."

Aaron watched her enter the elevator. He stood up, turned the key over, walked to the front desk, and dropped it on the counter.

Chapter 26

Aaron couldn't wait to get home. Upon entering the house, the first thing he did was to call Karen in San Diego.

"Hi," he whispered into the phone. "This is the start of an obscene phone call."

Karen laughed as she whispered back into the phone. "Why are you whispering?"

"I had such a great time this afternoon that I didn't want you to know it was me."

"What did you do?" she asked with feigned indifference. "I thought you were going to the gym to work out?"

"I did, and I met a most beautiful woman."

"Really!" Her tone changed ever so slightly.

"I certainly did. She was about five foot five, had blonde hair, and she came on to me like no one has. Well, since I first met you anyway."

"I don't remember coming on to you."

"They call that selective memory." He laughed into the phone. "How are you feeling?"

"I'm feeling fine. Are you going to tell me the rest of the story?"

"The rest of what story?"

"The one about a most beautiful woman coming on to you."

"There's really nothing to tell. Her name is Kebra Metcalf and she works for the California Behavioral Institute."

"Isn't she the person you're supposed to meet with who wants to interview Carl?"

"That's her. I have a feeling that maybe she knew who I was and was trying to compromise my position. She invited me to meet her at the Hyatt for a drink, and she then invited me to her room."

"Why'd she do that?"

"Probably to find out more about me."

"You're sure it's not your animal magnetism."

"Maybe it is, which brings up another question. When are you going to be ready to get married?"

"The doctor says I can be up and around by next week. How about three weeks from Friday?"

"Start planning. Just tell me where to be."

"How about I tell you where not to be, and before you ask, it's at the Hyatt with this Kebra person."

"Okay, let me write this down. Don't go to the Hyatt with Kebra."

"Aaron, I love you. Be careful."

"I'll call you tomorrow. I love you." Aaron listened waiting for Karen to disconnect first. He then called Scott.

Without announcing who he was, Aaron just started talking. "We're changing the play at the line of scrimmage. Tomorrow I want Michael to take Mai Ling with him to the hospital."

"Any special reason for the change?"

"Yeah. I met Kebra Metcalf tonight at the gym."

"So that's who she was. I was just reading through the first report filed by one of our men at the gym. It came in fifteen minutes ago. What did she want?"

"I'm not sure if she knew who I am. She came on pretty heavy and she never gave me her last name."

"Who did you tell her you were? Me?"

"You're half right. I said my name was Scott. I never gave her my last name. I'd like to hold off on seeing her again until we can take better advantage of the situation."

"What does she look like?"

"She's a knockout."

"Don't tell Karen about her."

Aaron started laughing. "Karen's not the problem. She thinks my name is Scott."

"Very funny. What's your plan?"

"You and Mai Ling go and try rattling their cage. Tell them we want Mai Ling there so that Carl's not inhibited by one woman. I'll have Michael down there early making sure Carl knows what he's supposed to say."

"How far are we going to let Carl go? Remember we haven't told the police yet about the yellow shirt with the name Sunrise Gym on the back and Paul on the front."

"Carl is going to remember nothing, just like he told the police, but if they ask the right questions, he will remember the yellow shirt. He's going to try and remember about the truck. I had a thought earlier today. What if it was a garbage truck?"

"A garbage truck?"

"They have those prongs on the front to pick up the baskets, and I doubt if anyone would have paid them any attention during the search."

"Where would the crooks get a garbage truck?"

"I don't know, but if he remembers seeing a garbage truck and a yellow shirt during this interview, we may shake someone up in a hurry."

"What are you going to do about Kebra Metcalf?"

"Depending on what happens tomorrow morning, I may show up at the gym again in the afternoon, but this time we'll play on my home court."

Chapter 27

"I was told your Mr. Carlyle would be here."

Scott looked at Kebra Metcalf. *She is certainly a good-looking woman,* he thought.

"He had some other business to take care of. He asked me to fill in for him."

"I would have thought that this meeting was important enough that he wouldn't have sent underlings." She made the statement with contempt in her voice.

"I hope we won't disappoint you. My name is Scott Miller, and this is Mai Ling. Mr. Carlyle has requested that she be in the room with you so that Carl can see a familiar face. I run the sales for Besafe and Carl works for me. Mai Ling is the administrative assistant and second in command of our detective agency division."

Kebra Metcalf looked at Scott and then said, "This town has an awful lot of Scott's living here, and the answer is no."

"What do you mean no? And do you know another Scott in the area?" Scott smiled as he asked the questions.

"She's not going into the room with us. And no, I don't know any other Scotts."

"I suppose I understand your position about Mai Ling. But, I did hear a story about some guy in the area telling people he is me. He's giving me a bad reputation."

"Why is that?" she asked with more than a little interest in her voice.

"I hear he's a big hit with the women. They seem to fall all over him. Regardless, let's get started."

"We would like you to sign this form," Mai Ling said to Jerry Whitney.

"What forms are those?" Carole asked.

"Nothing for you to worry about," Mai Ling replied coyly. "Since Mr. Whitney is the senior person in attendance, Mr. Carlyle would like a release from Interstate regarding anything that is heard today."

"What makes you think Mr. Whitney is the senior person?" Kebra asked loudly.

"That's obvious," stated Scott. "He works for the company and you're only a hired gun."

"That's bullshit!" Spit came out of her mouth as she raised her voice. "I'm the one in charge of this meeting."

"Well, let me call Mr. Carlyle. If he says it's okay, I'll let you sign." Mai Ling again spoke quietly.

"Tell you what, Mai Ling." Scott interrupted. "I can okay her signing. On top of that, I don't think they're going to learn anything from Carl anyway."

"We'll see," she said as she signed the paper in front of her without even glancing at the words.

"We're finished here. Don't forget to let us know if Carl remembers anything." Scott smiled as he turned to walk away. "And don't forget, if you see that other Scott, please let me know."

Kebra Metcalf, her face red with anger and embarrassment, turned and walked toward the hospital room.

Scott watched her take a deep breath and compose herself as she entered.

"Are you the people from Interstate?" Carl Rojas, sitting up in bed, asked.

"My name is Jerry Whitney. I'm from Interstate, and this is Kebra Metcalf. She's from the California Behavioral Institute."

"They told me about her."

"What did they tell you?" she asked in a most pleasant voice.

"They told me that you might help me remember some of the things I forgot about the night of the robbery."

"What type of things do you think you forgot?"

The door to the hospital room closed blocking Scott's view. The one thing he could tell was that she was in her element. Scott and Mai Ling went quickly to a room down the hall where Aaron and Michael were looking at a closed-circuit television.

"The reception is great. We'll be able to watch their every move." The four Besafe people sat back to watch the proceedings.

Jerry moved to the back of the room and sat down. He set up a tape recording device after first waving a wand at different parts of the room.

"Maybe how many men, maybe what they were wearing, maybe something about the truck. I don't know. Everything happened very fast." Carl's eyes were shifting from Kebra to Jerry and then back to Kebra.

"I understand. I've also been told that you are a very brave man. They think that you shot one of the crooks." She crossed her legs, making sure he could hear the nylon stockings as they brushed against each other. She had positioned herself so that he could see her legs from where he sat. Past experience had shown that she was able to distract men with this maneuver.

Carl looked at the ceiling. "Yes, they told me that. I don't know how. I don't remember aiming at him."

"You do remember pulling your pistol."

"I remember that part, but it wasn't to shoot at someone. It was before that. We were walking down the alley and I heard the truck."

Kebra looked at her notes. "It must have been a big one."

"You know, it's funny. I just now realized I saw the truck."

"You didn't remember seeing it before?" She glanced over at Jerry. He motioned with his fingers to keep Carl talking.

"Maybe I didn't see it."

Kebra couldn't make eye contact with him staring at the ceiling. She stood and walked over to the bed. She leaned across his body and said, "Let me adjust your pillow."

Carl's eyes moved from her face that now covered his view of the ceiling to her chest and very quickly up to her face again.

She smiled. "It must have had some markings on the side."

"I didn't see the side. All I saw was the back. It was a garbage truck!" he shouted convincingly

"A garbage truck? It couldn't have been very large."

"Maybe it wasn't a garbage truck, but I think it had something in the back that you threw stuff into."

"Maybe it was like a cement mixer?"

"Maybe! You know, it's odd. I didn't remember it before today, and now I'm sure, or almost sure, it was a garbage truck."

"We'll get back to that. Let's talk about the thieves."

"I never saw them."

"I know that, but sometimes the mind plays funny tricks. Let's walk through that night." She paused making sure she had eye contact. "You walked down the alley. You heard what sounded like a truck. Then what did you do?"

"We both pulled our weapons. We continued walking and then a man stepped out from around the building."

"That's good. What did he look like?"

"Couldn't tell. He had a gun and I dove to the ground."

"Then what happened?"

"Hank was shot and . . . wait a second. The man we were looking at didn't shoot him. The shots must have come from behind us."

"Why do you say that?"

"The man with the yellow shirt didn't get off any shots. He was wounded when Hank's revolver fired."

"So it wasn't you?"

"I knew it wasn't me. It was Hank who shot him."

Kebra looked at Jerry. He shook his head in a side-to-side manner that told her not to ask any more questions.

"They bought it," Aaron said to his people. "They don't want to bring attention to it. I can't wait for a copy of the tape."

Chapter 28

"May I have a copy of the tape?" Mai Ling asked.

"The machine must have malfunctioned. We didn't get anything. Sorry," Jerry quickly answered.

"Mr. Miller asked that I get a copy. Perhaps you could just brief me. I'm sure that will suffice."

Kebra sighed. "Unfortunately, he didn't remember much. He seems to think that it was a garbage truck that broke down the door."

Mai Ling looked at her note pad. "Well, that's something new. Why did he think that? Our records indicate that he never got to the back of the building."

"He said he saw the rear of what looked like something you throw garbage into."

"Anything else?" Mai Ling made a big show of writing down what was said.

"I have a question for you. It's personal, so you're not obligated to answer," Kebra said with a Cheshire cat grin.

"You can ask, but hat doesn't mean that I'll answer."

"We've heard a rumor that you're . . . involved with one of the bosses of Besafe."

"And?" Mai Ling asked.

"Is it true?" Kebra asked.

Mai Ling looked at Jerry Whitney. "Is she asking for you?"

"Me? Why me?"

"I thought you might be interested, and were afraid to ask on your own."

"No. She's not asking for me, but I could be interested."

Mai Ling turned back to Kebra Metcalf. "You must be asking for yourself. Either way, the answer is no. I'm not sleeping with any of the bosses. If your next question is if I'm a switch hitter, ask when Jerry's not around." She smiled suggestively, enjoying herself immensely.

Before Kebra could answer, Scott joined the group. "How did the interview go? You look a little flushed, Ms. Metcalf. Is there something I could get you?"

Kebra, her eyes throwing darts at a smiling Mai Ling, looked at Scott and replied, "Your second in command has the information. If anything comes of it, I guess I can get in touch with her." Without saying good-bye, she started down the hall.

"Sometimes when things don't go as planned, she gets a little upset. It was nice meeting you." Jerry nodded at Mai Ling and shook Scott's hand. "Kebra, wait up. Don't forget, I'm driving."

Aaron emerged from the room two doors away where he'd been waiting for them to leave. "You did great, Mai Ling. I don't think she's used to dealing with someone as quick as you. I'm going to say good-bye to Carl and head back to the office. Anyone need a ride?"

Mai Ling glanced at Scott. "Maybe you could go back with Aaron. I promised to meet Cassius and Michael for lunch."

"Anything important going on?" Scott asked.

"Michael wants me to get to know Cassius better. He says it's smart business to be on the good side of the regulars."

Scott nodded his head and said, "I'll go back to the office with Aaron."

Upon opening the door to Carl's room, they found him waving his hands above his head. "What's going on?" Scott asked, looking quickly around the room.

Carl, his eyes huge, pressed his finger to his lips and kept shaking his head.

Aaron walked over to the bed and leaned over Carl.

"I think they left some listening device attached to the underside of the chair," he whispered, pointing to the chair in front of the heating unit.

Aaron tiptoed over to the chair in the corner. He motioned for Scott to continue talking.

"Hi Carl! I understand that you didn't remember anything more than you told us, except for maybe you think it was a garbage truck."

Carl's tongue went nervously over his lips. "I'm really not sure. I think I saw . . ."

"Hold it!" Aaron shouted. "I think they put a bomb under the chair. Get Carl the hell out of here. Tell that cop outside the door to clear the floor."

"What's going on in here?"

Aaron and Scott both turned toward the voice.

"Barry!" Aaron yelled. "There's a bomb attached to the bottom of the chair."

Barry, rushing towards the chair, said, "Don't panic. Open the bathroom door and step back." He picked up the chair gingerly and slowly walked the chair into the tiled bathroom. He set it gently into the enclosed shower.

"Now you can start panicking. Get the officer outside of the door to clear out the rooms on this floor and the floor below." He took a small walkie-talkie out of his pocket, pushed down the send button, and started talking to his driver parked on the street below.

"This is Captain Sands. Get a bomb squad over to the UCLA Medical Center. Third floor, room 3052. Now!"

"Hang on, pal. We'll get you out of here," Aaron grunted as he and Scott lifted Carl off of the bed.

"It's not a big one," Barry yelled over the sounds of panic starting to rise in the hallway. "I think it's designed to only blow . . ."

The explosion threw the closed bathroom door almost off of its hinges. Alarms started going off all over the hospital as the sprinkler systems started spraying water over every one and everything.

"Shit!" Exclaimed Barry. "I just bought this jacket."

"Whatever happened to 'How are you guys?'" Aaron asked as he calmly sat down on the bed.

"It certainly made a big dent in the bathroom for not being a big one," Scott grumbled as he peeked through the door that swung comically from one hinge. "The tile absorbed most of the damage."

"Is everyone all right in here?" The policeman who had been guarding the door had returned holding a towel over his head and asked somewhat cautiously.

"We're all okay, but see if you can find some one to shut off this water. It's ruining my jacket."

The policeman looked at Barry and quickly retreated from the room.

"You guys certainly have a knack of making enemies. Would you like to tell me what the hell is going on?"

"I think my closest and dearest friend, Dennis Canon, has made this personal. If you want in on it, you know the rules."

Barry made eye contact with Aaron. Neither man blinked for a long moment until Scott moved.

"I'm going to alert the troops. You two decide what part Barry is going to play. I'll be back in about ten minutes." Scott looked down at his shoes. "These shoes probably cost more than that jacket he's so proud of."

Aaron smiled. "Be nice. I think it's just the color that makes it look that way."

"What's wrong with the color?" Barry asked his two friends. "My wife picked it out."

"It's not the color, it's your size, and make sure you tell her that it was Aaron that said it." Scott laughed as he left the room.

Chapter 29

"You guys are going to cost me my pension!" Barry paced the room as he spoke.

Aaron watched without saying a word. They had moved to a waiting room three doors away from Carl's original room. The Los Angeles Police and Fire Department were still searching the building and Barry requested some private time with his friends who he said "were in shock."

"How is she?" Barry asked Aaron, finally coming to a stop. There was no mistaking who "she" was.

"She's getting there, but she doesn't say much about the shooting. It's almost like she's blocking it out of her memory. It's been three weeks since it happened and I get the feeling she's trying to put it behind her, but it's tough."

"When are you guys planning to get married?" Barry continued.

"I don't know. She's stopped talking about it. The latest is a couple of weeks from Friday. I spoke to her mother and she asked me to give her some time." Aaron looked out the window before continuing, "Are you with us, or are we on our own?"

"Count me in. What do you want me to tell Cassius?"

"We're handling Cassius, I think."

"How are you doing that?" Barry asked, but before Aaron could reply, he answered his own question, "Mai Ling!"

"Yep! The two of them hit it off big time."

"What does Min say about it?"

Aaron smiled. "Sitting on the sidelines, it's like reading Romeo and Juliet. Min keeps getting in the way, but we think he is secretly orchestrating the romance." Scott entered while Aaron was talking. "Or he thinks he is. I think he's afraid that if he doesn't get involved, it won't come out the way he wants."

Scott closed the door to the room and said, "The police are down the hall with the fire department. What are we going to tell them?"

Aaron looked at Barry. "You're going to have to talk to someone. It would be great if the story was that a heater exploded."

"Do we want to say that Carl died?"

Aaron considered this. "What do you think?"

"How about just hurt again? It will save us from staging a funeral."

"Good point. Can you sell it?"

"I think I can get some professional courtesy on a case I'm working on, after all . . ."

"Is everyone all right in here?" The door swung open and in walked two firemen, obviously officers.

"My name is Captain Barry Sands. I'm with the Ventura County Police. Can I talk to the person in charge?"

"The explosion rocked the elevator. Luckily, it didn't get stuck. When I reached the first floor, alarms were going off and there was no way I could get back up." Mai Ling was explaining what happened to Michael and Cassius.

"Well, we think that everyone is all right. Captain Sands called in the request for help just minutes before the explosion. We haven't been able to get any other information. It's almost like there's a news blackout."

While Cassius was talking, Michael dialed the office. "Have you heard from your husband or Aaron within the last couple of minutes?" he asked Carole, the switchboard operator.

"No, should I? The last time I heard from Barry, he was going to the UCLA Medical Center to talk to Carl. I'm not sure where Aaron is; maybe he's on some kind of stakeout somewhere."

"Thanks. If you hear from either of them, ask them to call me."

"Is something wrong?"

"No, I don't think so. I just have to talk to one of them." As he disconnected, he turned at the sound of Cassius's ringing phone.

"It's them," Lieutenant Sizemore yelled to Michael and Mai Ling. "Yes, Captain, they're both with me now. Tonight at seven o'clock at Aaron Carlyle's home? Sure, I guess. Captain, is everyone okay?" He looked at the phone in his hand. "He hung up!"

"What did he say?" Mai Ling inquired.

"They want to see the three of us at seven o'clock tonight at Mr. Carlyle's home."

"That's all?" Michael asked.

"He didn't even say if it was for dinner."

Chapter 30

Aaron glanced at his watch as he entered the gym. He had three and a half hours before the meeting he had called was to take place. After walking through the entire workout area and not seeing Kebra Metcalf, he was trying to decide what to do when his eyes landed on a yellow shirt with Paul stitched across the pocket. The man was jogging on one of the machines while he mouthed the words to some song that only he could hear through the headphones attached to his Sony Walkman. Aaron retreated until his back touched the wall behind him. The man stood about six feet tall. He was slightly shorter than Aaron, but Paul's muscles showed years of workouts. There was an inch-long scar on the right side of his jaw. As Aaron stared at his face, he could understand why some women would consider him good looking. The scar gave him a look of mystery. He had a bandage wrapped around his left thigh that caused him to drag that leg about every eighth or ninth step, but it was his eyes that people would never forget. They were a deep shade of cobalt blue, and they never stopped moving. Now and then they would come to rest on one of the women working out. From Aaron's vantage point, he could see that Paul was undressing each woman and filing her away for future reference. The machine next to Paul's became available and Aaron quickly stepped on it.

Aaron set the machine for four and a half miles per hour and hit the start button. Looking over at Paul, he asked, “How long should the start-up period be?”

When Paul didn’t answer, Aaron tapped him on the shoulder.

Paul turned, pulling the earphones off his ears.

“You want something?”

“Yeah. How long should the start up period be?”

“Didn’t they have someone show you the equipment when you joined?”

“Some kid called Tommy started to show me some stuff, but I guess he got busy or something.”

Paul looked at the machine Aaron was on. “You have it set at four and a half. Do that for three minutes and then move it up to five and a half. How long do you think you can run?”

“An hour, if I have to.”

“What’s your name?” Paul asked.

“Name’s Scott. I see yours is Paul. How’d you hurt your leg?”

“I scratched it on a wire fence I was trying to get through. It took six stitches.”

“That must have hurt.” Aaron forced his eyes to wander around the room.

“Looking for someone in particular?” Paul’s eyes followed Aaron’s gaze.

“Willing would be good. Do you know any of the women?”

“Some of them.”

“Any of them willing?”

“Some of them.”

“Any hints, or am I on my own?”

“You’re basically on your own, but a suggestion would be to concentrate on the hard bodies.”

“How come?”

“They’ve already made the commitment, the ones that are out of shape may be still trying to make up their mind,” Paul said as he looked around, his eyes falling on a woman wearing black leotards. “Although that’s not always the case,” he finished the statement smiling.

Aaron watched the woman. She was about five foot two or three, and weighed about one thirty or forty. She was straining on a stair master machine and the sweat flattened her hair to the side of her head.

"Sometimes they have money." Aaron heard Paul, but did not look in his direction. "I gotta go and give some lessons," Paul said as he stepped off of the machine. "Good luck. Maybe I'll see you again."

"I'm sure you will." Aaron's lips pressed against his teeth as he forced a smile.

Aaron moved the speed of the machine up to five and a half and after thirty seconds, moved it up to six and a half. Sweat was starting to run down his face and chest when he heard her voice.

"Are you running to or away from something?"

He hit the pause button and turned to see Kebra Metcalf glaring at him. He took a deep breath and said, "Maybe a little of both."

"I have two questions for you. First, what the hell is your name?"

"And the second is going to be?" Aaron asked.

"What happened to you yesterday?"

Aaron took the towel from his neck and started wiping his face. "Let's take the second question first. I like to do the courting. I don't like to be, let's say, managed. As far as my name, if I remember correctly, you asked what people call me. The answer to that could be Boss."

"I asked you your name!"

"No you didn't. You asked me what people called me and I asked you if Kebra was your real name. When you said 'If it wasn't, what would people call me,' I said Scott. You then asked me what type of car I drove."

Kebra looked at him trying to remember the conversation. "What is your name?"

"I don't think it makes a difference now. I also remember you saying that I had ten minutes to make the right decision."

She looked at him. "Do you think you did?" she asked as she placed her hand on her hip in an exaggerated stance.

"Probably. How does that saying go? He who runs away today, lives to fight another day."

"What does that mean?" she asked, raising her voice.

"I'm still here, aren't I?"

"You two getting acquainted?"

They both turned as a smiling Paul, with the woman in black leotards on his arm, approached them.

Chapter 31

"No," Kebra spat at exactly the same moment Aaron replied, "Yes."

"Which is it?" asked Paul.

"I thought we were," replied Aaron. "I guess I was wrong."

Paul looked at Kebra, smiled, and said, "Give him a break. Scott's not such a bad guy."

"You know him?" she asked.

"We've met."

Kebra pursed her lips, looked at Aaron, and said, "Same place, thirty minutes from now, and don't stand me up again."

Aaron shook his head. "It's going to be the same result. I have a business meeting at seven o'clock that will probably last for two hours. How about we meet at nine thirty for a drink?" Looking at Paul, he continued, would you and . . ." He stopped and held out his hand. "My name is Scott and this is Kebra. Your name is?"

More than a little flustered, the woman answered, "Ellen Moore."

Aaron then continued, "Maybe you and Ellen would like to join us for a drink?"

"I couldn't make it," Ellen Moore stammered. "I have to get home."

"Maybe some other time then," replied Aaron.

"I can't make it either," Kebra responded.

"I guess this was never meant to be." Aaron smiled as he looked at Kebra. Turning, he asked Paul, "How about you? I can meet you here about nine thirty."

"That's strike three. I need my beauty sleep. I've got a tough day tomorrow. I'll see you around." Paul led Ellen by her elbow toward the locker rooms without looking back.

"She doesn't look his type," Aaron said aloud

"She isn't. Her husband is the top guy at a contract manufacturing place out in Simi Valley. They're not getting along, which is why Paul is involved."

"You obviously know Paul well."

"Not as well as you think. Just through business. He does things for the company I'm contracted with."

"What type of things?"

"I don't know, just things." Her eyes started moving and Aaron could see that she was getting agitated.

"Let me ask you a question. I asked before, but you didn't answer. Are you married?" Aaron asked smoothly.

"Why are you asking?"

"You can't meet me at nine thirty. It sounds like maybe you're married."

"I'm not. It's just that I have another appointment."

"Maybe next week then," Aaron said as he started to leave.

When he didn't hear an answer, he turned and watched Kebra walk to the locker rooms.

"Mrs. Williams, this is Aaron. Can I talk to Karen?"

After a slight hesitation, she replied, "Karen's lying down right now. Can you call back later?"

"How's she doing?"

"Not so good."

"What does that mean?" Aaron asked nervously.

"Why don't you try a little later?"

Now it was Aaron's turn to hesitate. "Is someone there stopping you from talking?"

"Karen's napping on the sofa and I really don't want to disturb her. Are you at home?"

"Yes, I am. We're having a business meeting at seven o'clock, but I should finish by nine o'clock. If I start out then, I could be in San Diego by eleven thirty. Will she be awake?"

"I don't think so, Aaron. Why don't you stay at home and I'll get back to you?"

"If you think that's best. I'll talk to you later." Aaron hung up and sat looking at the phone until there was a knock on the door.

"You look like you lost your best friend. You feeling okay?" Scott asked as he entered.

"I've got a little headache. It's nothing serious."

Scott looked at his friend more closely and then went on, "We ran that name you gave us, and I think we found the company. Barney Moore is president and chief executive officer of a small contract manufacturer in Simi Valley called MCD. It stands for Moore Contract Development. They've been in business since 1968. They're not public, so I couldn't find out how large or small they actually are, but their brochure says they have two hundred employees."

"How come we don't do their security work?"

"They're signed on with Interstate. We quoted the service three years ago but lost it. I don't know if you remember, but they beat our cost by over thirty percent."

There was a knock on the front door.

"I'll get it," Aaron said. "It's time for the others to arrive."

"You son of a bitch!" shouted Dennis Canon as Aaron opened the door. "You keep screwing with me and I'll destroy you and your entire company."

Aaron stared past Dennis Canon at the three men standing behind him. He could hear movement behind him and without looking, knew that Scott was positioning himself to help.

"Dennis, it's so nice to see you. What seems to be the problem?"

"What seems to be the problem?" Dennis Canon yelled. "The problem is you! You keep meddling in things that don't concern you."

Quietly, almost in a whisper, Aaron leaned forward and said, "If you don't take your three friends and get the hell off my front steps, it's going to get worse."

One of the men behind Dennis Canon took a step toward Aaron.

"One more inch and you'll be operating without a kneecap for the rest of your life," Scott warned as he emerged from behind the door with a pistol, causing the three men to retreat a few steps.

Chapter 32

"What happened when Scott pointed the gun at them?" Mai Ling asked, her eyes huge with astonishment.

"They left," Aaron responded and shrugged.

"You left out the part about their promise to get even," Scott said with a sandwich in hand.

"Everyone get something to eat and let's get this meeting started." Aaron looked around the room. Tom walked over and sat down next to Scott.

"How come I miss out on all the fun?" he asked, lightly punching his friend's arm.

Mai Ling had taken the seat next to Lieutenant Sizemore, but to their obvious annoyance Min had wedged his chair between them. Michael was standing against the wall with a Coke in his hand next to Captain Sands who had a Coors Light.

"Let me bring everyone up to date," Aaron said loudly to get everyone's attention. "The bomb that exploded was intended to kill Carl. The minute he mentioned the yellow shirt, even in passing, they had to get rid of him. The reason Canon is so pissed is that Barry had some of his men stop by to ask questions and to disrupt the flow of Canon's office. The men were instructed to say the reason they were there was because I personally filed a complaint.

"When one of Canon's men shot Karen, he made this personal. That's why I asked you all here today. Personal is not good when friends are involved. We still have a business to run, and families to protect. I would like each of you to re-think what is going on and if you decide to stay on the business side, just remember, you're not leaving me alone, you're just protecting from another angle."

Aaron looked at Min. "Old friend, we've been through a lot together. Maybe it's time for you to sit back and relax." To Barry he said, "If you still think you owe me, you're wrong. We both know you saved my life that night a long time ago." Looking at Mai Ling and Cassius Sizemore he smiled. "You two have your whole lives ahead of you. You became part of this through no fault of your own and if you walked out now, no one would blame you, and Michael, the same applies to you. We still need you to run the detective agency part of the business, which has no part in what is going on." Raising his bottle of water in the direction of Scott and Tom, "I know better than to try talking sense into you two. So everyone decide while I get a sandwich."

Aaron took his time getting a sandwich and when he returned, Cassius Sizemore was the first to stand. "I'm a police officer with one function in life, and that's to uphold the law. I get the distinct feeling that some laws are going to be, if not broken, pretty well bent. I'm sorry, but I couldn't participate in anything like this and hold my head up straight." He looked across Min at Mai Ling. "Saying that, I have to tell you that I wouldn't allow a woman I love to take part in something like this without me." He now turned solemnly to Barry. "Captain, I am tendering my resignation, effective immediately."

The room became silent. Mai Ling rose from her chair and walked around Min. She put her arms around Cassius's neck and whispered, loud enough for everyone to hear, "You wouldn't allow? A woman you love?"

As she planted a kiss on Sizemore's lips, Min rose. "This is inappropriate behavior!" he sputtered.

"Sir, I would like to ask your permission to marry Mai Ling." Cassius moved between Mai Ling and Min.

"You have not yet asked me," wailed Mai Ling from behind him.

"You must be quiet for one second. Your grandfather must give me his permission."

"And what will you do if he doesn't?" she asked.

"He does not have to answer that," Min interrupted. "I give him my consent, but he must understand that he is not getting a bargain. There is much he must teach you, and I will not allow him to change his mind."

Cassius turned to face Mai Ling. "Will you marry me?" he asked softly.

Mai Ling stepped back. "Since you now have my grandfather's consent, and my love, I must say yes, yes, yes."

Everyone started applauding at the same time. Min stood and walked over to Cassius and shook his hand. He hugged Mai Ling and then sat down in the chair Mai Ling had been sitting in, ensuring that Mai Ling and Cassius would now be sitting next to each other.

"Can I now have the floor?" Barry raised his voice.

Everyone turned.

"Just so everyone understands, neither Cassius nor myself will be indulging in anything illegal. We are sworn to uphold the law and there is nothing that I have discussed with Aaron that would change that. As long as we all understand, I will now refuse to accept Cassius's resignation. Good cops are too hard to come by."

"Min, I won't dishonor you by asking what you want to do. The same goes for Scott and Tom. If necessary, we can discuss this further in private. What we are planning is the destruction of Interstate Security and all of its subsidiaries. Let me change that to the 'legal' destruction of Interstate. Tom, why don't you hand out the game plan you've been working on? I would like each of you to study your part and how it connects with each other. If anyone sees any problems, let's put them on the table and discuss them now," Aaron concluded.

Tom handed everyone six pages. The first one to complain was Cassius.

"I don't like Mai Ling's part. I think it could be too dangerous."

"I was thinking the same about yours," Mai Ling countered.

"I will make sure nothing happens to Mai Ling!" Min's voice left no question that the matter was finished.

"If that's it, we start tonight. Good luck everyone, and keep in touch."

Chapter 33

"What the hell do you think they want?" The driver of an Interstate Security car looked down at his speedometer. "I was only five miles over the speed limit."

"You better pull over," the man riding shotgun lamented.

When their car came to a stop, both men started to exit the car. The spotlight from the police patrol car was turned on and pointed at the man on the passenger's side.

"Don't exit the car until we tell you to," the voice blared out of the bullhorn.

"We belong to Interstate Security," the driver yelled back, shielding his eyes from a second light now shining on him."

"Keep your hands where we can see them!" The command sounded ominous.

"We better do as they say," the man on the passenger's side said as he got back into the car.

"We're Interstate Security people!" the driver yelled at the voice before re-entering the vehicle.

When both men were seated inside the car, the two policemen approached them.

"Don't make any fast moves. Very slowly remove your identification from your wallets."

The officer that approached on the passenger side continued for his partner, "I see you're carrying weapons. Slowly take out your licenses and permits to carry those weapons."

"Is something wrong?" the driver of the Interstate vehicle asked.

"We've been alerted to the fact that there are some phony's driving security vehicles, and we're checking out the tip."

"Shit!" the driver exclaimed.

"What's the problem?" the senior officer asked.

"I don't have my license with me."

"Step out of the car, please."

"If you let me make a call, I'm sure we can straighten this out."

"You're entitled to one call—at the station." The police officer reached over and took the pistol out of the driver's holster. "You have the right to remain silent. If you give up this right, anything you say or do, can be held against you."

"This is bullshit!" the driver screamed.

The policeman turned him around, pulled his arms behind him, and placed his hands in handcuffs. He asked the passenger, "You do have a driver's license, don't you?"

"Sure I do." As he started fumbling through his wallet, he dropped it on the floor of the car.

After finally retrieving the license and handing it to the officer for inspection, the second officer said, "When you get back to the barn, you can tell your supervisor that your partner is at the Olson Road station. You can also tell them that we'll be checking all security vehicles from all the independent companies. They may want to spread the word. We're really not hard to get along with."

Putting the driver into the back seat, they drove off, leaving the other man still sitting in the passenger's seat.

As the taillights of the police vehicle disappeared, the man jumped into the driver's seat and pressed the speak button on his car radio.

"Base! Base! This is Darrell. Jeff's just been arrested." After a moment's delay, he started again, "Base, this is Darrell. Can you hear me?"

"To the person calling himself Darrell on this frequency, please be advised to use regular procedures, such as car number and last names." The female dispatcher sounded stressed.

"This is car sixteen. My name is Darrell Huffman. Jeff . . . I don't know his last name . . . he the driver of this vehicle . . . and was just taken into custody by the cops."

There was a silence that was followed by a male voice. "This is Paul. Go to a landline and call the station. I'll advise you then what you should do next. Do you understand?"

"Yeah, I understand. Give me ten minutes."

Paul Kiesler sat at his desk contemplating his next move. "The asshole must have been speeding," he said aloud as his phone rang.

"This is Paul."

"This is Sharon. Another car just had someone arrested."

"What?" he yelled into the phone.

"Car thirteen just had Rick arrested. He's not the driver, he's the assistant. I told the driver to go to a landline and call in. What should I tell him when he calls?"

"Put him through to me." Slamming down the phone he looked at the ceiling. "What the hell is going on around here? There must be a full moon or something."

His phone rang again. "It's Sharon. Car three's driver has been arrested. I've given the same instructions to the assistant. This looks like it's going to be a screwy night. Hold on, we've got a problem."

"Tell me something I don't know," Paul answered.

"The alarm has just gone off at the donut shop in Agoura. That's one of the buildings covered by car thirteen."

"Send one of the others to check it out."

"The two cars that would normally be backup are cars sixteen and three."

"Call the police, and divert the next two closest cars we have. Make sure you connect me to the guys that call in quickly."

"Will do."

Paul reached over and picked up another phone on his desk. He didn't want to make this call, but was afraid not to. "Dennis, this is Paul. We have a problem."

Chapter 34

"Jeezus, I'm tired!" Paul said to Dennis Canon as he looked at his watch. "I'm glad this night is over. It's six thirty and I'm supposed to meet Ellen at ten o'clock."

"How's that going?"

"Not bad. I think by the end of next week I'll be able to get her into the hotel and we can take some pictures."

"You must be losing your touch. This one's taking longer than usual."

"She's nervous as a long tailed cat in an home with two dozen rocking chairs. She's getting close; I almost had her yesterday afternoon. Ask Kebra."

"What's Kebra got to do with it?"

"She was talking to some guy at the gym when I walked by and he asked Ellen and I to join them for a drink."

"Did you?"

"No. She said no, Kebra said no, and I said no. The guy got left empty handed."

"Who was he?"

Paul hesitated a second. He thought Kebra was screwing around with Dennis, but he didn't think it was anything serious. "His name is Scott something. I met him on the machines. He thinks the gym is a good place to find some quail."

Dennis stood there thinking when the phone rang. Paul picked it up.

"This is Paul . . . what buildings? Okay, I'll take care of it."

"What's wrong now?" Dennis asked.

"Three of the buildings didn't get cleaned last night. One of the trucks got a flat tire and they couldn't finish their route."

"Which three?"

"MCD is one of them. The other two are small. I'll have to get someone out there this morning."

"We seem to have had a shitload of bad luck last night. What's going on?" Dennis Canon asked as he looked at his fingernails.

"Coincidence, nothing more. I spoke to a Lieutenant Sizemore and he told me a story about their getting a call complaining about some men who worked out of a security company car. All the local security cars will be getting stopped over the next two weeks or so and everyone inside of the cars will be checked out. I'm sending out a memo today telling our guys to carry I.D. and avoid arguments."

"What about the three guys they arrested last night?"

"We have a problem with one of them. He's an ex con and can't be allowed to carry a gun. I told the cops he must have lied on his application and it slipped through."

"What did Sizemore say?"

"He said that since it was an unsubstantiated phone call, they might not have had enough probable cause to stop and arrest, but after the results of last night, they now have more than enough. They're going to let him go, but starting tonight, they're going to get tougher."

"One guy is probable cause to keep this thing going? That cop Sizemore must be as dumb as he sounds."

"I got the impression that your friends over at Besafe had a tidy amount of violations. I also got the feeling that he's a pretty bright cop."

"Couldn't have happened to nicer people." Dennis chuckled, but was interrupted by the ringing phone.

"Dennis here." His smile instantly disappeared. After listening to the person on the other end, he said, "Tell me again slowly what they found."

"I've never been through an inspection like that one," the driver of car eleven said to his partner.

"I understand that three of the guys were stopped last night by the police and violations were found in all three cars."

The driver looked around the empty car before he answered. "I heard that Dennis Canon found out this morning that the health department closed down the gym he owns. You know, that place called Sunrise Gym."

"No shit! What happened?"

"During a routine inspection, they found pieces of dead rats laying around."

"Dead rats? What the hell were they doing with dead rats?"

"I don't want to know. I've eaten in the restaurant area of that place and it makes me sick just thinking about it."

"I don't know. Shit just happens." Dennis Canon was listening to the voice of someone he had never met and never wanted to.

"Yeah, I've met Aaron Carlyle, but I haven't had any dealings with him." Dennis thought, *This guy is eerie. How does he know about Carlyle?*

"I know you told me to stay away from him and the Besafe organization, but he just got in the way one night." Sweat started to run down the side of Canon's face.

"Listen, if you don't like the job I'm doing, come on down and we'll discuss it face to face." As the words left his mouth he felt his chest start to constrict. There was no doubt in his mind that this man, whoever he was, could inflict more damage to him than he could imagine. This man spoke like he was used to having his orders obeyed.

Three thousand miles away in a non-descript office two blocks away from Dupont Circle, a man with short-cropped gray hair and a thin white scar that ran down the side of his face sat staring out the twelfth floor window. He turned to the two men seated on the opposite side of his desk.

"Every operation we have is working, except for the one in Southern California. We're going to have to do some housekeeping."

Chapter 35

The two men looked at each other, but they knew better than to say anything. They would be told exactly what to do and when to do it.

Aaron Carlyle has always been a pain. He screwed up an operation for us in Cambodia about seven years ago, hurt our stock manipulation deal two years ago, and now he's gotten in the middle of our moving into the high tech manufacturing arena."

The younger of the two men seated at the desk asked, "Are those people from Interstate capable of handling Carlyle?"

After a moment, he answered, "Probably not, but I know they're going to try, even though I told them not to."

"Do you want us to give them some help?"

The man with the scar glared. "Don't you listen? I told them not to get involved with Aaron Carlyle or his people."

"But he did! We've got a lot of money invested out there. We've got to protect what's ours."

"Aaron Carlyle is one of the good guys. He could bring this whole operation down around our heads. We might be better off just walking away with what we already have." He ran his hand across the top of his crew cut and looked at the two men. He realized that he would have to let them try and help that idiot Canon or lose some of his control. "Let's try and give Canon some help, but we can't let him know we're doing it. He doesn't know who we are and we're better off keeping it that way. Carlyle's got some friend who's a police captain, and another with connections to the Vietnamese Mafia, if that's what they call it. Whoever you send out there to help, tell them to be careful."

"I'm going to go," said the younger of the two men.

The man behind the desk touched his scar. He knew how the youngster felt. Looking at the other man, he asked, "Is he ready?"

"Probably not, but he's got to go. It's called on-the-job training."

He stared at the youngster for almost thirty seconds before he whispered, "Be careful." He turned his back on both of them and returned to staring out the window.

It took almost fifteen minutes before he saw them leave the building and get into the back seat of a waiting limousine. He took a deep breath and closed his eyes, waiting for the rush of sentiment to retreat. He left the window and walked over to a mirror where he straightened his tie. Looking at the mirror, he could see the American flag against the back of the office.

"Watching your son go on his first mission is like being in the reviewing stand as the American flag is carried past," he said to his image in the mirror, explaining to himself why his eyes were red. He walked back to his desk, picked up the phone, and started barking out instructions.

Chapter 36

"It's been three days since we started screwing with Canon. What do you think he's doing?" Tom waited for Aaron or Scott to answer.

"Min told me this morning that he's put seven of Canon's cleaning trucks out of commission. Nothing serious, just some sugar in the gas tanks, slow leaks by the valves in the tires, and draining the oil," Aaron told his two friends.

"That'll only keep them out of action for a couple of days. I would've thought between Min and Tuloc, they would've been more creative," Scott said and laughed.

Aaron smiled. "Don't sell them short. They've followed the workers home and have done the same things to them, keeping them away from work." He turned his head as there was a knock on the conference room door. "Come on in."

Michael entered with a single sheet of paper in his hand. "The police have arrested eight of Interstate's men during the past twenty-four hours. They've also handed out citations on five vehicles, which will keep them off the road for a couple more days. Cassius thinks it would be a good idea for you to call Canon and complain that his sloppy work is causing you grief. We've also had four people apply for jobs that either work for or used to work for Interstate. They're all saying the same thing—it's chaos over there."

"You haven't hired any of them, have you?" Aaron asked.

"No. We can't take a chance that they're spies for Canon, but we are starting to get calls from some of the companies that he services. We're going to have to hire more people."

"Where are you going to get them?" Scott asked.

"I'm thinking of going to the colleges. With summer break coming up, I think I can get some students that are looking for work. I also put out the word through the regulars that we're looking. Morale is pretty low and I might get some of them to give us a try."

"Let us know how you make out," Aaron said. It was obvious from his voice that he expected Michael's hiring of people to be part of his job responsibilities.

Michael nodded and left the room, closing the door behind him.

"He's a good man," Scott said to no one in particular. "I'm glad he's on our side."

"Tom, tell us where you stand with Providence." Aaron looked up from the paper he had in front of him.

"I ducked all the calls from Canon's lawyer for a little over a week. I then told him we were prepared to sell, and the asking price was fourteen million."

"What'd he say?" Aaron asked.

"That I was out of my mind. They might be willing to go to three and a half, but even that was a stretch. He reminded me that without shipments, they could be bankrupt by this time next month."

"Could they?" Scott asked.

"What he doesn't know is that with the money we put into the place, Lan was able to negotiate a deal that will get her parts within the next four to five days. Her material director fired the cleaning service run by Canon's guy and hired Min's company as their replacement. Min leaves some men inside the building after everyone goes home. He's done the same thing at Active Components, the company that is making the chips. Someone trying to break into either building is going to run into a bunch of screaming Vietnamese men with guns."

"When are we taking care of Kebra Metcalf?" Scott asked Aaron.

"Tonight around eight thirty."

"Any changes on who's going to be there?" Scott continued.

"No, we're going as planned. Cassius isn't happy, but I think it works."

Tom hesitated, and then decided to just ask. "Scott and I have been wondering how Karen is doing?"

"She answered the phone when I called earlier. It's not what she's saying that bothers me—it's what she's not saying. I get the feeling that she's still reliving that night and can't put it behind her. I'm going down this weekend to see what I can do."

"Are you going to call Canon?" Scott asked

"Yeah, I might as well do it now. I need the lift."

"Put him on the speaker, I'd like to hear his voice," Scott said as he moved closer. "I think he telegraphs his outbursts with a catch in his voice, or something like that."

"Hold on a second," Tom said as he stood up and left the room. He returned with a tape recorder, put the plug in the wall, and nodded his head. "Ready!"

Aaron dialed the number and asked for Dennis Canon.

"Canon, here."

Before he could say anything else, Aaron started yelling into the phone, "Canon, you no good piece of garbage. I'm sick and tired of you and your company! It's bad enough I have to put up with your coming to my house, but when you can't even do simple maintenance on your vehicles, it's creating a major problem that I don't want or need."

"Who, who is this?" Canon sputtered into the phone.

Scott held up his thumb.

"This is your worst enemy. Listen carefully, if just one more of my cars gets stopped, you'll regret it."

"I'll regret it? Listen to me. I'm done with you threatening me. Why don't you and I just meet in a parking lot and have it out?"

"I'd love to meet you, but I don't trust you. You'd probably bring three or four of your goons like last time."

"Just name the time and place!" Canon was now screaming into the phone.

Aaron, smiling at his two friends, tapped on the phone. "Hello! Hello! I guess he hung up."

"I can hear you! I can hear you!" Canon was screaming at the top of his lungs as Aaron ended the call.

"Aaron," Tom started, "you're going to have to be careful. I don't think it'll take much to push him over the edge."

"I'm not worried about him, I just hope he'll somehow lead us to his boss," Aaron replied.

"I hope I'm wrong but, every once in a while, there's something in his eyes that tells me he could be dangerous. I just don't want us to underestimate him." Tom turned to Scott for his input.

"I think Tom's right in wanting us to be cautious, but he seems to send other people to do his dirty work. I'm more concerned with this guy Paul Kiesler." A knock on the conference room door stopped their conversation.

Michael spoke as he entered the room. "Aaron, I have someone I'd like you to meet."

Chapter 37

"Gentlemen, meet Pamela Haviland," Michael said as the three men rose from their chairs.

"My friends call me Pam," she said as she held out her hand.

"Pam and I worked together in San Francisco when I was on the force. She recently moved to San Clemente and stopped by to say hello."

"That's almost a hundred percent true. We really didn't work together, I worked for Michael, the last two years he was on the force." She smiled at Michael before continuing. "My father took ill and I had to move back to Orange County to help out about six months ago." The smile left her face. "He died last month and now I need a job. I hadn't seen Michael since he got involved with some Vietnamese in Ghirardelli Square a couple of years ago and when I heard you were hiring, I came looking. Michael said he wanted me to talk to you three." The smile returned as she said, "I didn't want there to be any confusion as to my being Michael's friend and that's why you would hire me. I'm a pretty good cop. I was up for my gold shield when my dad took sick."

Aaron looked at Michael. "Is there some reason you brought her into meet us except to say hello to a new employee?"

"Yes there is. I've already had Mai Ling start on the paperwork, but with your approval I was going to assign her to watch over Karen."

Both Tom and Scott sat down and watched Aaron as he stared at Pam.

"Have you ever shot anyone?" Aaron asked.

Pam looked at Michael, who nodded.

"Yes" she said quietly. "During the four years I spent on the force, I shot five people—three men, one woman, and a seventeen-year-old boy. The seventeen-year-old died." Her voice, which had started quietly, was almost down to a whisper.

"What did the review board have to say?" Aaron asked.

"They were all justifiable shoots. Two of the men were shot attempting to rob a drug store. The other was shot while trying to drive away in a stolen car." Her voice got stronger and she started talking faster. "I shot the woman as she was carving up her pimp, and I put three bullets into the seventeen-year-old as he ran when I stopped him in the middle of raping a six-year-old little boy."

The entire room was silent. Pam looked at the three men in front of her. They were all absorbed in thought.

"If it will make a difference in what you're thinking about me, I wish he hadn't died. I'd have preferred the system handle him," she hesitated, "where they could have used him the way he used that poor kid."

Michael motioned to her. "Come and finish the paperwork. You can start tomorrow. We'll figure out the best place for you."

"Michael, when you get a second, come on back. I want to talk to you." Before they were gone, Aaron added, "And Pam, welcome aboard. I think you'll like it here."

"Who's Karen? Pam asked as they left the room.

"She's the boss's lady friend. She got shot by two guys who were trying for Aaron."

"What happened to the two guys?"

"One of them didn't make it and we haven't found the other one yet."

"Is she okay?"

"Physically, I think yes. Mentally, I'm not sure. I haven't spoken to her, but the rumor mill says something's wrong."

"What would you expect me to do?"

"Watch over her. I'm using twelve men around the clock. If

Aaron can talk her into it, I can reduce it to six men and you. I can use those six bodies to cover other locations."

"I'm not a baby sitter."

"If you accept the job, you're what we tell you to be. A few years ago, we had two men break into her house. The guards we had on duty killed one of them and no one ever heard from the other. Besafe is a law-abiding firm that doesn't put up with any . . ." Michael interrupted himself. "You haven't told me if you're signing on yet."

"Michael, I'll take your word. I don't want to waste away. I liked being on the street. Tell me this is more than just checking doors at night."

"Pam, when you were on the force, some days you were the dog and some days you were the hydrant. Come to work for Besafe and you'll never be the hydrant."

Chapter 38

"You wanted to see me Aaron?" Michael asked as he entered the conference room.

"Has she signed on?"

Michael nodded. "Mai Ling is having her fill out the rest of the paperwork."

"How did you plan on using her?"

"That part gets a little tricky. I was hoping that you would talk to Karen and have her agree to let Pam stay with her for a couple weeks. I'd still have two men around the clock, but with Pam around, I could then get by with six and put the other six back covering some of the new places that Scott is signing up."

"Is she as good as she seems?"

"Better. If she were a man, she would already have her gold shield."

"Can we trust her enough to bring her along tonight? Mai Ling might like the company, and it would certainly relieve Cassius's mind."

"Aaron, let me ask you a question about tonight. I haven't heard a word from Min or Tuloc. I can't believe this operation is going down without their involvement."

"They're starting to worry me a little also, but they said they would stay out of the way. If you're comfortable with Pam, let's get her and Mai Ling in here and make sure we have our plan down tight."

Kebra Metcalf threw her keys to the valet standing by the door of the Hyatt. "I won't be needing it tonight. You can park it somewhere."

He nodded his understanding of her instructions. She gave him twenty dollars each Friday for listening. He only had to hear two things, she was either coming back, in which case the car was left nearby, or he could park it because she was in for the night.

Kebra strode across the tile floor, her high heels attracting everyone's attention as she headed for the bar at the rear of the hotel. Just before she started up the three steps, she noticed Mai Ling sitting at a table in the corner with another woman. *Bitch,* she thought. *What the hell is she trying to pull?*

Mai Ling looked up from her conversation and waved at Kebra. She stood and walked over to where Kebra had stopped.

"Who's that?" Kebra asked.

"Her name's Pam. She's waiting for some guy she met at the lounge in Westlake. We're having a drink. Come on in. She won't be here long. I promised you that the two of us would have some time together, didn't I?"

Kebra looked at Pam across the room. She had dark hair, a pretty face, and a nice body. As she got closer, Kebra noticed that Pam's nose was a little crooked and that she had a small birthmark on her neck. Pam stood as they got closer, but then waved at someone behind Kebra and Mai Ling. Kebra instinctively turned and felt her face flush as the man she knew as Scott entered.

Pam walked up to where Mai Ling was standing and said, "Mai Ling, it was nice having a drink with you. We'll have to do this again when we have more time." She nodded at Kebra and then walked off to join Scott who had remained standing at the door.

Aaron smiled and waved at Kebra as he took Pam's arm and directed her toward the elevator.

"Keep smiling," he said to Pam as the elevator door closed. "She's doing a slow burn."

The elevator stopped on the fourth floor where Aaron and Pam got off. Aaron led Pam to the stairwell and walked quickly down to the third floor where he had reserved the room next door to Kebra's.

Upon entering, he knocked softly on the door that connected the two rooms. He expected one of Min's people, but almost didn't recognize Sookie in a maid's uniform when the door opened.

She bowed her head slightly toward Aaron. "I'm leaving now. I don't think she will notice the door between the two rooms is unlocked. The camera in this room is hooked up to the television in the room you're in. Channel twenty-five will give you the ability to see what is happening. I have been told to remind you that nothing must happen to Mai Ling."

"I understand," Aaron replied. "How are your people coming with their search for the room with the other camera?"

"Tuloc is in charge and has finished inspecting all the rooms on the first and second floors. He thinks they will be finished by tomorrow night. The hotel is very busy and it is sometimes hard to get into the rooms." She started to close the door between them. "Uncle Aaron, I know that Mai Ling is without fear and has helped you in the past, but please take care of her." Without waiting for a reply, she closed the door, leaving Aaron and Pam alone.

"She called you uncle," Pam commented as Aaron sat down on one of the two chairs in the room.

"It is mostly ceremonial, although I'm the godfather of their son."

"Obviously there's a lot I don't know about the cast of players and the events leading up to tonight, but I do understand that nothing happens to Mai Ling. What about Kebra Metcalf?"

"She was there when they planted a bomb in the hospital. I don't know how involved she is, but I don't want her around helping them. I'm not looking to have her hurt physically, but mentally is another story."

Through the door, they could hear voices. The first one was Mai Ling's.

"This is a nice room."

"It's adequate. It's not as nice as the hotel I stay at in when I'm in Washington, D.C. or San Diego, but it serves its purpose."

Aaron and Pam were staring at the television. Mai Ling had taken off her jacket and was looking out the window. Kebra walked up behind her and placed her hands on Mai Lings shoulders. Her fingers brushed aside Mai Ling's long black hair as she leaned forward and lightly kissed her neck.

"You smell nice. What are you wearing?"

Mai Ling turned around to face Kebra. "I feel a little uncomfortable. Besafe and Interstate, the companies we work for, are having problems with each other and I feel like a traitor."

"Don't be silly. What we do when we're alone has nothing to do with what our companies are doing." She spoke as her fingers were unbuttoning Mai Ling's sweater.

Mai Ling raised her hands to Kebra's face, forcing Kebra's hands to stop what they were doing.

"Do you really believe that?" Mai Ling asked.

"Of course I do. I've had a relationship with the big boss back in D.C. for a couple of years and that has nothing to do with what I do out here. My allegiance is to me."

Aaron stood up and walked closer to the television.

"What's wrong?" Pam asked.

"I don't want to miss a word of what she's saying."

"We are making a copy of the video, aren't we?"

"I need to freshen up. Why don't you get into bed and I'll be out in a minute." Mai Ling's voice interrupted Pam's question.

Kebra placed her hands on each of Mai Ling's cheeks and pulled her face closer. She lightly kissed each of her eyes before kissing her on the mouth. Her hands started massaging Mai Ling's back, moving faster and faster until they reached the base of her spine.

Mai Ling stepped away and said, "I'll be right out. Why don't you get into bed?"

As the door to the bathroom closed, Kebra started to discard her clothes in a frenzy.

"You ready?" Aaron asked.

Pam nodded that she was and stood next to the connecting door, waiting for Aaron's signal.

When Kebra got into bed, Aaron walked over and opened the door.

"How the hell did you get in here?" she shouted, recognizing Aaron. "Get out! You had your chance and blew it."

She started to get out of bed when Pam walked in behind him. Kebra sat back and looked intently at what was happening.

Aaron banged on the bathroom door. "Get out here, now!"

The door opened and Mai Ling walked out fully clothed.

"Mr. Carlyle!" she stammered.

"Mr. Carlyle?" Kebra sat up, the blanket falling to her waist. "You're Aaron Carlyle?"

"I knew someone at Besafe was leaking company confidential information, I just didn't think it was you, Mai Ling."

"I'd never tell anyone information about our company," she cried.

"We've got you on tape with this bimbo talking about the big boss in Washington, D.C."

"Who the hell are you calling a bimbo? What tape?" Scanning the room she yelled, "It's against the law to tape someone without their permission." Kebra started to get out of bed.

Pam stopped her. "Stay put! We don't need your naked butt parading around the room."

"Who the hell do you think you're talking to?" Kebra said as her feet hit the ground.

"Someone who'll be under arrest for commercial espionage, and accessory to murder. That's who." Kebra turned as Barry walked into the room.

"My name is Captain Sands of the Ventura County Police. We've been investigating the break-in and murder at Active Components, and you fill the bill as an accessory. I would suggest that you don't say anything else until you consult with your lawyer. Anything you say can and will be held against you."

Kebra put her hands on her hips as a show of defiance.

"I would get dressed if I were you. You stay like that and I'll add prostitution to the rest of the charges."

"This is a setup!" Kebra cried out. "I want to make a phone call."

"You're entitled to one down at the station. Are you going to get dressed or am I taking you in that way?"

"Barry, can I talk to Ms. Metcalf alone for a second?" Aaron asked.

"What for?" Barry responded loudly.

"She may be an unwilling accomplice, in which case I'd be prepared to drop charges against her."

"Out of past friendship, I'll give you ten minutes, but I'm holding on to this one," he replied, pointing at Mai Ling.

Closing the door to the adjoining room as they left Aaron turned and looked straight at Kebra, who hadn't yet put on her clothes.

"Are you just looking or do we have time for a quickie?" Kebra sneered.

"Listen carefully," Aaron interrupted. "I want Paul. I'm positive he's the one that killed one of my men. I also want his boss. I don't believe Canon's smart enough to pull this off, and I think you know who the real boss is."

"You're crazy. Even if I knew what you were talking about, I wouldn't say a thing. Guys like them have connections beyond what you could imagination."

"Suppose I could guarantee no one would ever know what went on here today. Could you come up with enough information to make it worthwhile?"

Chapter 39

Kebra reached down and pulled a pair of black panties from the pile of clothes. “I don’t think you have enough evidence to put me in jail.” Her insolence was gone and she was left with questions that she was afraid to ask. She hooked her bra and pulled the straps over her arms as she glared at him.

“Kebra, let me tell you a story. I don’t know if there really is a big boss in Washington, but let’s for a second consider what happens if there is. We are going to leak enough information so that he believes you have told us what we want to know. He’s going to have to make sure you never talk to a jury. If you help me get Paul, he’ll give me his boss, and you’re off the hook.”

Aaron watched her face and could tell she wasn’t convinced. He had no other cards to play except for the wild thought going through his head.

“This guy you met in D.C., the guy with the crew cut and the scar on the side of his face, I don’t want him.”

Kebra looked up, startled at his reference to the man she had met in D.C. “You know Simon?”

“We’ve met a few times. Does he still stand like he’s got a broom handle up his spine?”

“Where did you meet him?” she asked.

“I’m sorry, but I never discuss him with anyone, and I mean anyone. If I ever need to talk to him I use a private number.”

Kebra sat down on the bed. “I don’t know if Paul is the one who killed your man, but I can tell you he’s capable of it.”

“What’s with him and Ellen? Is he trying to get a foothold in MCD or something.”

“Where do you get all your information?” she asked, genuinely surprised.

“Simon calls me from time to time and fills me in.”

In the other room, Barry, Mai Ling, and Pam stood silently staring at the screen.

“Who’s Simon?” Pam asked.

“No one Aaron knows. She gave him that name and he’s using it like a professional.”

“Maybe you can tell me something,” Kebra said as she pulled her blouse over her head. “When I met Simon, I was at a convention in Washington on behavioral science. I got the impression he worked for the government. Do you know who he works for?”

“Yes, but I’m not allowed to mention it. I can tell you the first time I met him he was in the Marines.”

“That figures. His body is like a rock and he’s got a two-inch scar under his rib cage.”

“Have you seen him out here in California?”

“No. I’ve only seen him twice since I first met him two years ago. I ran into him at a meeting in Austin, and again in Detroit when he suggested I start California Behavioral Institute. He even helped me get the funding. He set me up with Dennis Canon as my first client with the understanding that I could call him if I needed help.”

“Have you?”

“I’ve called him twice with little problems, and within forty-eight hours, the problems were taken care of.”

“What kind of problems?”

Kebra buttoned her skirt as she stood and walked to the window. “Nothing I want to talk about,” she replied without turning around.

“Tell me about Paul. Why do you think he’s capable of murder?”

“He’s got a mean streak.” When Aaron didn’t reply, she continued, “He was one of the problems. When I first started working with Interstate, Paul asked me out." She sat down on the edge of the bed and looked at the ceiling.

"Something's bothering her," Pam said to Barry. "Something she doesn't want to remember."

"Or trying to forget," Barry responded.

Aaron poured a glass of water and handed it to Kebra.

"I'm not a prude, but I guess you already figured that out," She smiled at Aaron. "We went out for dinner and after, things got a little out of hand. When I objected to what he wanted to do, he started using his hands. I called the number Simon had given me and told him what happened. Two days later, Paul sent me flowers and apologized. He's never bothered me again."

"Tell me about that guy Jerry you were at the hospital with."

"I never met him until the day before we visited your man Rojas. He told me what questions he was after and said he would give me a high sign when I should stop."

"You know he left a bomb in the room."

"Where would he get a bomb? The only thing he had with him was the tape recorder."

Mai Ling whispered in the other room, "She didn't know?"

"Have you heard anything about a company called Providence?" Aaron continued the questions.

"There was a joke going around about the lady that owns the company. It seems they sent her a one-year free membership in Sunrise Gym, and she raffled it off to her employees. It didn't make a lot of sense because they already did her cleaning."

"Time to go!" Barry sounded impatient as he entered the room.

"Captain Sands, I find I must ask you a favor," Aaron replied looking at his watch.

"I would like you to hold off charging Ms. Metcalf with anything criminal. How about keeping her as a material witness?"

"Why would I do that?" Barry asked, looking at Kebra.

"First of all, we're friends, and I wouldn't do anything to compromise an ongoing investigation. Second, I don't think she knows anything about any criminal activities, but can certainly help you with her insight into some of the people."

"How do I know she'll cooperate?"

"Would you take her word . . . if I vouch for her?"

Barry looked at Kebra. "Ms. Metcalf, do I have your word?" Kebra nodded and Barry continued, "Pack your clothes and let's get out of here."

Chapter 40

"I'm headed down to San Diego tonight, and I should be back late tomorrow or the next day, depending on how Karen's feeling."

"Constance spoke to her yesterday. She said she sounded better, but Karen told her she wasn't ready for visitors yet," Scott told both Aaron and Tom.

"I spoke to her this morning. She told me she was going back to work on Monday and would like to see me before then. I don't know exactly what that means, but I couldn't pass up the opportunity."

Scott and Tom looked at each other, but didn't say a word.

Michael entered the room, closing the door behind him. "Captain Sands has Kebra Metcalf stashed away near Santa Barbara. We had everything she said transcribed and she signed it. That along with the video we took will at least prove conspiracy. We just have to find the people to tag it on."

"Did she say anything else about Simon?" Aaron asked.

"She gave us the phone number, but it doesn't exist, according to the phone company. Aaron, I have to ask you a question," Michael hesitated. "I've watched the tape and it's almost like you and Barry know this guy. Is there something I should know?"

"We don't know him," Aaron replied and paused. "Actually, maybe we do. About nine or ten years ago, I had a problem when I left Vietnam. A colonel helped me. Two years ago when we were involved with those guy who were trying to fix the stock market, we got a little help from a guy in Washington. We never figured out where he fit in, but when she started talking, I just gave it a shot."

"Have you ever tried to find him?"

"Barry tried, but came up empty. We're sure he's out there, but we don't if he's a friend or an enemy."

Michael turned toward Tom and handed him four sheets of paper. "These are some new hires. The background checks were clean. Pam you've met, Fred and Jeff are ex police, and Troy is Princeton graduate. He graduated with a degree in criminology. He's looking for experience, which we can give him, but I think he'll ultimately go on to bigger and better things."

Tom, looking over the personnel forms, mentioned, "Both Troy and Pam have the same birthday. He's just a year older."

"They'll be getting to know each other better. I'm sending him down to San Diego with her."

Aaron looked up. "He doesn't have enough experience to be on that detail."

"I think he'll do fine," Michael responded quickly.

After a few seconds, Aaron said, "I'm sure he will. Will it be okay if I say hello to both of them before they leave?"

Michael smiled back. "Come on, I'll introduce you."

After they left the room, Tom said to Scott. "I wonder what kind of name Ewing is?"

"Ewing? Sounds familiar. Maybe Scandinavian?" Scott thought for a second, "Maybe English."

"Pam's last name is Haviland. Maybe that's English also?" Tom replied, turning over Pam's paperwork.

"Now you're going to be a matchmaker!" Scott said as he left the room.

Walking toward his office, Scott noticed Aaron talking to Pam and the person he assumed was Troy. He muttered, "They are a nice looking couple."

Chapter 41

"This is Aaron."

"Are you alone?" Barry asked.

"Yes, is there a problem?"

"No, I just didn't want anyone listening to this conversation. I think we've gotten as much out of Kebra Metcalf as we're going to get. I tried to have the number she had for this guy Simon traced, but came up empty. I'd swear it sounds like that guy Webster we were trying to find a couple of years ago."

"I think you're right," Aaron responded quietly.

Barry continued, "We've pulled thirteen of their cars off the road and arrested eleven of their people. The health department is allowing them to re-open the gym next Monday. That's when I'll have the fire department go in and look around. I spoke to Tuloc earlier and he told me that he has hired sixteen of their cleaning crew and has taken over seven of their accounts. I've pulled in some favors, and starting today, police cars are going to swing by their liquor stores and start checking the ages of the people buying alcohol."

"They've got to be bleeding all over the place." Aaron slowed his car down and looked into his rearview mirror. "Their stock has fallen over ten points in the past three days. Someone has got to be selling out."

"Speaking of stock, how's my favorite stock advisor doing?"

"I'll know better after I see her today. Gotta go, traffic is getting heavier."

"Be careful," Barry said as he disconnected.

Aaron was now positive he was being followed. He had noticed the light green Oldsmobile earlier and even though he switched lanes twice, it was still three cars behind him.

Aaron looked at the sign he was approaching. The Palomar airport was only fifteen or twenty minutes from where Karen lived. Moving from the number four lane to the number two lane, Aaron watched the green Oldsmobile. It had gotten caught in the number three and was now stuck in the flow of traffic. Aaron hit the gas and cut off the car next to him as he abruptly left the freeway for the service road. He followed the flight of the Oldsmobile as it tried to exit—unsuccessfully. The traffic light turned green as Aaron approached and he impulsively decided to get right back on the freeway and hopefully get a chance to follow the followers.

Twenty minutes later, he pulled into Karen's driveway. Looking up and down the empty street, he decided whoever was following him was lost in the maze of lights and exits between Palomar and Carlsbad.

The front door opened as he approached. "Hi, Aaron." Dorothy Williams held out her arms.

"Hi, Mrs. Williams. Is everything okay?" Aaron returned her embrace.

"Everything is fine. I'm going out with some friends and I wanted to say hello before I left."

"How's Karen?"

"You can ask her yourself. She'll be out in a second. I'm staying at my friend's house tonight, so don't worry about me." She picked up an overnight bag, kissed him on the cheek, and walked out.

Aaron was watching her leave when he heard Karen behind him.

"Are you going to stand there all night or are you going to say hello to me?"

He turned as she moved into his arms. "I've missed you," she whispered.

"You've missed me? I've been worried sick about you."

She stepped back. There was a sad smile on her face.

"Aaron, we have to talk." She led him by the arm into the den. "I've ordered some food, but we can go out if you want."

"No, I'd just as soon stay in. Is there anything specific we have to talk about or can I just tell you how much I love you?"

"How about I tell you what's bothering me, and then you tell me how much you love me."

"First can I have a kiss?"

Karen started to walk into his arms and then stopped. "I think I should talk first."

Aaron lowered himself to the sofa as Karen started pacing.

"First, let me tell you that I love you," she paused. "But, I'm scared stiff. I've had plenty of time to think about what happened and what I think I need is a shrink. I'm pretty self-sufficient, but this business you're in could get you killed, and I couldn't live with that as a possibility."

"Karen . . ." Before Aaron could say anymore, she held up her hand.

"Please let me finish."

Aaron sat back, his heart beating so loudly he was positive she could hear it.

"Besafe means too much to you for me to ask you to give it up, but I can't live with the alternative. I think we should cancel the wedding."

There were tears in her eyes as she watched him struggle to come up with the right words.

Before he could say anything else, there was a knock on the door. He watched as Karen retreated into a corner.

"I'll get it," he said automatically.

Before opening the door, he looked out the window. "They're my people," he called to Karen over his shoulder. "You should meet them. They're new."

Opening the door, Aaron motioned for Pam and Troy to come in.

"Karen, I'd like you to meet Pam Haviland and Troy . . . I'm sorry, I don't remember your last name." His voice sounded strange to his ears and he hoped they wouldn't notice.

"Ewing. Ms. Williams, my name is Troy Ewing."

Aaron's face clouded over.

"Something wrong, Mr. Carlyle?" Pam asked, looking at Aaron and then at Troy.

"No. It's just Troy's last name. It sounds familiar, but I can't place where I heard it before." Shrugging his shoulders, he turned toward Karen. "We've got twelve men around the clock watching you, your house, and your mother. I'd like to have Pam stay with you for a little while and reduce that number to six."

"You've got twelve people watching me?"

"Not only you. Like I said, you, your mom, and your house."

"I've never seen them."

"You shouldn't. We don't think there's a problem, but I would rather err on the side of caution."

"You've got twelve more people outside?"

"No, Ms. Williams. Since Troy and I came down, we've gone to six people working eight-hour shifts. The two people on this shift followed your mother to wherever she's headed."

Every one turned at the sound of the chimes from the front door and Karen said, "It's probably the deli. I hope I ordered enough food for four of us."

Aaron started to look out the window as Troy asked, "Who's there?"

"Delicatessen!" was the reply.

Troy opened the door as Aaron yelled, "Don't!"

Three men pushed their way by Troy with guns in their hands.

"Don't anyone move!" shouted the first man in the door. He motioned for the man behind him to open the door leading to the back yard.

Two more men entered, one of them quickly going up the stairs. "No one up here," he shouted.

"You thought you lost us, didn't you?" The heaviest of the five men pointing at Aaron asked. "Who are these two?" he asked, pointing his chin at Troy and Pam.

"They're neighbors," Karen answered.

"Neighbors my ass. They're probably security." The man coming down the stairs said, "Someone better search them."

One of the men walked over to Aaron and another headed in the direction of Troy. As he passed, Karen lashed out screaming, "Keep your rotten, filthy hands off of him." Everyone turned to face her. Troy grabbed the man who was approaching him and Aaron punched the one closest to him. Karen was bending over to pick up the pistol that was dropped by the man she attacked when she and everyone else in the room heard Pam.

"Don't anybody move!"

As if in one motion, every eye turned toward her voice. The man that had been near her lay on the floor and she stood with both hands clenched around a pistol.

"Troy, take their weapons! Mr. Carlyle, Miss Williams . . . are you both all right?"

Karen quickly turned to look for Aaron. He smiled and acknowledged with a nod of his head.

Pam kicked the intruder lying on the floor in front of her. "Get up and join your friends. Troy, search them one at a time. We need guns, knives, and any identification they have on them." Turning to Aaron, she asked, "Mr. Carlyle, please keep an eye on these amateurs while I contact the men following Ms. Williams's mother."

"Do they have to involve her?" Karen asked.

"No, they won't say a thing. I just want to alert them to the problem."

Aaron looked at the men sitting on the floor. "What were you supposed to do?"

No one answered.

"Troy, go out and see what kind of car they were driving."

Troy looked at Pam. The look on his face said he didn't understand.

"Now!" she barked.

As he reached the door, he turned and looked at Pam.

She walked over to the man closest to her and kicked his leg. "The next time you're asked a question, someone better answer." She looked at each of them in turn and then nodded at Aaron.

"Now that I have your attention, what were you going to do once we were under your control?"

"We were supposed to tell you to stay the hell out of ISCC's business."

"And who told you to tell us this?"

"Jerry Whitney."

"I've been looking for him for over a week. Where do you think I could find him?"

"Don't know. These guys work for me and I contracted with Jerry over the phone."

"How'd you find me?"

"When we lost you on the freeway, I called Jerry and he gave me your girlfriend's address."

"You didn't have it when you started?"

"I asked for it just in case I lost you, but he said there was some reason they didn't want to start up with you at home. We were supposed to stop you where it was deserted and give you the message."

"Why so many people?" Aaron motioned to the five of them on the floor.

"He said you might have help, either with you or close by."

Troy had entered while Aaron was asking questions and in the lull said, "It looks like they got here in two cars. There's a green Oldsmobile and a black Chevrolet out in front."

"I have another question. How did you know about the deli food?"

"The kid pulled up in front the same time we did, and I and paid him for it. It seemed like a good way to get inside."

"I guess that means I should thank you for buying us dinner." Aaron looked around the room. "I now have a problem. You five know the address of this house. If I were to let you go, how would I be sure that you would never bother Ms. Williams again?"

"Shit man! We're long gone."

Troy, who was watching, was fascinated by what was going on.

"I don't think so. I have another idea, though. Suppose I cut off the pinkie on your right hands. It would be a reminder that if anything ever happened to her, the rest of your hand would be next. Even if it wasn't your fault."

"Mr. Carlyle, why don't you let Troy and I handle this for you? I think the loss of a pinkie might be a little extreme. The small toe would be the same reminder and it wouldn't show."

Aaron looked at Pam and winked. She was good.

"Okay, Troy, you have their names and addresses. Why don't you and Pam take them out of here and handle it any way she sees fit?"

The five men on the floor were squirming. None of what they heard made them feel good. Pam motioned for them to rise.

"Good night Mr. Carlyle. If you need us for anything, you have our number."

When the door closed, Aaron turned toward Karen. "That was a dumb thing you did earlier."

Sitting, she looked up at him and said, "Aaron, I was prepared to tell you that we should stop seeing each other for a while, but when I thought he might hurt you, all I could think about was what I would do if you weren't here. I couldn't let that happen. I realized that without you . . ." She stopped as Aaron leaned over and kissed her. ". . . there would be no one to . . . " He kissed her again. ". . . keep saving your ass."

Putting his finger on her lips, he whispered, "Your mother said she wouldn't be home tonight, and we have a lot of catching up to do."

Chapter 42

"This is Troy."

"Where the hell have you been?" Troy recognized the nasal voice of the colonel's aide.

"I'm in California. I told you I was going and you said okay."

"And I told you to report in on a regular basis. The colonel is all over my butt."

"What's he so concerned about?"

In his office, the aide looked at his boss, who shook his head no.

"He doesn't like operatives in the field running wild and not reporting in. This is your first assignment and I feel like dragging your ass back here and sending someone else. Your assignment was to give aid to Canon without letting him know who's helping."

"Let me stay out here . . . I'll report in on a regular basis, I promise. It's just that things got a little hectic.

"Tell me what's happening."

"I got myself a job with Besafe. They assigned me to work with another new employee and . . ."

"This is Colonel. Make your report correctly. What is her name?"

"Pam, Pam Haviland." Troy sat up straighter as he heard the colonel's voice.

"Tell us about her," the aide continued.

"Not a lot to tell. She's from San Francisco. She was a cop

whose father took sick and she had to come back to Southern Cal to help him."

As Troy spoke, the colonel looked through a file on his desk.

"What does she look like?" the aide asked.

"Sort of a plain Jane. Darkish hair, maybe five foot five, mostly nondescript is how I would describe her."

The colonel held up Pam's picture for his aide to see. They both smiled.

"What else is going on?" the aide asked.

"We were assigned to watch over Carlyle's girlfriend and her mother."

"And?"

"Some of Canon's men . . ." Troy stopped. "Let me rephrase that, some men that were hired by one of Canon's men broke into the girlfriend's house while we were there."

"What were you doing there?"

"Carlyle was introducing us to his girlfriend."

"Go on." This time it was the colonel urging him to continue.

"Karen jumped one of the men . . ."

"Who the hell is Karen?" the colonel barked as he opened another folder.

"Karen's the girlfriend."

"Tell me about her."

A look of concern crossed Troy's face. The colonel was now asking all the questions.

"She's good looking. She seems in pretty good shape. I had the feeling something was wrong with her, but she handled herself okay. She was shot a few weeks ago, so maybe that was it. She has beautiful eyes. You get the feeling that she's looking right into your soul."

"Go on."

"Well, she jumped one of the guys. Aaron hit another one . . ."

"Aaron?"

"Mr. Carlyle hit another one and all of a sudden Pam has a gun out and is threatening to shoot them."

The colonel was reading through a third folder. "Did she?"

"No. These guys folded like an accordion. Mr. Carlyle, after he asked them a bunch of questions, wanted to cut off their pinkies as a reminder not to come back."

"Who stopped him?"

"Pam suggested that cutting off of one of their toes would have the same effect and he told the two of us to take them outside and do whatever we felt was right."

"Which was?"

"I had all their names and addresses, so she just scared the shit out of them and sent them on their way."

The Colonel ran his hand through his crew cut. "You said they were hired by someone who worked for Canon. What's his name?"

Troy looked at his notes. "I forgot to write the name down. I remember it sounding like the name of a mountain. I'll see if I can find out from Pam."

"Do that, and keep in touch." The colonel disconnected the call and turned to his aide. "Find Whitney and get him the hell out of California."

"I've already done that, Sir. I told him to use a different name and fly to Colorado. When he gets there, he'll check in and I'll have new papers and tickets for him to fly to Costa Rica. He'll help out on the banana project and it'll keep him occupied for about eight months."

"When that project is finished, cut him loose. He knows the rules—no killing unless I sanction it. Trying to kill Carlyle's man was stupid."

At the other end of the country, Troy looked at the phone and said, "I don't know how Mom was able to live with him."

Chapter 43

"Aaron, I'm glad you called. Min has been trying to reach you for a couple of hours." Scott's voice sounded strange.

"Why didn't you tell him where I was?"

"Pam checked in last night and when she told us what happened, I wasn't about to call. I take it that everything is okay with you and Karen?"

"Better than okay." Aaron smiled at Karen.

"Well, as long as everything's fine. Call Min. He'll only talk to you. Then call me back."

Aaron hung up and dialed Min's number.

"Who is calling?" Aaron could never tell who answered the phone.

"This is Aaron Carlyle. Can I please speak to Min?"

"Please hold. I will see if he is available."

As always, in less time than it took her to say please hold, Min answered the phone.

"Aaron. It is nice of you to return my call. Tell Karen I said hello and await our next visit together."

Aaron thought, *Min is showing off his new toy.* Tuloc had told him about something they put on the phone that told them the phone number calling them.

"I'll tell her. Meanwhile, what is so urgent that I had to call back regardless of the time?"

"Do you remember that picture you gave Tuloc of the man called Whitney? The one that was taken when he was at the hospital."

"I remember. I hoped that one of your people might see him in one of the plants they worked in."

"Tuloc, at my suggestion, sent the picture to our family in Colorado. Tuloc had them, again at my urging, check all incoming flights from the Los Angeles area. Early this morning, they found him arriving on Delta Airlines from LAX."

"Did they follow him to see where he was going?" Aaron asked.

After a slight hesitation, Min continued, "Tuloc, without asking my advice, had our relatives take him to one of our warehouses."

"You kidnapped him?"

"Kidnapped is a strong word. Maybe you should talk to Tuloc and have him explain his actions."

"Mr. Carlyle, this is Tuloc."

"Tell him what happened." Min was speaking from an extension.

"Tell me you didn't kidnap him," Aaron interrupted.

"Okay, I didn't kidnap him, but someone from my family did."

"Were you listening to Min as he told me what happened?"

"Yes, and everything he said is true."

"Tuloc, I'm ashamed of you," Aaron replied.

"See, Tuloc, I told you that was what he would say," Min exclaimed. "Aaron, tell him what he should have done."

Before Aaron could speak, Min continued, "It is very hard to teach new generation what they should do."

Something was wrong. Aaron sensed a mood of agitation in Min's voice. It was not like his friend to seem this upset.

"Tuloc, on second thought, maybe what's happened is not such a bad thing. His people sent him there for a reason. Maybe we can find out what it is."

"Mr. Carlyle, a little problem developed. When they took him to the warehouse he tried to escape and was shot."

Aaron sat back in his chair. "Shot?"

"I told Tuloc you would not be pleased," Min spoke.

"Min, you have connections in Denver. Is there somewhere they can take him? A private hospital, a clinic, somewhere where he can be taken care of?"

"Like a mortuary?" Tuloc responded.

"A mortuary? He's dead?"

"I'm afraid so. My relatives are telling me it was an accident."

Karen moved over to where Aaron was sitting and put her hand on his shoulder. Aaron looked up at her as she mouthed the words. "Who's dead? Anyone we know?"

Aaron shook his head. Taking a deep breath, he spoke somberly into the phone.

"Min, Tuloc, it's time for damage control. I'm not going to mourn for the bastard, but I would've liked to talk to him. Have your relatives make it look like a mugging and let's move on. Let's not cry over spilled milk."

"See, I told you Aaron would come up with plan, now hang up your phone so that I may speak in private."

"Good-bye, Mr. Carlyle. Say hello to Karen for me."

Aaron heard the click and then Min continued, "Aaron, what is happening with Lan's company? I have not heard from Tom and I am getting concerned."

"There has been an offer, well below what Tom thinks it is worth. There should be a delivery of parts that will allow her to make her commitments, and hopefully a nice profit. At that point, she will be back in the driver's seat." The silence on the phone told Aaron he was getting close to finding out what was really bothering his friend.

"Aaron," Min whispered, "I have become very fond of her. I would not like to think that our actions have put her in any jeopardy."

"What actions?" Aaron asked.

"The taking away of that woman, the replacing of their cleaning service with mine, the harassing of their patrol cars, and this man that will disappear."

"We knew what we were getting into when we started. Nothing has changed. We have both had people who work for us die and loved ones threatened. One of your jobs is to make sure your people, including Lan and her son, are protected. Can you do that?"

"Of course I can. It is just that I have a feeling." Min paused a moment, thought, then replied, "Of course I can!"

"Let me know about the final disposition of our friend in Denver," Aaron said and hung up.

"Who's dead?" Karen asked.

"The man who planted the bomb in the hospital. Some of Min's relatives found him in the Denver airport. They tried to take him somewhere, he resisted, and he ended up dead."

"What was Min so concerned about? I've never known him to be squeamish."

"I think our friend Min is in love, and is having a problem handling it."

Karen smiled and sat down next to Aaron. She put her arm around his neck and leaned over to kiss his ear. "How would you like a double wedding?"

"I'd like to be part of a single one. I want to go on a honeymoon," he replied as he turned his face toward hers.

"We can start practicing now," she said as she ran her tongue across her lips.

"All you ever think about is sex." Aaron laughed as he put his arms around her.

"Anyone home?"

Both Aaron and Karen jumped like high school kids caught by their parents as they heard Karen's mother enter the house.

Chapter 44

"Karen, I've got to get back to Los Angeles, and I need your special talents."

She laughed. "You are insatiable."

"That's not what I meant." Aaron was surprised to find he was blushing.

"I'm only kidding, change that to I'm serious, but I know that's not what you meant."

Aaron smiled. It was good to have the old Karen back. "This stock, ISCC, has gone from over one hundred dollars five weeks ago to a little over sixty-five yesterday. Can you find out who's selling?"

"I don't know if I can get the name of the person, but I can probably find out which firm is handling the transactions. What do you think is happening?"

"I think we're starting to hurt someone, and that someone is cutting his losses. I never believed that Canon was smart enough to run this operation and whoever the boss is, he's getting out."

"That's good, isn't it?"

"It could be, but Canon is a little crazy. I would hate to be the one he tries to get even with when he realizes that he's been left high and dry."

"Do you think it could be you?" Karen's voice was tinged with more than a little concern.

Aaron held out his arms. “No, I don’t think so. I’m the enemy, not the person he will think betrayed him.”

“Lunch is ready,” Karen’s mother called from the kitchen.

“I’m not hungry. I’ll say good-bye to your mom and I’ll call when I get back home. Start planning the wedding and let me know what the date is so I can tell the guys.”

Aaron was kissing her when her mother came in. “I said lunch, not dessert.”

“One more thing, sir. Whitney never got on the flight to Costa Rica.”

The colonel, who was lost in thought staring out the window, turned and asked, “Did he call in?”

“No, he picked up the new tickets and then disappeared.”

“You don’t think he’s running, do you?”

“I wouldn’t put it past him. I’ve had other airlines checked, and no one has turned in the tickets for credit. If he was running, he wouldn’t throw away six thousand dollars. Shall I put out an alarm?”

“No, not yet. I’d rather not set off any bells or whistles until I know what’s going on. This operation is starting to unravel quickly. Start the disconnect procedures.”

The aide looked at the clock on the wall. It was nine forty-five and he hadn’t eaten dinner yet.

“Pam, what was it like being a cop?”

Pam put her drink back down on the table. “To tell you the truth, it gave me a high. People were afraid to make eye contact and I could feel their nervousness as I would stare at them.”

“Did you ever shoot anyone?” Troy tried to look straight at her, but he felt his face get red and looked down at his drink.

“Why are you asking?”

“I don’t know. Maybe because you’re the first cop I ever sat down and talked to.”

She nodded her understanding of what he said.

“You are also one of the prettiest women I’ve ever met.” He couldn’t believe he said that.

Pam looked up from the table with a surprised look on her face.

"Are you married, or in a relationship with someone?" Troy spoke quickly, hiding his embarrassment.

"Pam smiled. "No, no, and no, I don't date people I work with."

"I would quit this job in a second. They know I'm not long term."

"Troy, you're nice, but you don't know a thing about me. You don't know what I'm like off the job or what I want for my future."

"I could learn. I know we're about the same age. We're both interested in police work and I think we're attracted to each other. The rest we could learn as we go forward."

"What would your folks say? You do have parents, don't you?"

"My mom died a few years ago, and my dad . . . he works for the government."

"Sorry about your mom. What's your dad doing?"

Troy looked at the ceiling. "Would you like a refill?"

"I don't think so. The way this conversation is headed, I better stay sober. You were going to tell me about your dad."

"My dad was an officer in the Vietnam War. He doesn't talk a lot about what he does, except that it's something in finance. He sent me to good schools, made sure I had clothes on my back, and he's always around if I need him."

"And what would he think if you got involved with an ex-cop?"

"I don't care what he thinks. I think it would be great."

Troy watched as Pam drew diagrams on the table with her finger, using the water that sweated off the drinks. She drew a heart with an arrow that pointed straight at him and then used her hand to erase it. Aside from the music that came from the jukebox, the bar was silent. When Pam stood, the scraping of the chair on the floor made Troy jump.

"Where's your car?" she asked.

"It's parked at Besafe."

"Let me drive you home," she said as she picked up her coat. "We'll decide in the car where to take this conversation."

Chapter 45

"Mr. Carlyle, when my relatives were disposing of Whitney's body, they found another ticket for a plane leaving yesterday for Dallas. From Dallas, there was another ticket to Costa Rica. The tickets were made out in the name of Jordan and he had a passport, driver's license, and social security card for the same name."

"Tuloc, are you sure they got the right guy?"

"I'm sure. I had them take a picture and fax it to me. It's him."

"I'll talk to Michael and get back to you."

"Min said that I should tell you that he thinks this man had connections."

"He's probably right. Talk to you later."

Contemplating what he had just heard, Aaron subconsciously hit a speed dial button on his phone.

"This is Karen."

Aaron smiled. "I hit your speed dial number by mistake."

"I bet," Karen replied. "As long as you're on the phone, let me tell you what I found out about ISSI. The amount of stock being traded has doubled over the past ten days. The company went public eighteen months ago, and their sales and profits have risen by over thirty percent per quarter. They've gone from a twenty-million-dollar a year company to more than a one-hundred-million-dollar a year. Their quarter, which closes in six weeks, is expected to be over thirty million in sales. They came public at twenty and in a year and a half, the stock has grown to over one twenty. It looks like someone has sold over five hundred thousand shares in the ninety to one ten range. Either they're going to miss their numbers big time, or you're right, some one is getting out."

"Thanks, I owe you one."

"I love it when you talk dirty." Karen laughed as she hung up the phone. Picking up her interoffice phone, Karen spoke quickly, "Sell ten thousand shares of ISSI at the market." After listening to the person on the other end, she answered, "I know that's six hundred thousand dollars, just get it done in a hurry." Hanging up, she punched in the symbol on her computer and watched as the sale streamed across her screen. Her phone rang. "You sold five thousand at fifty nine fifty and another five at fifty nine seventy five. Which accounts do I take it from?"

"I'll split it up among twenty of them. Give me fifteen minutes and I'll send you the paperwork."

Karen hit the refresh button and the price of ISSI was now fifty-seven. She had made $26,250 for her clients in five minutes. She thought, *If I had heard the information from someone connected to the company, I wouldn't have been able to take advantage of it.*

"Listen!" Dennis Canon shouted into the phone. "You don't tell me to be calm. My payoff for all the work I've been doing was supposed to be in the millions. The stock is going down and all I have is restricted paper. We're losing accounts to Besafe and that Vietnamese cleaning service. Our restaurants are being harassed unmercifully and you tell me to be calm. I don't even know who the hell you are. What I do know is that you were supposed to keep my back protected." He took a deep breath and continued, "I want to meet face to face, and I want to do it now!"

"That's impossible. I'm too busy now. Maybe next week."

Canon's face turned red with rage. The faceless voice sounded bored, which infuriated him even more.

"You listen carefully. If you don't make time to meet with me tomorrow, I'm taking off the kid gloves. If you think I'm going to let this Carlyle guy get away with pushing me around, you're crazy."

"Listen to me." The words shot through the phone with the

force of ice picks being inserted into his ear. "It's your starting up with Besafe that caused this problem. You were told not to get involved with them and you disregarded orders."

"Disregarded orders? Who the hell do you think you are? Some general or something?"

"I know who I am, and let me repeat, if you fool around with Besafe or Besafe people, you will get hurt. They are tough and well connected."

Canon hesitated. "You have until tomorrow. Either meet with me or I'm cutting myself loose from you. You have my phone number." Slamming down the phone, he took little solace in the fact that he had had the last word.

The colonel turned to his aide and asked, "Where do we stand as far as getting out of that operation?"

"We've turned some of the stock into cash and we have some interest in buying the cleaning service. I'm prepared to sell the casino to one of our other enterprises. It would almost be a transfer. It's a cash cow and we should keep it."

"What about the gym and the electronic plants?"

"I'd let them stay with the company. Neither one of them are making big money. The problem is Interstate Security. That's been a moneymaker and the hub of the entire operation. If we pull that, we're going to have the SEC and probably the IRS breathing down our neck."

"If we keep it, we're stuck with Canon," the colonel concluded.

"Sir, would you mind if I shared my opinion?"

"Go ahead," said the colonel.

"The way I see it, you have three choices. The first is to support Canon and help him get rid of Besafe. Either buy them out or . . ." He let the words hang in midair. "The second choice is to get rid of Canon and turn the business straight, or, and I think this is the best, just get out. We let Canon do whatever he wants and we just walk away. If Carlyle is as good as you think, he'll take care of himself. If he's not, we still own over one hundred thousand shares of the stock."

The colonel walked over to the window. Standing at the corner he could see the Vietnamese Memorial. *Things seemed a lot clearer back then,* he thought.

"Okay, pull Troy out and let the Besafe people take care of themselves." He turned toward the desk as the phone rang. "It's Troy, that's his number. Put him on the speaker phone."

The aide punched the button and answered in a monotone voice, "Go ahead."

"This is Troy. I've just been assigned to fly to Denver and track down some guy called Whitney."

"We heard that Whitney disappeared," the aide said as he shrugged his shoulders.

"He changed his name to Jordan. I'm supposed to meet some people there and they'll point me in the right direction."

"This is the colonel. When you get to the airport, we'll have tickets for you to fly home. We've got another assignment for you."

"I don't want to come home."

"I don't give a shit what you want. Get on the plane back to D.C. and do it today."

"Please take me off the squawk box."

The colonel picked up the receiver. "You're off."

"Dad, I'm not coming home today. These people have assigned me an important job and I won't let them down."

"It's that girl Pam, isn't it?"

Troy's eyes lit up. "For almost a week, something's been bothering me, and I just realized what it was. When I called last week and told you that they teamed me up with a cop, you knew it was a woman. I never mentioned it, but you knew. You've got a spy out here."

"We'll talk about that when you get home. Just be on that plane."

"Or?"

"Or? What do you mean or?"

"Dad, I'm not coming. Since I've been a kid, even before Mom died, you've taught me to do what's right. You better decide what you're going to do if I don't come home today, because I'm not coming." Troy hesitated waiting for his dad to say something else.

"Troy, be careful. This operation is starting to turn ugly. Don't turn your back on Canon for a second, and trust Carlyle. Call me when you're ready to come home."

"Colonel, from the half of the conversation I heard, maybe we should go to Plan B, which is getting rid of Canon."

"No. I'm sure Carlyle can handle it, and we never have to be involved. I'm concerned about what happened to Whitney. It seems they know about his name second identity. Carlyle's got better sources than we do. Can they trace the tickets back to us?"

"I don't think so. I used the agency account to purchase them, but the name I used was Interstate."

"Make sure we're not connected to whatever happens out there, and get someone else to Costa Rica."

Chapter 46

Mr. Troy Ewing, please go to a white courtesy phone. Mr. Troy Ewing," announced a voice over the loud speaker.

Troy looked around and spotted a courtesy phone walking over, he picked it up and said, "This is Troy Ewing. You have a call for me?" Troy hoped it was Pam calling to say good-bye. She had kissed him long and hard when she dropped him off two nights ago, but hadn't said a thing about the two of them since then.

"Mr. Ewing, where are you standing?"

"I'm in the Delta terminal, right across from the sports bar."

"We have a package for you. Please stay where you are and we'll bring it to you.

"Who's it from?"

"Sorry, I don't know that, Sir. We were instructed to make sure you had the package after you passed through security, but before you boarded the plane."

"I'll wait, but please hurry. The plane will be boarding any second now."

I can't believe they're sending me with a gun, Troy thought as he continued watching people enter the boarding area from the front of the building. He never saw the two men approach from behind him.

"Mr. Ewing?"

Troy turned. "Yes, that's me. You have a package?"

"What you'll have is a knife in the ribs if you make a wrong move. Start walking toward the exit sign."

"That's an alarmed door," Troy stammered.

"Just walk toward it. It'll open when we get close."

He just couldn't leave me alone, Troy thought and said, "Look, we both know you're not going to stick that knife in me. Why don't you just go tell your boss I wouldn't go with you?"

"I don't know any such thing. I was told bring you or leave you dead. You can decide. Either start walking or say good-bye."

Troy started walking. Something wasn't right. "Who is your boss?"

"You'll meet him in twenty minutes, if you're still alive."

Twenty minutes? Dad's in Washington, Troy thought frantically.

"Troy! Troy, wait for me."

He turned and saw Pam running across the marble floor.

"Keep walking," the man threatened

"It's Pam," Troy whispered unbelievingly.

The man holding the knife pressed against Troy's back muttered, "I said keep walking."

The exit door opened as they approached and a man dressed in a janitor's uniform walked into the terminal. He looked around and held the door open waiting for Troy and his escorts to get there.

"Troy, wait up a second," Pam yelled louder.

People started turning, looking first at Pam and then at Troy and the two men.

Troy pushed the man closest to him and yelled, "Pam look out!"

The man that had just entered through the exit door pulled a gun.

This isn't happening, he thought in slow motion. Troy felt a tug before he heard the shot. He raised his hands and yelled, "Not Pam!"

Chapter 47

Michael burst into Aaron's office. He bent over to catch his breath, which seemed to be eluding him.

"Are you all right?" Aaron rose and rushed toward him.

He straightened. "No, I'm not. Troy's been shot."

"Troy? I thought we sent him to Denver."

"I just heard from Pam. She went down to see him off and saw him being held by two men. When she called his name, some guy in a janitor's uniform shot him. She had left her gun in the car to avoid airport security problems, so all she could do was call 911."

"What's his condition?"

"I don't know. She was going to the hospital in the ambulance with him and said she would call in when she arrived."

"Did they get the guys that shot him?"

"No. According to Pam, they ran out the security door and disappeared."

"Do our men know where Paul Kiesler is?"

"We haven't been able to find him. I'll stick a rod up their butts and tell them to put it into high gear. Do you think he's our man?" Michael asked, as he headed out of the office.

"Right now he's my first choice."

Scott came running in. "I guess you heard."

"Yeah, bad news travels fast. Have personnel contact his family. As soon as they find out when they'll be arriving, let me know. I'll want to meet with them."

"Michael, how many people knew Troy was going to Denver on that flight?"

"I don't know. I told Tuloc and he had to notify his family to meet the plane. A secretary bought his tickets." Michael stopped, looked at his fingers, and then continued, "Me and I guess Pam, but I don't know who told her."

"I'll call Tuloc, you check with the secretary and Pam." Aaron turned to Scott. "Why don't you check with the travel agent that was used and find out if anyone else called asking the question."

When they left his office, Aaron picked up the phone and dialed Barry. His conversation was short. All he wanted was the whereabouts of Paul Kiesler and Denis Canon, and the status on the condition of Troy Ewing.

His second call to Tuloc wasn't as easy.

"None of my people here knew. Michael told me what flight he was leaving on and I called a relative in Denver to meet the plane. It's the same relative that found Whitney. I trust him explicitly."

"I know you trust everyone explicitly, but I want them all checked again."

"Mr. Carlyle, I don't think you know what you're asking."

"Tuloc, you tell Min I am not asking. This is the third Besafe man shot. I want it to be the last."

Sixty minutes later, information was starting to come together.

"Troy made his own reservations. I spoke to Pam and she told me he called from his car and told her he was leaving and wanted to say good-bye."

"I checked with the travel agency. Troy called in this morning and got himself an E ticket travel voucher."

"What's an E ticket travel voucher?" Aaron asked

"No need to have a ticket. They put you in the computer and you check in at the gate."

"When Pam called in, how was he doing?"

"She didn't know. He's in the operating room."

"Have we notified his parents? When no one answered, Aaron asked again, "Have we notified his parents?"

Michael cleared his throat. "We seem to have a little problem. The number Troy gave us has been disconnected and when I sent someone over to the house, it was empty. Three weeks ago, people lived there. I had Mai Ling call Cassius and ask him to run a trace for us. So far, there's no answer."

Aaron leaned forward with his elbows on the table and his fingers entwined. "Start a background check on Troy. Check out everything he's told us, every school he's gone to, every recommendation he gave us. Something stinks."

"I've already started. Aaron, I'm sorry. We ran the standard checks three weeks ago. If he was put here by Canon, they did a damn good job."

"That doesn't make sense," Scott jumped into the conversation. "If Canon put him here, why would he have him shot?"

"Maybe it has something to do with Pam. His calling her might mean that he switched sides and they had to keep him quiet." Michael continued, "Unless we're missing something that's as good a reason as we've got."

The phone on the desk rang and Aaron picked it up. "I thought I said to hold all calls."

After listening for a few seconds, he said, "Put Troy's father through in about ten seconds."

Putting down the phone he said to Michael, "Get a trace on this call, and leave me his personnel records."

As Michael ran out the door, the phone rang. After three rings, Aaron pushed the speaker button. "This is Aaron Carlyle."

"This is Troy Ewing's father. I understand he's been shot. I want to know how and where he is."

"Mr. Ewing, I'm sorry to put you through this but we've been getting some strange phone calls. We think it's the press trying to get information, so I'm going to ask you a few questions to verify that you are Troy's father."

"Those bloodsuckers. Go ahead, ask what you want."

"I'm reading from his personnel file. Your wife's name is?"

"My wife's name was Theresa. She died over ten years ago."

"You live where?"

"Right now, I'm living in a motel outside of Bakersfield. I moved from Southern California last week."

Michael tiptoed back into the room and laid a piece of paper in front of Aaron.

"What business are you in, Mr. Ewing?"

"What did Troy say I did?"

"He neglected to fill in that section."

"I doubt he'd do that. I work for the government in the taxation department. We don't tell people that, but he would have put down that I was employed by the government."

"Have I ever met you?"

"Why would you ask that?" The voice became steely. "That question's not on the form, is it?"

"Your voice sounds familiar," Aaron spoke slowly waiting for his memory to click in.

"Mr. Carlyle, just tell me about my son?"

"One more question, how did you know he was shot?"

The colonel's voice got louder. "Mr. Carlyle, don't be cute. Of course you know we've met in the past. You may not remember exactly when or where, but you do know we've met. Just tell me, how is my son, and do you know who did the shooting?"

"I'm not sure how your son is. I've got people standing by waiting for the doctor's report. The other answer is, I don't know who did it, but I get the feeling that you know who's responsible."

"Why do you think that?" The voice now sounded wary.

"I would've asked who was responsible, not who did the shooting."

"I'll be in touch." The phone went dead.

"Do you know him?" Michael asked.

"I think I've met him, but I don't think I know him. I'm learning more about him with every call, even from Alaska." Aaron wadded up the paper Michael had given him.

Chapter 48

Aaron was waiting for the ten o'clock news to begin. He was stretched out on the sofa with his hand in a bag of potato chips as his phone rang.

"Aaron, I've got to tell you what I did today." Karen's voice sounded like she was on a high.

"You set the wedding date!" He sat up, wiping his hand on his sweatshirt.

"No, not that. Now promise me you won't get upset."

"Okay, I promise I won't get upset unless you did something crazy."

"After I spoke to you, I sold ISSC short."

"How'd you make out?" Aaron had learned that stockbrokers got highs the same way salespeople did when they closed a big deal. Her voice had the same energy to it that Scott's had when he signed a new client.

"I sold ten thousand shares at about $59.50."

"And?" he asked as he wrote on a piece of paper in front of him $595,000.

"It closed at $38.75."

Aaron wrote $387,000. "That's over $200,000 in profits."

"Isn't that great?" Her happiness was infectious.

"Now you can set the date and we can really have a great honeymoon."

"It's not my money. I do this for my clients. Ten of them made over twenty thousand dollars today."

"Does that mean that Barry gets to go on our honeymoon with us?"

"It means he could afford to, but I'm not going to tell him where we're going."

"Where are we going?"

"That's your job. I get to set the date. You do the rest."

"How about you set the date and we discuss the rest."

"I'm looking at my calendar, and the date I pick is . . . no that's not so good. I'll have to keep looking. How was your day?"

"Not as good as yours, but interesting. I'd rather not discuss it on the phone just in case the phones have ears."

"Do you think that's possible?"

"We're checking the office ones and I had this one checked two days ago, but you never know. By the way, as I'm sitting here looking at the numbers, how come you didn't buy, or I guess sell the stock for yourself?"

"It wouldn't have been ethical. I buy and sell for my clients first and myself second."

"Makes sense. I'll talk to you tomorrow."

"That's all you have to say?"

"What else?"

"You could tell me how you feel about me."

Aaron thought for a second and then said, "I feel pretty good about you. Good night." After hanging up the phone, he dialed Karen's number.

"Yes?"

"I love you."

She didn't respond for a few seconds and then said, "Who is this?" She hung up the phone.

The news came on and the lead story was the shooting at the airport. He saw Scott, Pam, and Michael at the hospital as a doctor told the television reporter that the patient was still in critical condition. As the television camera panned the hallway, he saw Tuloc with a mop, cleaning the hall. He was sure other people from Min's cleaning service were also in the hospital. He turned off the television and the lights, and lay there thinking about the events of the day when the phone rang.

"You love me, too?" he spoke into the phone before he heard the steely voice of Troy's father.

"Not likely, but I do want to meet you."

"Who is this?" Aaron asked.

"You know who this is. Thirty minutes from now in the Denny's off Kanan Road. Pull into the parking lot and if you're not followed, I'll contact you."

"Bad spot to meet. My men use that location for coffee breaks."

"Where then?"

"How about my house in ten minutes."

"Why there?"

"You must have seen my lights go out, so you know I'm alone, and ten minutes gives me time to put on some clothes and make a pot of coffee."

"Do I have your word that you won't put out a call for some of your people?"

"You don't need my word. I have no reason to think I'm in any danger from you, do I?"

"See you in ten minutes."

Aaron ran into the shower and turned it on full blast cold. "Son of a bitch," he said as the icy water cascaded down his body. He counted to fifteen and then turned it off and toweled himself dry. Deciding that he should at least have a gun when they met, he put on his pants that were laying over the back of a chair and went to the closet for his pistol.

"You weren't looking for this were you?" he instinctively jumped back, falling on the bed. In his closet, the man stood ramrod straight. He had close cut gray hair and a thin white scar glowing eerily down the side of his cheek.

"How the hell did you get in here?" Aaron asked, keeping his voice steady.

"You invited me."

"I said ten minutes and people usually knock before they enter."

“I decided there was no need for formality since we’re old friends.”

“What makes you think we’re old friends, or for that matter even friends?”

“Webster says that friends are nothing more than acquaintances or contacts. I think you’ll agree we are at least that.”

“Is your name Ewing?”

“Why do you ask?”

“A few years ago, we were looking for someone called Webster. I thought that might be you also.”

“Yes, your friend Captain Sands, I remember. Maybe this is the time for some truths. I think you understand I can’t give you all the information you seek, but I will try not to lie.”

Aaron stood there contemplating the value of this man’s word as the phone rang.

“Let it ring,” the colonel said.

“I can’t. If I don’t answer it, someone will come by within ten minutes.”

The colonel shrugged. “Go ahead. Just be careful what you say.”

“Hello.”

“Aaron, this is Scott. I’m at the office with Michael and I think we have a problem.”

“What kind?”

“I started doing some checking after our meeting this afternoon and I came up with some inconsistencies in Pam’s folder.”

“Like what?” Aaron kept his voice flat and his eyes on his guest.

“First, she quit the Frisco police two years ago. Her father never lived in Orange County, and in fact is still alive. For the past two years, she’s been on the payroll of a company called Guident Technology.”

“How’d you get all this information?”

“Mostly Michael and Barry. There are still some blanks, but they’re all leading toward some sort of government involvement.”

“Do we know where she is?”

“Last we heard, she was at the hospital.”

Aaron watched the man who was now looking out the window as if he had stopped by to enjoy the view. "Tell Michael to keep an eye on her and I'll get back to you in a little."

"Aaron, you know she could be our only lead to this guy in Washington."

"I've got one another idea, trust me. I'll get back to you soon."

Aaron put the receiver back in the cradle. "Is Pam one of yours?"

"Do you have anything to drink?"

"Water, juice?"

"Preferably Johnny Walker Black, on the rocks."

"I have some Glenlivet. Will that do?" he asked with a trace of sarcasm.

The colonel nodded his head.

As Aaron went downstairs to the bar, he asked over his shoulder, "What do I call you? Are you still a colonel or should I just use your last name?"

"My name is Lawrence Ewing, and my rank is unimportant. I answer to colonel."

Returning with the bottle of scotch and a bucket of ice, Aaron asked, "Your friends don't call you Larry?"

"My friends don't call me. I call them."

"Tell me about Pam. Is she one of your people?"

"She works for the same organization that I do, if that's what you're asking."

"Look, if we continue to do it this way, I'm going to lose a good night's sleep. Why don't you just tell me what you want me to know?"

The colonel poured a half glass of scotch, took a sip and said, "This is a little difficult. I live in an environment where we don't ever give out information. We get it, store it, and use it when it best suits our needs."

"Pardon me for not making it easy, but I seem to recall you were around when I was in trouble in Singapore, when I was having a problem a few years ago with that maniac who thought he was a general . . ."

"He was," interrupted the colonel with a small smile.

"And now you're back, when two of my people have been shot and another killed. If I thought for one second that you were also responsible for Karen's getting shot, we wouldn't even be having this conversation."

The colonel exhaled, refilled his glass, and sat down in a recliner facing Aaron.

"Singapore was a long time ago. That operation you broke up was supposed to net the government hundreds of millions of dollars. The plan was simple, from that part of the world; drugs were going to end up in Russia, China, and any country that the U.S. was having a problem with. What the geniuses didn't plan on was the drugs ending up in the United States. When you closed it down, you saved many people from being embarrassed, including some elected officials that should have known better."

"Which officials?" Aaron asked.

The colonel smiled and shook his head no.

"I convinced the powers that be to take care of you and your friends in exchange for your silence. Our real problem was General Waldman. He was a certifiable schizoid. It was decided to set him up with men just like himself and with help supplied by my office, he would make millions buying and selling stocks. Inside the government, it is not unusual for people in Office A not to know what people in Office B are doing, which is what happened. Your getting accidentally involved again saved some people's bacon."

"It also cost some people their lives," Aaron countered, his anger rising.

"Casualties are a way of life in my world. In retrospect, we are probably better off with those people gone."

"You can't set yourself up as judge and jury." Aaron raised his voice.

The colonel smiled. "I didn't. If I remember correctly, you became the judge, jury, and executioner."

Aaron looked down at his feet. "Tell me about Canon."

"It was decided that the government needed a better handle on the manufacturing of certain items. My office was charted to buy into businesses that were on the cutting edge. We made sure they got sufficient contracts and made enough money to keep them healthy. It didn't take long for us to realize that their stocks were making us more money than the companies were making. As usual, we hired people to run the operations that had nothing to do with us. I guess deniability is what we were after. Canon fit the bill perfectly. He wasn't the brightest bulb on the Christmas tree. He could take direction, and he was on the fringe of being honest. We gave him the names of the companies we wanted to become part of and he did the rest. When we started, the companies were all located on the East Coast. The 128 corridor outside of Boston was our testing ground. When we realized that California was where everything was headed, Canon was given specific instructions to stay away from anything or anyone that had any attachment to Besafe."

"What changed?"

"I don't know. All of a sudden, the reports we received showed him competing with you for security work. He started pushing your friend Min around, but since I hadn't given him any instructions about him, there was nothing I could do."

The colonel stood and poured himself another drink.

"Would you like some food to go along with those drinks?" Aaron asked half jokingly.

"How about a steak, medium rare, with a side of French fries?"

"How about some crackers or pretzels?"

"How about telling your guest not to move a muscle or I'll shoot his kneecap off?"

The colonel and Aaron both turned to face Scott standing by the kitchen door with a pistol aimed at the colonel.

"Took your time about getting here," Aaron said as he walked over to the window to look outside. Returning, he smiled and said, "Let me introduce you to Colonel Ewing, Troy's father. We've been having a conversation about how our lives have crossed over the years and it was just going to get interesting."

"Mr. Miller, it's nice to finally meet you." The colonel extended his hand, which Scott ignored.

Scott looked at Aaron and shrugged his shoulders.

"Are you alone, Colonel?" Aaron asked.

"Are you alone, Mr. Miller?" the colonel asked.

The phone ran before Scott could answer. Aaron picked it up.

"Is everything okay in there? Tom and I don't see anyone else in the vicinity." Barry's voice was crisp and business like.

"Colonel, anyone else outside?" Aaron asked.

The colonel shook his head no.

"I don't think so, come on in," Aaron told Barry.

"That must be Mr. Greenberg," The colonel said and took a sip of his drink.

"And Captain Sands," Aaron replied.

"The gang's all here. It's probably better this way."

Chapter 49

"Before we start, Mr. Carlyle, let me ask how they knew I was here."

"They didn't know it was you. It could have been anyone."

The colonel closed his eyes. "Of course. When you said you had one other idea, you were telling them one person was in the house. You also said, trust me which meant trouble of some kind." He opened his eyes and smiled. "Correct?"

"The years haven't dimmed your thought process. You're almost a hundred percent correct." Aaron filled his friends in on the conversation he had before their arrival and then said to the colonel, "You're on."

"I told your friend earlier, I have a little problem discussing anything that's not on a need to know basis, so please bear with me." The colonel looked at each of the four men and then continued, "Canon had a number to call when he needed anything. A few weeks ago, his ranting reached a level that made me more than a little concerned about what was happening. I dispatched two of my people to passively help him along."

"What does that mean?" Barry asked.

"What that was supposed to mean was they were to give aid and comfort to Canon without his knowing they were helping.

"Who were your two people?" Scott asked.

"One was Pam Haviland and the other was my son, Troy."

"Did they know each other?" Scott asked.

"No. They had never met, and the way things were set up, they probably never would. It was a stroke of luck that they both ended up on the same assignment. They both reported in and gave us information from two different angles. I decided to close down the operation when I received a threatening call from Canon. I told Troy to come on home. He told me about your assigning him to look for Whitney . . . by the way, how did you find out about the name change to Jordan?"

Scott looked at Aaron and then at Barry.

Barry, looking back at his two friends, rubbed his forehead and asked, "Is this something I would rather not know?"

"It's outside of your jurisdiction, but it's not one of our finest hours," Aaron admitted.

Barry shook his head. "Good thing Karen's watching out for me. You're going to cost me my pension one of these days."

"We had his picture and we gave it to Min's people. They located him at the Denver airport, and after a little disagreement, he died. They found the tickets and passport made out to Jordan in his pocket."

"He died?" The colonel asked.

"There was a scuffle and he was shot."

"Are your people crazy?" Ewing raised his voice, shocked.

"It wasn't my people, but in their defense, he had tried to kill one of my people."

"What did they do with the body?"

"I understand that the body will turn up, and it will look like a robbery."

Barry walked over to the bar, "Anybody want one?" he asked.

"I'll take a refill." The colonel held out his glass.

"That brings up an interesting question," Scott said to the group. "Why did he attempt to kill our man if you were only giving passive help?"

"I don't know if he did try to kill your man. If he did, he exceeded his instructions," the colonel answered with a frown on his face.

"This is getting us nowhere. Who do you think shot your son?" Aaron's tone said that he had had enough.

"I was hoping you had some idea."

"Our thoughts were headed in the direction of Paul Kiesler, one of Canon's men. If Whitney hadn't met up with an accident, I would've added him to the list."

"Why would they try to harm him? If they wanted to get even, they would have gone after Pam. She was the one that made fools of them."

"How did you find out about what was going on out here?" Scott asked.

"I was getting information from Whitney first and then Pam."

"You forgot your son!" Barry exclaimed from the bar as he poured a glass of scotch.

"Troy, too, but the real info came from the others. This was my son's first assignment, which is why we also sent Pam in. She was supposed to watch over him."

"Did she know why?" Aaron asked.

"No, she didn't even know he worked for us. Like I said earlier, many times the people in Room A don't know what the people in Room B are doing. In most cases they don't even know who they are."

When the phone rang again, the colonel looked at his watch and said, "Who's not here?"

Aaron answered the phone and recognized Michael's voice.

"I got a call from Cassius. The Denver police found Whitney's body and have put in a request for the local cops to hold Troy. They have reason to believe that he's somehow involved in his death."

"What?"

"I said . . ."

"I heard you. What is Cassius going to do?"

"It's not his call. L.A.P.D. called him as a courtesy. He's just the bearer of news. He's trying to locate Captain Sands and ask for instructions, so far no luck."

"Thanks, Michael. Go home and get some sleep. I'll talk to you in the morning.

Aaron hung up the phone and relayed the conversation to his friends and the colonel.

"I need a ride back to your office. That's where I left my car," Barry said as he threw two breath mints in his mouth.

"I'll take you, Captain." The colonel answered. "I'm going to do some checking on my own."

"How do I get in touch with you?" Aaron asked looking at the colonel.

"You don't. I'll be in touch with you."

After they left, Scott asked, "What do you think?"

"I think he's a concerned father who's in the business of not giving a damn and it's playing havoc with his mind."

Chapter 50

"You and Carlyle go back a long way."

"Look, Colonel, or whatever the hell you are, thanks for the ride. If I have to make nice talk, just let me out here," Barry said as he unsnapped his seat belt."

"What's got you so upset?"

"I'm not like Aaron and the Besafe guys. I work in law enforcement and that makes you one of the bad guys."

"What have I ever done to make you think that?"

"You forgot that shit you pulled saying you were Webster?"

"Captain, I'm ashamed of you. My name may be Webster. What makes you or the Besafe guys think my name is Ewing?"

"Because Troy . . ." Barry stopped, looked out the passenger side window, and shook his head. "You're right. The name that you use doesn't mean anything, but . . ."

"But what?"

"You do things I don't like, or approve of."

"I'm sorry you feel that way, but I've never hurt you or your friends."

"That's bullshit! Every time you pull a scam, or one of the people you're using breaks the law, you're hurting my friends."

"That's a pretty big brush you're using to paint me with."

"You think so? What about Kebra Metcalf?"

"What about Kebra?" The Colonel's voice turned wary.

"You set her up in business as a behavioral specialist and then you hang her out to dry."

The colonel didn't say a word. Barry looked at him and thought he saw a strange expression cross his face.

"Well?" Barry persisted.

"Well what?" the colonel asked.

"You think leaving her to deal with that psychopath Canon isn't hurting someone?"

The colonel thought for a second and then replied, "I said your friends! I didn't know Kebra was one of your friends."

"She's not, but I have . . ." Barry stopped himself. "You're right, she's not one of my friends."

They drove in silence until they approached the Besafe building.

"Look, Captain, I know you don't like me, or for that matter even understand what I do for a living, but I am interested in what is happening to my son. Aside from the four of you, no one out here knows he's my son, and I'd like to keep it that way."

"Don't worry. If the word gets out, it won't come from us."

The colonel again sat quietly. "Can I at least expect you to notify me if you need anything?"

"I would think with all your connections you could get better and quicker information through your own sources."

"I'll be trying, but I don't want to bring any more attention to him than necessary."

"How do I get in touch with you?"

"I'll give you a number. It only works once and then I'll have to give you another one. If anyone tries to trace the number, it'll go on to an automatic disconnect."

"If something happens, I'll call you. I still consider you an enemy, but I like your son and Pam."

"You think they're an item?" The colonel smiled.

Surprised by the question, Barry hesitated before answering, "I did until this second. If you're . . . no even you wouldn't do that."

"Do what?"

"Nothing, just let me out here. If something happens, I'll call you. If not, do me a favor and forget I exist."

Without waiting for a reply, Barry got out of the car and slammed the door.

As Barry walked to his car, the colonel picked up his phone.

"This is the colonel. I'll be in the office by four o'clock this afternoon. Be there!"

Chapter 51

"It wasn't my fault" Canon spoke loudly into the phone. "I gave those guys instructions and the kid wouldn't play ball." After listening for a minute, he continued, "I think the bigger problem is this guy Min and his people, but if you want, I'll tell my guys it's open house on Besafe people, including that pompous ass Carlyle."

Canon leaned back in his chair and adjusted the volume on the television across the room. He watched Alan Ladd ride out of town as Brandon de Wilde sadly calls out, "Pa's got things for you to do, and mother wants you, I know she does. Shane. Shane. Come back. Bye Shane." A knock on the door brought him out of his reverie.

"Who's there?"

The door opened and Paul Kiesler walked in and looked at the television.

"You like that movie?" he asked as he sat down in front of the desk.

"Yeah I like it. I think Alan Ladd should have gotten an Academy Award," Canon replied.

"He probably would have if he shot Van Heflin and stayed with the wife."

Canon shook his head. "He wasn't that type of guy. He had what they call 'inner strength'."

"What he doesn't have is the Academy Award"

Canon nodded and then asked, "What's going on?"

"I can't find Kebra Metcalf anywhere. Did she go somewhere for you?"

"No, she didn't, but I just got a call from the boss and he's asking the same thing."

"Who is this boss?"

"Beats the hell out of me, but he's taken off the wraps on getting even with Besafe."

"What do you mean getting even?"

"It turns out that they were behind all the problems we've been having, and it's time to stop them."

"How rough can we get?"

"It would be stupid to get the law involved with a murder, or even an accidental death, but anything short of that is okay."

"I'll have the boys start tonight." Kiesler picked up a pen from the desk. "Any feedback on the shooting of the kid?"

"I haven't heard anything yet. If I do, I'll let you know. When it happened, he almost came through the phone, but he seems to have calmed down. He asked if we heard anything about Whitney. It's really strange. I wonder how he knew about him?"

Kiesler rose and said, "What's even stranger is that he knew he was missing. Do you think the boss works over at Besafe?"

Canon contemplated Kiesler's question. "I don't think so, but nothing would surprise me. He seems to know an awful lot about those people. Maybe it's Miller or Greenberg wanting to take over the whole company and using us to do it."

"You got us protected, don't you?"

"Don't worry, our problem is the falling price of the stock. It's gone from over a hundred to less than forty today. That's where we make our money, on the stock."

The colonel looked at his watch as he waited for the door of the 727 to open. The door to the pilot's cabin opened and the pilot walked out and said to the flight attendant, "We must have a VIP aboard."

She turned and replied, "Why do you say that? No one asked for or received any special attention."

"The gate attendant just called and said there are three men from the government outside waiting for someone."

The colonel looked around and stepped back to let the other passengers off first. As they filed off, he noticed the door opposite the exit open and the cleaning service enter. He quickly moved to that portal.

"I'm sorry, Sir, but you have to use the regular exit," the man in coveralls said as he emptied one of the trash containers.

The colonel flashed his badge and said, "I'm on special assignment, and I have to get to the front of the terminal before the second man that left the plane. If you can't drive me there, get me to the ground in a hurry. This could be a national emergency."

"Captain?" The custodian motioned towards the colonel. "This gentleman has a problem."

"How can I be of assistance?" the pilot asked.

"I'm in the Secret Service." He flashed his badge and continued, "I've been following a suspected spy. My men are waiting in front of the terminal in a cab. I just heard the stewardess say that there are three men outside waiting for someone on this plane. They must be there to help the spy. I've got to get to the front of the terminal before they do. My men won't be expecting four of them. You've got to have your man here either drive me to the front or at least get me to the bottom and I'll make my way there. I can't let them know they're being followed."

The captain inspected the badge and the credentials the colonel produced and said to the custodian who was standing there with his mouth open, "Get him as close as possible, as quickly as possible."

"Thanks, Captain. I appreciate your help."

After being let off at a door that led to the front of the terminal, the colonel hailed a taxi at the back of the line.

"You have to use one of the cabs up front," the driver yelled through the open window.

Flashing his badge, the colonel replied, "Zip it up and start driving. Marriott Hotel. Midtown."

The red eye from Los Angeles arrived at JFK before the sun, and traffic into the city was light. The driver attempted to start a conversation three different times, but the non-response from his passenger never let it develop. Upon arrival at the hotel, the colonel leaned over and handed the driver two one hundred dollar bills.

"These are yours if no record of this trip is logged onto your trip sheet."

"That's against the law!" The driver answered, looking at the money in his hand.

"So is not reporting the exact amount of tips you get."

The driver rubbed the bills together, stuck them in his shirt pocket, and asked, "What tips?"

The colonel exited the cab and entered the ground floor of the building that housed the hotel. He walked across the promenade and purchased a newspaper. None of the stores located on the ground floor were open yet, although some lights showed that people were reporting for work. He glanced over the headlines and then walked out the side entrance down into the subway system that traveled from one end of the city to the other. Boarding the first train that he came upon, he traveled one stop and then exited. Years of training had given him a sixth sense of when he was being followed, and he felt that there was no one behind him. The same years had taught him never to trust his feelings. He was now on Thirty-Fourth Street and the light of day that started on Long Island and worked its way across the borough of Queens was reaching over the tall buildings of Manhattan. He walked halfway up the block and dialed an eight hundred number. The phone was answered on the second ring.

"Go ahead."

"This is the colonel."

"Good morning, Sir." After a slight hesitation, the aide continued, "I thought you wanted me to be here early."

"The only flight I could get to the east coast was one to Atlanta. I'm trying to connect from here to D.C. as soon as possible. I'll let you know what flight I'll be on."

"I was going to, but after I checked in, a problem came up and I missed the plane."

"That's a shame. How is Troy?"

"As well as can be expected. Have you heard from Canon?"

"No, but I expect I will soon. I think he's going to be tough to cut ourselves away from. Colonel, I've been scrolling while we've been on the phone and I find a Delta flight out of Atlanta that leaves in about thirty minutes. Should I make a reservation for you?"

"What time does it arrive?"

"Nine forty-five. Should I have you met?"

"No, I'll grab a cab. See you in a couple of hours."

The colonel stood on the gray street and watched the people scurry up and down. Everyone was in a hurry. He dialed another number.

"It's me. I'm going to need some help. Arrange for a private plane out of Tetaboro Airport. I'll be there in about forty minutes." He listened and then replied, "One way, New Jersey to D.C. And by the way, don't contact my office until further notice."

Chapter 52

"Where's Pam?" Aaron asked as he followed Michael and Scott from the hospital lobby to a quiet corridor.

"I don't know. She was gone by the time I arrived. I've alerted the office that if she's seen, to contact me immediately."

"We just had a meeting with Troy's dad. He works for some arm of the government and Pam works for him."

"While she was working for us?"

Aaron nodded his head. "How's Troy?"

"Not good, not bad. I guess he's doing as well as can be expected." Michael glanced up and down the hall before continuing. "I haven't heard from Cassius. Have you spoken to Captain Sands?"

"Not yet. He's going to try and find out why the Denver P.D. thinks that Troy shot Whitney."

Michael's foot made circles on the tile floor of the hospital as Aaron started talking.

"Something's bothering you. Why don't you just spit it out?"

Michael looked at Scott before turning his attention on Aaron. "There are a lot of things bothering me. Pam is one; Troy's dad is another; Whitney's death is the third; and the Denver Police thinking its Troy is just the whipped cream on a pile of dog shit."

Aaron glanced at Scott who nodded. "Is there a cafeteria around here?" Aaron asked Michael.

"Down the hall."

"Let's get a cup of coffee and I'll try to bring you up to date."

The cafeteria was a large room with about thirty tables. Each table had eight stackable chairs, four on each side. Ten machines serving everything from coffee to sandwiches lined the walls. Aaron motioned to a table in the rear of the room.

"How do you want your coffee?" Scott asked Michael.

"I take it black."

Aaron sat with his back to the wall and waited for Scott to arrive with the coffee.

"I almost didn't get us any," Scott said as he carefully put down the three cups. "There's a little sign on the machine that says distributed by ISSI."

"Think it's the same company?" Michael asked.

"Probably, but I figured, what the hell, it's only coffee."

Aaron looked around the room. "Michael, let me bring you up to date before someone decides to sit next to us."

Scott said, "Too late. Tom's just walked in and he looks agitated."

They watched as Tom hurriedly weaved between the people and arrived at their table slightly out of breath.

"Three of our cars have had accidents. One of our men reported that he recognized the driver of the car that ran him off the road and it was one of the men that work for Interstate. In another incident, a garbage truck had a malfunction and unloaded its entire load of dirt in our parking lot. They're apologizing like crazy, but it will be at least four hours before they can get it cleaned up. We can't get our cars out or our people in."

"What kind of garbage truck?" Michael asked.

"It belongs to a nursery in Newbury Park. It's one of those small ones that have two pincers in front that move platforms around, and they have plenty of room inside to haul away garbage and debris."

"Any of our men in the accidents get hurt?" Michael asked.

"One of the guys who went off the road got a bloody nose, but that's it."

"Tom, have one of our people find out how close to Active Components they garage that truck," Aaron interjected.

"You think that could be the truck used in the break-in?"

"Could be. We were never able to find that truck, and it may have been right under our noses. At the same time, it might be a good idea to find out who owns that nursery."

"I'll get on it at once." Michael stood.

"Michael, I haven't forgotten why we were sitting here." Aaron rose and looked at Michael meaningfully. "You have my word that we'll finish this conversation some time in the very near future. Meanwhile, for the record, Pam and Troy are under contract to someone else besides us. Troy's dad is very well connected in some government agency, and as far as Whitney, I'm sorry he's dead, but I know it wasn't Troy who did it."

Michael smiled gratefully. "Don't worry, the *Reader's Digest* version works for me, but I would still like to sit down and find out how you get so involved."

Chapter 53

The twin engine Cessna landed at an airstrip used solely by government aircraft eleven miles from C.I.A. headquarters in Virginia within three minutes of its intended arrival time. Two women dressed in business suits met the colonel. They stood about five foot seven, had shoulder-length dark hair, and wore polarized sunglasses. One of them held open the rear door of a new stretch Lincoln Continental and the other walked to the driver's side.

"Any luggage, Sir?" the one holding open the rear door asked.

"No, just this overnight bag."

The inside of the car had a glass partition between the front and rear seats with a telephone and mini bar in the back.

"Is this line secure?" the colonel asked.

"It was checked this morning. We have the capability of changing the address if you want." The driver responded as if she had been asked these questions many times before.

"What address will it show?" the colonel asked.

"Right now it will show Florida."

"I would like it to show a terminal at Dulles."

The woman sitting in the front passenger seat picked up a phone located on the dashboard and spoke into it. In less than a minute, she turned back to the colonel.

"It's done. The call will look like it is originating right outside of the Delta terminal."

The colonel sat back and said, "Take me to the phone booth at

Dulles." He closed his eyes and sat back. *I'm getting too old for this,* he thought as a smile crossed his face. *But I wouldn't change it for anything else I know.* The smile turned to a frown. *Except maybe for Troy.*

"We're approaching the airport," one of the women up front called out.

The colonel picked up the phone and dialed his office. On the second ring, his aide answered, "I'm here."

"This is the colonel. I'm at Dulles waiting for my luggage. Have you heard from Canon?"

"No. Are you coming here?"

"Why?"

"I was going to dispatch a car for you."

"Don't bother. I'll take a taxi. The bags are coming out. I'll call you back in five minutes." The colonel looked at his watch. "Why don't one of you go over and use the phone. I would like to see if it's in working order."

The woman on the passenger side got out and ran to the booth. She put some coins in the phone and dialed a number. The phone in the car rang.

"This is January," the woman behind the wheel said before turning around and addressing the colonel. "July says the phone is working."

"Talk to her for a couple of minutes."

Before January could relay his request, he watched as two men pushed open the phone booth door. They were both wearing overcoats, which gave them an odd look in the midst of a crowd dressed for summer. They handed July something and pulled her out of the booth. She shrugged her shoulders and walked into the terminal without a backward glance.

"What was that all about?" January turned and asked the colonel.

"We'll know in a minute. July will come back here, correct?"

"She'll call and ask for instructions."

"Tell her we'll meet her upstairs in about ten minutes."

The two men stood twenty to thirty feet away from the phone booth scanning the crowd. Before long, three more men arrived dressed the same way and entered the terminal through the departure doors leading to the baggage area.

"It looks like you drew a crowd."

"It certainly does. Let's go get July."

"Canon, this is Aaron Carlyle. Three of my cars have been involved in accidents today and the word I'm getting is that it's your men causing them."

"Only three? You're at least twenty minutes behind. I think you'll find that the number of accidents your men have had is closer to six."

"Really? Well if that's so, it's too late for me to tell you that if there was a fourth accident, I would take it personally."

"Who cares what you take *personally*. As far as I'm concerned, the wraps have been taken off."

Aaron put the receiver back on the phone.

"Every couple of years, something comes up that takes us back in time."

Scott rose from the conference table he was sitting at and poured a cup of coffee. "Want one?" He motioned to Tom who was sitting across from him.

Tom shook his head. Looking at Aaron he inquired, "What did that idiot say?"

"He said the wraps had been taken off. He also said we have three more accidents."

"Odd choice of words," Scott said aloud. "It's as if someone else gave him the go-ahead."

"That's what I thought. Advise all the men to be careful. I'm going to call Min and let him know what's going on."

"Reset this phone for another phone booth in the area, maybe the next terminal." The colonel made the request of July after they had picked her up and were headed to his office.

"I have one about half a block away. Will that do?"

"Yes, that'll do fine. How long before we reach my office?"

"Less than fifteen minutes," January replied

The colonel looked at his watch and smiled. "What are your instructions?"

"We were told to transport you wherever you requested and to give aid if required."

"Do you have backup available?"

"Sir, we've never needed help before."

"Do you know who I am?" The colonel smiled as he asked.

"We've been instructed never to ask."

"But if you had to guess?" He continued to smile as he played along.

"The only thing we can surmise is that you are with the mother organization. The speed at which the plane was put at your disposal and the instructions we were given would lead us to believe that you're very high up. They didn't tell us your name, and the building your office is in has well over two thousand people."

He nodded in satisfaction before dialing his office number. "How far away are we now?"

"Less than five minutes."

"I'm here," The colonel's aide said, answering his phone.

"This is the colonel. I can't find a taxi. How long will it take to get someone here to pick me up?"

"Which terminal are you at?"

"I'm about a half block away from Delta."

"Someone will be there in less than ten minutes."

"Have you spoken to Canon?"

The colonel detected a slight hesitation before his aide replied, "No."

"I'll see you soon," The colonel replied and disconnected.

Chapter 54

"I will have Tuloc advise our workers about what you have told me. Have you any news about what is happening with Lan's company?"

"If you would have asked me two hours ago, I would have said not to worry. Troy's father gave me the impression that he was cutting all ties with Canon. When he left yesterday, I thought it was over. Now I'm not too sure."

"The parts she needed are to be delivered tomorrow. I have told Tuloc that we are to double the amount of cleaning people at Active Components."

"Min, there's something wrong. Active is getting the parts from the company that manufactures them, when?"

There was no answer from Min.

"Min, did you hear me?"

"Yes, I heard you. I am trying to put everything in place. For Providence to get the parts tomorrow, they would have to be shipped today. That means they are at Active now."

"Min, I will have Michael get some people over there immediately. You call Mrs. Burnett and tell her to request a pick up of the components today. My men will escort her back to Providence and that's where you can double your cleaning crew."

"Thank you, Aaron. I will make the call."

Aaron sat in his office staring out into space when his private phone rang.

"This is Aaron."

"Hi, it's me." The sound of Karen's voice made him smile.

"Hi Me." He responded. "I was going to call you."

"When?"

"When what?"

"When were you going to call me?"

"You were next."

"That sounds like a business call."

"It was going to be. There's a company called Active Components. I was going to ask you to find out if they are a public company and if so, who their officers are."

"That's why I called you," Karen said breathlessly into the phone. "I bought back the stock that I sold short at thirty-four dollars. Later in the day, ISCC announced that they were spinning off their electronic group. The group included three contract manufacturers, and this company called Active Components. The press release says that they expect to buy the stock they don't own in a company called Western Amplifier. I never heard any mention of Active Components before and then I remembered that was where Carl was shot."

"That may answer a couple of outstanding questions," Aaron replied.

"What questions?

"The stolen parts never appeared on the gray market, and Active Components was able to replace them in half the quoted time."

"You think the crooks are part of Active Components?" Karen asked.

"Or somehow involved," he answered.

"You sound like you're busy. Call me when you have time to discuss the date I picked for the wedding. Love you!" Karen hung up the phone before Aaron could answer.

He started to call her back, but stopped and dialed Min instead.

"Who is it you wish to speak to?"

Aaron recognized Soo Kim's voice. "Sookie, it's Aaron Carlyle. I must talk to Min."

"Uncle Aaron, he has left with Tuloc to pick up some parts for Mrs. Burnett. They are in the car and can be reached there."

"Sookie, contact them and tell them not to go to Active

Components. I am leaving my place now and they can call me through the switchboard at Besafe."

"What is your number? I will have them contact you directly."

"I'll probably be on the phone, so tell them to do it my way. I'm leaving now."

Aaron's first call after getting in his car was to Barry.

"Barry, get Cassius over to Active. I just found out that the same people own them that own Interstate. The parts that Mrs. Burnett needed to keep the lines going are supposed to be shipped today and I have a feeling that they are the same parts that were supposedly stolen."

"What do you want Cassius to do?"

"Help out. I'm on my way there now. Min and Tuloc and a crew of their people are also on the way there. I have a feeling that a problem could develop."

"I'm twenty minutes away. Can you keep a lid on it until I arrive?"

"No promises, but I'll try. Tell Cassius to hurry."

"Aaron, this is base, I have a call from Tuloc." Aaron turned down the volume of the closed circuit radio.

"Put him through," Aaron replied.

"Mr. Carlyle, what's the problem?"

"Is Min with you?"

"No. He is in the car ahead."

"Can you stop him?"

Tuloc yelled something in Vietnamese and then replied to Aaron, "We missed the light. He is now a block ahead of us. I will try calling, but he doesn't like to answer the phone."

"Don't let anyone enter the Active plant until I arrive. I'm about ten minutes from there."

"I will try and stop him."

Aaron kept looking at the clock on the dashboard. L.A. traffic always seemed the worst when he was in a hurry.

"Aaron, this is base."

"Go ahead, base."

"Aaron, this is Scott. What's going on?"

"Karen called me with some new information. The same people that own Interstate own Active. I had already told Min to get his cleaning service people over there and I'm now trying to get there before a problem develops."

Scott didn't answer for a few seconds. "Do you think the parts were never stolen?"

"Either that or they were stolen and given back at a later time. The whole thing may have been done to force Providence into a position that would make them ripe for a takeover."

"Where did Karen get this new information?"

"ISCC announced a reorganization today and Active Components was listed as a part of the reorg."

"Do you think Ewing is behind this?"

"I wouldn't put it past him, but I still can't figure out why Troy got shot."

"Aaron, I'm going to send two cars over to Active Components as a backup. Keep me in the loop as to what's going on—and be careful."

"Aren't I always?"

"No, you're not. I'll talk to you later."

Aaron could see the Active building up ahead. Tuloc was standing in front waving his hands in an obvious disagreement with Min. Aside from the two dark Lincolns, there were two panel trucks with at least eight men standing around. Pulling into the parking lot Aaron jumped out and walked slowly over to Min and Tuloc.

"Why am I waiting? Do you think I am afraid to enter?" Min was yelling at Aaron.

"If you would answer your phone, I could have told you why I asked you to wait."

"What's going on out here?"

Everyone turned toward the voice.

"I asked, what's going on out here?"

"Who are you?" Aaron asked.

Chapter 55

"Colonel! I didn't expect you for another hour."

"I found another means of transportation." The colonel stared at his aide until the silence in the room became uncomfortable. "Did I ever tell you what my real rank is?"

The aide now standing replied, "You said colonel and that's what I thought you were." The ringing of the phone broke another elongated stillness.

"Answer it," the colonel said to his subordinate.

"I'm here." He answered the phone, but his eyes never left the colonel. "No, it's all right, he's here." His hand shook as he hung up the phone.

"Was that the man you sent to pick me up?"

"Yes it was. He couldn't find you. How did you get here so soon?"

"How many men did you send?"

The aide picked up a bottle of water on his desk. "I sent two. Why?"

"Five came to get me."

"That's strange."

"I thought so." Silence again filled the room. "Why did you do it?" the colonel finally asked.

The aide took another sip of the water as he looked questioningly at the colonel.

"Don't insult my intelligence by saying 'do what'." The colonel spoke with contempt in his voice.

"If you're asking about the three extra people, I didn't want you to know I was worried about you."

The colonel took a pistol out of his pocket. "Canon didn't know Troy was going to Colorado. Troy told us when we had him on the speakerphone, and I didn't tell Canon."

"What makes you think I said anything?"

"Canon was doing things differently than I had told you to pass on. I was prepared to chalk everything up to chance, but when Whitney started doing things other than what I had instructed I knew there was a problem. Only you and I knew Canon's role and how to contact him, and it wasn't me."

The aide opened one of the drawers in his desk. "Look at these numbers," he almost shouted. "There's a fortune to be made. All we have to do is let him continue. Even the selling of the stock worked in our favor. We can buy it back today for half of what we sold it for."

The pistol in the colonel's hand looked like it became heavy as he lowered it toward the floor. "You're right, there's only one problem."

"What's that?"

"Troy. You knew he was my son and you still gave the orders that almost killed him."

"That was a mistake." The aide was now shouting, not so much to make himself heard, but as an act of bravado.

The colonel raised his pistol and pulled the trigger once. The aide gasped, closed his eyes, and slumped back into his chair. Nonchalantly taking out his cell phone, the colonel dialed a number, which was answered on the first ring.

"My aide just died of a heart attack. I'll be moving to new quarters later today and will call you with my new address. When I call, please let me know about his funeral arrangements."

The limousine was waiting at the front door of the building in the no parking zone. January was sitting behind the wheel and July was standing by the door. As she opened the door, July said, "We have been asked to take you to the wall before the airport. We were told you would know what part of the wall to let you off at."

He ducked his head and entered the car. He sat back and closed his eyes before dialing Aaron Carlyle's private number in California.

"How's my son?" he asked as if it was an order not to be answered incorrectly.

"As well as can be expected," was Aaron's reply. "I have to talk to Pam. Do you know how to reach her?" Aaron continued before the colonel could hang up.

"Why do you need Pam?"

"I think she may have answers to some of our questions."

"She'll call you in three hours." The colonel disengaged before Aaron could ask anything else.

July turned and said, "The wall's up ahead. Where should we drop you?"

"Here's fine. What are your instructions?"

"We're to let you off and come back in thirty minutes."

The colonel put his thumb in his mouth and chewed on his nail. "Make it twenty minutes," he said aloud.

The limo stopped and July got out and opened his door. "We'll pick you up at this spot in thirty minutes."

"I told you twenty."

"I know what you told us," she replied as she closed his door and re-entered the front seat. The car pulled away almost before the front door was closed.

The colonel looked both ways before walking to the wall. Stopping before one of the sections, he ran his finger over one of the names. *It seems like such a long time ago,* he thought.

"You're going to wear it out!"

The colonel turned. "How are you, Sir?" He held out his hand.

"You're getting old, Raymond. I never would have gotten this close in the old days."

Smiling, the colonel replied, "In the old days, I would have wondered why you stood behind the wall by the A section when we were supposed to meet by the W section."

"Touché! I'm glad to see you're still in practice. Suppose you tell me what's gone wrong."

It took almost twenty minutes for the colonel to explain what had happened and what he saw as the fix. The man he was talking to looked at his gold Rolex watch. "I can see why you told the girls twenty minutes. You never were one to waste any time."

"It's all right. I can use the extra time to look up some old friends."

"Raymond, this is the last one. I'm bringing you inside." The words were said quietly, but with unseen power behind them,

"We've been carrying you on the books as a deputy director in charge of South East Asia. When you finish cleaning up this mess, I'm going to promote you to director and you can get out of the field. I owe you at least that."

The two men stood looking at each other. The colonel again extended his hand.

"My ride is here. How about letting me have the driver and shotgun rider as back up? They're very good."

"Where will you be tomorrow?"

"In California."

"So will they."

Chapter 56

The man was huge. Two of Min's "nephews" stepped between Min and this giant. Aaron, who stood six foot three, felt dwarfed. He reminded Aaron of Andre the Giant, the wrestler that no one could beat.

Tuloc stepped forward and said, "We are from the cleaning service. We're here to clean the building."

The giant's face showed concern and confusion. "I was told not to let anyone in the building."

"That didn't mean us. We come every night. I've never seen you here before. When did you start working here?" Tuloc's steady stream of questions had the giant confused.

"Mr. Canon hired me today. He said to not let anyone in the building."

Tuloc stepped forward and held out his hand. "My name is Tuloc. I am the man in charge of cleaning. I feel much better now that I find you here. There have been some robberies in the neighborhood. With you out here, I can send some of my men home. I have three extra for protection."

The giant held out his hand. Tuloc's hand disappeared inside of it as they shook.

"My name is Frederick. I'm glad to meet you. The other people who were here didn't even say hello to me." After releasing Tuloc's hand, he continued, "You do, of course, have proof that you are the cleaning service."

Tuloc turned to Aaron. "Show him your badge." Turning back to Frederick he said, "That man is in charge of security. You can see the name of his company pasted on the door. He is here to ensure our safety."

The giant looked at Aaron's badge and then looked back at the door. He slowly matched the Besafe logo to that in Aaron's wallet.

Smiling, he asked, "What do you want me to do?"

"Please stay on watch out here while the building is cleaned. With you here, I can now go inspect other buildings in the area." Motioning the men to enter the building, Aaron looked up at the giant. "What did you do for a living before Mr. Canon hired you?"

"Mr. Canon never hired me."

Aaron waited for him to continue. When he didn't Aaron asked, "What is your name?"

"My name is Hubbard, William." It sounded like he was going to add something, but didn't.

"My name is Aaron Carlyle." On the spur of the moment, Aaron added, "Former lieutenant, U.S. Army."

The giant snapped to attention and saluted.

"Staff Sergeant Hubbard at your command, Sir."

Aaron held his hand out. "Glad to meet you Staff Sergeant. I thought you said your name was Frederick to Tuloc."

Hubbard again had a confused look on his face. A wide grin erupted, showing wide spaces between his teeth.

"Did you serve in Nam, Sir?"

"I was there. Lost some friends, made some friends, but I guess the good news is that I made it home. Were you there?"

"Yes, Sir. I served with . . ." he stopped. "I forgot. I'm not allowed to talk about it."

"I understand, Staff Sergeant. I spoke to the colonel last week and he still doesn't discuss Nam in public." Aaron was talking on instinct.

"You know the colonel, Sir?"

"The colonel and his son, Troy."

"I didn't know he had a son. I was captured while the colonel and I were on a patrol. He was only a captain then and he hid out in the swamp for three weeks before he was rescued. Two years later when I was released, he was a full bird. He was waiting at the gate when they carried me out and made sure that I received good service. He rode in the ambulance with me and told me about changing his name and swore me to secrecy. He's been there whenever I've needed anything."

"Is that why you didn't give me your real name?"

Hubbard blushed and nodded his head.

"What are you doing here?" Aaron continued to probe.

"He told me that I would be doing odd jobs for Canon and every week I write him a report about what goes on."

"Does he have you send your reports to the post office box in D.C.?"

"No, it's in Tulsa."

Aaron was fascinated by what he was hearing. This giant of a man was obviously mentally hurt in Vietnam, but the colonel took care of him. *He may have a soft spot.* Aaron rolled the thought around in his head. *The colonel certainly has many different sides to him.*

"We have the parts," Tuloc exclaimed as he rushed out of the building, followed by Min and three other men.

"What parts?" Hubbard asked.

"The parts the colonel wants us to deliver to Providence," Aaron shouted as he jumped in the vehicle.

The Staff Sergeant backed up, looking first at Aaron and then at Tuloc and Min. "Are they Vietnamese?"

"Of course they are. The colonel wouldn't use anyone else for this job. While we're at it, the colonel needs you to do something else."

"What's that?"

Chapter 57

"Michael, this is Pam. I heard you were looking for me."

"Where are you?"

"Does it matter where I am?"

Michael could feel his face getting red. "I guess it doesn't. It's just that I thought," he stopped and started again. "Aaron thought you might be able to help us catch the guys who shot Troy."

"How would I do that?"

Raising his voice he answered, "Why don't you just get your sweet ass down here and talk to us?"

"Don't get upset. I gave you a full days work every day I was with you."

"You know that's not the reason I'm upset. I vouched for you, and you sold us out."

"Grow up. We're not children. My job was to help you and make sure Troy didn't get hurt while I was doing it. I did my job to the best of my ability."

"I bet your boss was upset."

"I don't know my boss. He's just a voice on the phone."

"And that voice told you to call me?"

"No. Today I got a new voice. He had all the right conventions and wanted me to call Aaron. I figured I owed you the call first."

"Aaron would like to talk to you at the hospital in an hour."

"How did he know when I would be calling?"

"Your faceless voice told Aaron you would call in three hours, exactly three hours ago."

She was silent for a few seconds and then asked, "How's Troy?"

"You can see for yourself when you get to the hospital."

"Michael, I'm sorry."

Michael was about to respond, but changed his mind and hung up the phone, biting down on his lower lip.

From behind him, Cassius said, "No one ever said this job would be easy."

"One of the reasons that I left the force was that I was starting to feel sorry for people." Michael paused and took a deep breath. "After twenty years, it was starting to get to me . . . and now her. It just pisses me off."

"Hello, Mr. Carlyle."

"Hi Pam. Thanks for coming."

Pam acknowledged him and looked down the tiled hall. "Which room is Troy's?"

"I thought you of all people would be able to get that type of information."

"Normally I can. It would only take a phone call, but you people have this hospital closed down tight. They're so paranoid at the front desk that they won't put any calls through to anyone unless you're on some type of list."

Aaron smiled. Michael had done a first class job of shutting down the flow of information.

"My contact told me to give you a call. You need some kind of help in locating the people that shot Troy."

Aaron pointed to one of the rooms. "I have this one reserved."

The room had a standard hospital bed, two chairs, and a television on the wall. There was a door that connected to the adjoining room. Aaron noticed the walls were painted Granny Smith Apple green.

"I guess some things never change," he said aloud as he sat down on one of the chairs.

"What can I do to help you?" Pam asked as she looked out the window.

"We're trying to figure out who knew Troy was going to be at the airport."

"I knew."

"Besides you."

"People at Besafe."

"No one else?"

Pam turned and faced Aaron. "I've asked myself the same question a dozen times. The only person I spoke to was . . ." She stopped speaking and closed her eyes. "Bastard!"

"Who?" Aaron asked.

"I don't know."

"Would it help if I told you that I spoke to Troy's dad and he said that you work for him?"

She shook her head. "It wouldn't matter. I don't know whom I work for. I was hired and trained by the C.I.A., but was put to work in a special branch. Until I was assigned here, I did mostly guard duty. I drove people around as they came in from overseas or from other parts of the country. Every once in a while, I would be assigned to infiltrate some group, just to keep the company up to date on what was going on."

"You never met Troy before you came here?"

"No."

"Did you ever meet Whitney?"

"I don't know anyone called Whitney."

"How about Jordan?"

"I'm not sure what I'm supposed to tell you."

"Let me tell you what we know, and then you can decide what you can or cannot tell me."

It took ten minutes to brief Pam on what Aaron knew or what he thought he knew. When he finished, he asked, "Can you help us?"

"Pam, if you know anything, help them. Please."

She turned as Troy entered. "You're okay!"

"Thanks to you," he replied, with the bandages showing through his open shirt.

They stepped hesitantly toward each other, but stopped two feet apart. They stared silently at each other until Pam said, "The hell with it!" she put her arms around him.

"Who is this woman?" Staff Sergeant Hubbard came through the door and pulled Troy back. "I'm on duty here, and no one gets to see Troy unless I know about it."

Chapter 58

"Mr. Canon. Some men walked into Active Components and walked out with those parts we were storing."

"Which parts?"

"The ones that you said we were supposed to destroy."

Dennis Canon's face turned red. His eyes turned opaque as his tongue wet his lips.

The man that had given him the news started backing up, holding his hands up in front of him

"Start again from the beginning, and don't leave anything out."

"I don't know very much. I just received a call from Paul, and he said when he got there, he was told the parts were already picked up."

"Where is Paul?"

"He said he was going over to the cleaners."

"He's going *where*?" Canon shouted.

The man took another step backward. "I think he must have some clothes at the cleaners. He said to tell you he was going to the cleaning service."

"You idiot! That's who probably took the parts—the cleaning service." Canon took a deep breath in an attempt to calm himself. "How many men did he have with him?"

"Two."

"Get me three or four more men and let's get over to Providence. That's where the parts are headed."

The man turned and ran out the door, shouting over his back, "They'll be in the parking lot in five minutes."

Canon picked up his phone and dialed the number he'd been trying to reach all morning. "How could this number not be in working order?" he muttered to himself as he walked out the door.

He stood in the parking lot, checked his watch and tried the number again. When the recording came on informing him, "This is not a working number," he turned and in frustration yelled, "Where the hell are you guys?"

"Pam, I would like you to meet one of my father's only friends, Staff Sergeant William Hubbard. He's been assigned to watch over us until the people that tried to shoot us are found."

"Us?"

"Actually me, but I'm including you."

"Who is your father?"

Troy glanced around, took Pam by the arm, and led her out of earshot. "My father heads up a secret government operation that both you and I belong to. I don't think there are even ten people that know who he is or what he does, but he is powerful. This giant, Hubbard, knew him in Vietnam. He saved my dad's life, which is probably why he has a job for life. Mr. Carlyle also met my father in Nam. They are not friends, but I wouldn't say they're enemies either."

"But I was told to talk to Mr. Carlyle, nothing else."

"I'm pretty sure we can arrange another call and you can get new orders."

Pam roughly combed her fingers through her shoulder-length hair. "I'll stay with you until I get further instructions."

Troy smiled. "Great!"

"Wait a second. When I said stay, I didn't mean move in with you. I meant . . ."

"I know what you meant," Troy said before she finished, but he was still smiling.

"When we get there, if Paul hasn't gotten them back, I want the men to put on their masks and make it look like a robbery."

"What do we do if they put up a struggle?"

Canon glared at him impatiently. "I want the parts back, period! Whatever it takes just get it done!"

"Staff Sergeant Hubbard, I would like you to meet . . ." Troy thought for a second and then continued, "my very good friend Pam. She was sent by the colonel to watch over me and now we are both under your protection."

"I'm glad to meet you, Pam. You don't have to worry. I'll take care of you both."

"There's Paul," the driver said and motioned toward the front gate of the Providence building.

"Pull up beside him!" Canon barked.

"Paul, tell me what's going on," he shouted

Paul approached the car quickly. "There's a car and two vans in front of the building. The two vans belong to the cleaning service and I'm guessing the car does as well. I don't know how many of their people are inside, but it shouldn't be more than eight or ten."

"I've only got five guys with me. Think it's enough?"

"These are only janitors for Christ's sake. When did we start worrying about them?"

"I've heard stories about that guy Min." Canon looked uncertain as he spoke.

"I'll take him out first and then there's no one to worry about. You have five and I have two. We're ready."

Canon sighed. "Let's get started."

"Let's get some things straight." Pam planted her hands on her hips and stared at Sergeant Hubbard. "I'm trained in the use of guns and hand-to-hand combat. I don't need someone looking after me. I'm going along with this because I was ordered to report to Mr. Carlyle and help him in any way I could."

Hubbard smiled and held out his hand. "I'm sure you're capable, and I won't interfere in your daily activity, but . . ." Hubbard grabbed Pam by the throat, put his leg behind hers, and pushed. She fell to the ground and felt the point of a knife pressed against her chest. ". . . I am good to have around in a pinch."

He held out his arm and helped her off of the ground. As she rose, she produced a gun and pushed the muzzle under his chin.

"So am I, you sneaky son of a bitch."

Chapter 59

Paul and one of his men walked through the front door and found themselves in a small waiting room with a phone, two chairs, and a door that proved to be locked when he tried it. Having sent the balance of the men through the warehouse entrance, he immediately felt alone and a sense of foreboding swept over him. Picking up the phone, he dialed the operator.

"We're here to see Mrs. Burnett," he almost shouted into the phone.

"Mrs. Burnett is not here today. Please leave your card and I will see that she gets it."

"Can you please open the door so that I can talk to the plant supervisor in person?"

"May I please have your name, and the name of your associate?"

Paul turned and looked at the ceiling. A video camera pointed right at him. Before he could answer, he heard shots from what he imagined was the rear of the building.

"Shit! Let's get out of here!" Paul pulled on the handle of the front door and found that it was now locked. He pulled out his pistol and rapidly fired three shots into the glass door. He used one of the chairs to bang out the glass and jumped through, followed by his associate.

"Let's get around to the back," he shouted as he started running.

Before he reached the corner of the building, a car with Dennis Canon at the wheel careened across the parking lot and stopped beside him.

"Get in!" Dennis shouted. "It was an ambush. They were waiting for us."

"What about the rest of the men?"

"They're all down. Get in or I'm leaving you here."

"Aaron, there's been a shooting at Providence. I have no further information, but I sent Cassius over there to take charge. I'll be there in less than ten minutes."

"Min picked up the parts from Active Components about two hours ago. He's probably right in the middle of whatever's going on. I'm at the hospital and it'll take twenty minutes for me to get there. I'm leaving now."

"Don't get stopped for speeding," Barry said and laughed as he disconnected the call.

"How many guys can we lay our hands on?" Canon asked Paul as the car sped along the freeway.

"We have six on the payroll and I can get us another dozen or so by tonight. What do you want to do?"

"I can't reach the people in Washington, so I guess we're on our own. The first thing I'm gonna do is get even with that Vietnamese cleaning guy."

"What happened?"

"The guys walked up the ramp and all of a sudden the cleaning crew opened fire. Our guys didn't have a chance."

"Did they have their masks on?" Paul asked.

Canon nodded. "What happened to you two?"

"They had us on a television camera and locked the door behind us. As soon as I heard the shooting, I shot out the glass and headed to the back. That's when I ran into you."

"I'm also going to get is that big, tall idiot they sent to help out." After a moment's thought, he added, "And that kid we shot at the airport."

"We still have to watch out for the Besafe crowd."

"I'm not worried about them," Canon said emphatically.

"We weren't worried about the cleaning people either," Paul responded.

"That was you. I told you I heard stories about that guy Min."

"Mr. Min, could you please tell me what happened?" Cassius had Min and all of his men lined up at the far end of the parking lot.

Min looked at Cassius without responding.

"You're going to have to tell someone eventually, so why not me?"

"You show no respect to your elders."

"What does that mean?"

"You have not visited my house socially with Mai Ling."

Cassius closed his eyes and rubbed his forehead. "Arrest all of them!" he yelled over to his men.

"All fourteen?" one of the men shot back.

"What do you think, Mr. Min, all fourteen?" Cassius asked quietly.

Min glanced at Tuloc. "I cannot imagine any reason for Mai Ling to continue seeing this person on a social basis, can you?"

"I promised Soo Kim I would be home for dinner," Tuloc replied. "If you have no objection, I will tell him what happened here and then he doesn't have to arrest me."

"If you speak to him, will I have to go to jail?" Min was now excluding Cassius from the conversation.

Tuloc looked at the Lieutenant, who shook his head.

"If I speak to him, and then invite him to dinner this Sunday, you will not have to go to jail."

"Where did the dinner part come from?"

"It will be in the form of a bribe."

Min smiled. "This I understand. You may talk to him."

Tuloc now smiled. "Lieutenant Sizemore, I would like to take this moment to invite you to dinner at Mr. Min's home this Sunday."

"I would be only to happy to accept. Now, if you could tell me what happened, I would be most grateful," Cassius Sizemore replied.

"Due to the recent rash of robberies that have been taking place, we have had some of our most trusted men get permits to carry guns. We had just picked up some very hard to get parts from Active Components when it was noticed that men with masks were coming in the back door. We shouted for them to stop outside and when they didn't, the shooting started."

"Who fired the first shots?" Cassius waited for the answer with a pen in his hand.

"It is very hard for me to know. One of our men said the others did, but another thought we did when the men in masks showed their shotguns."

"Were any of your men hurt?"

"Two were wounded, but not badly."

"You know all six of the men in masks are dead. Your men are good shots."

"I think we were lucky. There were two more in the front of the building, but they just shot out the glass," Tuloc replied.

"Those two got away?"

"Yes. The two from the front were picked up by someone driving a car, but we have pictures of them."

"There'll be an inquest, but if what you have told me is what happened, you'll have nothing to worry about. However, I will need the names of the men that fired their weapons." Cassius looked around. "I'll also need the weapons themselves to determine who did what to whom."

"Aaron, the news just came across the television." Karen started talking before Aaron had a chance to say hello. "There was a shooting at Lan's building. Six are dead and two were wounded. Do you think any of the dead are people we know?" Karen's voice was trembling.

"No, but I hope you're out of ISCC. They are losing management people as we speak."

"I'm out."

"Talk to you later." Aaron turned to Pam and Troy. "Things are about to get very dicey. Why don't you two and the sergeant go down to San Diego and watch over Karen?"

"You're just trying to get us out of town," Pam answered.

"How was your flight?" The colonel asked his two new assistants.

"On time," replied January.

Chapter 60

"Aaron, Min's a disaster waiting to happen." Barry walked in circles waving his arms like a bird in flight. "Six of Canon's men dead, and we don't even know who fired first."

"Cassius, what did he tell you?" Aaron asked.

"He told me . . ."

"What difference does it make what he told Cassius? It probably was only a half truth anyway," Barry interrupted.

"Captain! The six men were wearing masks. They were carrying guns, and based on the video from the front waiting room, they were going to use them. His men have licenses to carry concealed weapons, and if we arrested them, all they would have to say is they were fired upon. There's no one to deny their story."

"Did we check all of them for licenses?" Barry continued his pacing.

"Only seven have licenses, but they say they were the only ones to use guns," Lieutenant Sizemore replied.

"Barry, look at it this way. There's six less pieces of shit walking the streets. Trying to prove something against Min or his family will only give you an ulcer."

"I think I've already got one." Staring at his shoes he continued, "Let them go!"

"Captain, there's one more thing you should know."

"What's that?"

"We're both invited for dinner Sunday night."

"Where?" He looked up at Cassius. "Don't tell me. Min's?"

Cassius nodded. "The invitation includes your wife."

"To what do I owe this honor?"

"One of the first things we have to get done is to locate Pam Haviland."

"I remember her," January said from the front seat of the car. "She used to work the banquet circuit."

"Here's her last known address. I spoke to her yesterday, but haven't been able to contact her since." Passing a piece of paper to the front, he continued, "If she's not there, I'll have to contact Aaron Carlyle."

"We read your reports on the plane. Do we consider Mr. Carlyle a friend or an enemy?"

"For the time being, he is not an enemy, but I wouldn't call him a friend."

The two girls glanced at each other.

"What does that look mean?" The colonel's voice told them that either one could answer, but it had better be quickly.

Without missing a beat, July replied, "Those tend to be the worst kind. They make you hesitate because you're not sure and you often end up hurt."

The colonel broke the silence after what seemed an eternity. "If you have to pull your weapons, treat everyone as an enemy."

The car continued along the Pacific Coast Highway with the colonel looking at the sun going down over the Channel Islands when he started laughing.

"The banquet circuit! That's pretty good."

"What did you do before you went to work as a policewoman in Northern Cal?" Karen asked as she served Pam and Troy iced tea.

"Ms. Williams, I have to let you know how funny I feel not being able to answer your questions, but I still work for someone else."

"I wasn't looking for any state secrets, I was just interested in you."

Pam started chewing on her lower lip. "I worked the banquet circuit."

"What's that?" Karen asked with a smile on her face. "It sounds like something I could gain a lot of weight on."

A smile appeared on Troy's face. "I'd love to know also. I'm sure you could tell her what the banquet circuit is. Just don't give any names or dates."

After a few seconds, Pam said, "Whenever a visiting dignitary, regardless of his status, had to attend a dinner, the government made sure they had a female driver. Many of the men, and sometimes the women, felt more comfortable, and said things they wouldn't have if there had been man driving."

Troy continued, "There is a feeling that many foreigners still consider women as furniture and talk openly in front of them."

Karen sat down on the chair across from Troy and Pam. "I hope our government doesn't make plans based on what these people say in front of the drivers. Foreign governments can't be that dumb. They have to know what we are doing."

"You'd be surprised at some of the decisions that are made," Pam replied.

"Carlyle, was Pam able to help you?"

"I wondered when you'd be back."

"Maybe I never left."

"That's true. Did you?" Aaron asked.

"Did she help?" the colonel asked again without answering Aaron's question.

"A little. The investigation is ongoing."

"Did she say where she would be?"

"Why? Did you lose her?"

The colonel didn't like the way this conversation was going. "I had to change my number and haven't been able to give her my new one yet. There's a fall back number, but it doesn't get used for seventy-two hours."

"Give Troy a call. He knows where she is."

"That would be great, but Troy has been out of the loop for six days. He doesn't have a number either. By the way, how is he?"

"He's fine. I hired an ex-staff sergeant to watch over him."

"I'm losing your signal. I'll have to call you back." The colonel hung up the phone and searched through his book for Staff Sergeant Hubbard's number.

"The first thing I want to do is take care of that guy Min and his family. How many men do we have?"

Paul Kiesler looked at his boss and realized that he was starting to unravel. "Dennis," he started hesitantly, "our information used to be pretty good. If we've lost that edge, why don't we just pull back and wait?"

"We can't let them think they're beating us. I don't need those guys that operate over the phones and never get their hands dirty." He shuffled some papers around on his desk and then continued, "Are you with me?"

"Of course I am. I know that you'll take care of me when this is all over."

"Good. Do we have his home address?"

"No. We have his office address, and I've got two men watching it now. I told them to follow both him and that guy Tuloc you met in the parking lot. The story I hear is that he's a son--in-law, or a grandson-in-law. They're related somehow."

"Staff Sergeant Hubbard, this is the colonel. Please call me at 800-999-2001. I am back in town and would like to get together."

"Is Sergeant Hubbard someone we should know, Sir?"

The colonel looked up from the backseat of the limo. "I can't keep calling you January and July. What are your real names?"

"My name is Sharon," replied the woman he had known as January.

"Mine is Elaine. The names we were using are the months we were born."

"What would you have done if you were both born in the same month?"

The two women looked at each other and laughed.

"Aaron, we hit pay dirt. Switching Hubbard's phone was a stroke of genius. We programmed all the numbers he had stored so he wouldn't know the difference and we were prepared to forward any call he got after whoever sent it left a voice mail." Scott stood there looking very smug.

"And?" Aaron asked.

"The colonel just called asking him to call an eight hundred number. I called it into Barry, and he's having it checked right now."

"We're finally one step ahead of that S.O.B. Keep me informed. I've got Michael trying to keep an eye on Canon. Hopefully he'll lead us to Kiesler."

Chapter 61

Canon sat with his feet up on the desk watching his favorite movie. He thought, *Paul would never understand. He could take a lesson from Shane. You can't back down when things don't go your way.* The ringing of the phone interrupted his reverie. With a scowl, he hit the mute button and answered with a grunt.

"Boss, I just wanted to make sure you want us to go ahead."

"I was just thinking about you," Canon replied.

"I hope it was about how much you're going to pay me when this is finished."

"All you ever think about is money. Of course I want you to go ahead. Let me know when you're finished."

"Call you back in an hour." Hanging up, Paul Kiesler looked at the nine men that were sitting around inside the closed gym. "It's a go! He wants them hurt, so let's go get it done." The men headed toward the door. Paul could see they were not enthusiastic about their latest assignment.

Canon watched Joey tell his mom, "He's so good. Don't you like him, Mother?" His mother answered, "Yes. I like him too, Joey."

He could feel tears welling up in his eyes. *I wish my mother only gave me one name.*

Cassius Sizemore poured himself a cup of coffee while he waited for Tuloc to finish handing out assignments to the night shift crew. He had been told to keep an eye on what was going on with Min's people. Almost half of them here were women.

"Wood City has been complaining about the trash cans not being emptied." Tuloc read from a sheet of paper, "Make sure they all get done tonight, and everyone remember we have men over at Providence, so as soon as you finish your regular building, call in and find out which one hasn't been covered. Things should be back to normal by Friday. See you people tomorrow. And remember, no sleeping on the job." Everyone laughed and started putting together their cleaning paraphernalia.

"Do you have a given name?" Cassius asked.

"Tuloc," he answered.

"Tuloc what? You're like Alan Ladd in that western movie. They only used one name throughout the whole picture."

"My family name is Giac. Why do you ask?"

"Well, you can probably tell it's getting kind of serious with Mai Ling and myself, and I was wondering . . ." Both men turned toward the garage door as it splintered inward from a truck being driven through it.

Tuloc screamed in Vietnamese as his people started running for cover.

Before Cassius was able to pull his gun out of his holster, he saw five of Tuloc's people lying on the ground. Of the half dozen or so men that had jumped off the truck and started firing, two of them fell from someone returning their fire behind him. Cassius opened fire and hit two more. The firing behind him stopped and he started inching his way to the back door when he heard more firing ahead of him. It looked like they had broken in both the front and back. He only had one more clip of bullets in his pocket and realized he needed a way out.

"This way!" He heard Tuloc yelling above the noise, but couldn't locate him through the smoke that was coming from three different places in the warehouse. The highly combustible cleaning material was exploding like bombs and the sprinkler systems were adding to the confusion by not fully putting out the flames and creating smoke.

"Cassius. Behind you!"

Turning, he saw Tuloc with a pistol on top of a rack that housed cleaning equipment. He was firing at the men in the truck while his people scampered for cover.

"Tuloc! Get down from there," Cassius yelled at the top of his lungs.

The men that had broken into the warehouse had started running out. With only himself and Tuloc returning their fire, most of them were gone without a scratch. It was then that he heard the approaching fire engines.

"Tuloc! Where are you?" he shouted as the roof caved in. When he didn't receive an answer, he yelled again, "Is anyone still here?"

Two men emerged from behind some boxes.

"Help me drag these people to safety," he ordered the two men. They would only carry their own friends out of the burning building, refusing to pull the three men that he and Tuloc had shot.

"Is anyone in here?" Came a shout from one of the firemen that arrived on the first truck.

"Over here. I'm a policeman and need some help."

The firemen had the blaze under control in minutes. The fire chief, talking to one of the reporters, mentioned, "This is the second time we've responded to a fire at this location. A few years ago, we had one where five homeless people died of smoke inhalation." Looking at the bodies lying covered on the ground, he finished by saying, "It's a shame."

Cassius was explaining to Barry, "Captain, we were just talking when the truck knocked down the door and they started firing. Tuloc and I were the only ones here with guns."

"Where is Tuloc?"

"I don't know. The roof fell in and they're still looking for bodies. He was behind me on one of the racks."

"Captain!" one of the other policemen called out. "They've found two more bodies. They're bringing them out now."

Cassius looked at his captain. "God, I hope he's not one of them. Min will never rest until he evens the score."

"Lieutenant, the person you don't want to be is the guy responsible for this. We don't have enough men to stop the streets from running red with blood."

The firemen carried out the two bodies and went to lay them on the floor. They were covered by tarpaulin except for one arm that was outside and swung loosely.

"That's a total of eleven so far—three of them women."

Chapter 62

"I am not happy with my course of action!" Tuloc raised his voice to Min, which was an unheard of thing inside of Min's home.

"You did the right thing. First reports are telling us that at least five of our men and three of our women are dead. There are another five hurt. As father to my great grandson, your duty was to come home. It is from here that we will plan our counterattack."

"I am not used to running."

Soo Kim entered the room carrying a tray with hot tea. "This will calm everyone down." She served her grandfather first without any emotion on her face, but smiled as she handed her husband his tea. "I added a little extra sugar. I am glad you are here."

Tuloc smiled before he asked in a quieter voice, "Do we know if Cassius is okay?"

"Not yet," Min replied. "The reports from our men are not yet very clear. We do know that four bodies that are not ours were found." With a twinkle in his eye, he asked, "How many of those did you account for?"

"I think Cassius shot at least two that are no longer moving, maybe three. I know that I hit at least three, but one or two of them might have been able to get out."

Min closed his eyes and rocked back and forth. "It will be good when Cassius becomes part of our family."

"Dennis, we lost six of the guys."

"How about them? How many did they lose?"

"More than us, but I get the feeling they have more men to lose than we do."

"Go hire more. I just found out where Min lives."

"Not before tomorrow. I got two wounded that have to get fixed up, and it's not going to be easy to get guys to sign on with us."

"Offer more money—anything. Just get more people."

"Aaron, this is Barry. Have you heard from Tuloc?"

"No. What's he done now?"

"There been a shooting at their warehouse. We've already found eleven dead and God knows how many wounded. We can't round them all up. Anyway, Cassius was there when it happened and he and Tuloc were the only ones with guns. Now Tuloc can't be found."

"He probably took off rather than trying to explain what happened."

"I hope so, but the place burned to the ground and we're still looking for bodies. I'm afraid he may still be in there."

There was no sound on the phone until Aaron asked, "Has anyone contacted Min yet?"

"You know it wouldn't be me. He and I are like oil and water."

"How about Cassius?"

"He'd rather not. In case Tuloc is still inside, he doesn't want to be the messenger."

"And if he got out?"

"He doesn't want to be the one that has to start screaming about leaving the scene of the crime."

"I'll make the call. Have you found out about the colonel?"

"I haven't gotten an answer on that number yet."

Aaron looked at the phone in his hand. There was something being left unsaid. "Barry, is there something you want to tell me?"

"I'm not sure. Let's see what happens with Tuloc. We'll talk later."

Aaron sat at his desk for a moment and then went to his bar. He poured himself a large glass of scotch and then dialed Min.

The phone was answered as always on the first ring. “Who is calling Min?”

Aaron was positive it was Sookie, which almost surprised him. He was sure they had heard about what happened and if there was any doubt as to Tuloc’s whereabouts she wouldn’t have answered the phone. “Soo Kim, this is Aaron Carlyle. I would like to speak to your grandfather.”

“Mr. Carlyle, it is good to hear your voice. Please hold.”

“Aaron! You have heard of the trouble?” Min’s words jumped out of the phone.

“Yes, I heard. Please tell Tuloc to call Lieutenant Sizemore immediately if not sooner.”

“What does he need with Tuloc?”

“Tuloc left the scene of a crime. They think he is buried under the debris of the building.”

“How do you know he’s not?” Min countered.

“If you are trying to hide him, tell Soo Kim not to answer the phone.”

“I will tell her. Meanwhile, what are we going to do about this?” Min asked.

“We have about forty-eight hours to put this to bed. After that both Troy and Pam will be able to contact that pain in the ass colonel.”

“Holding his son hostage should ensure his cooperation, don’t you think?”

“If he’s behind this, the threat hasn’t done it so far. We’ve got to deal with Canon and Paul Kiesler before we find out whose side he’s on.”

“Aaron, I get the impression that you harbor a good feeling for this person.”

“It’s funny, but I can’t help but like him, although I have a hard time agreeing with what he does for a living,” Aaron replied.

“I would not be so fast to judge what he does. The government gets involved in many strange enterprises. Without people like him . . .” Min’s voice trailed off.

“Min, have Tuloc call Cassius. He can’t leave friends hanging like this.”

"Aaron, I have a rule that I will not allow to be broken. In times of danger, my family is to return here immediately. Until such time as Cassius is part of my family, even his friendship must be put at risk for the greater good."

"Old friend, this is not a conversation to be held over the phone, but you realize what you are saying is that in a time of danger, I have to watch my own back."

"Aaron, you are family!"

"And my family extends to . . .?" Aaron let the words hang in the air.

"You are right. This is not a conversation to be held on the phone."

Chapter 63

"Are you awake?" Karen touched Aaron's shoulder.

"Almost. What time is it?"

"Ten after five."

"In the morning?"

"Yes, in the morning. I'm going out for a run. Are you up to it?"

"Sure. Can you give me an hour?"

Laughing, she replied, "You have ten minutes. I'll be downstairs."

"What time did you tell everyone to be here?" Canon looked at his watch as he asked Paul Kiesler the question.

"Five thirty. They still have fifteen minutes."

"For the money we're paying, you'd think they'd come a little early."

A van pulled into Sunrise Gym's parking lot. Six men wearing golf shirts and sneakers got out and walked to the front door. Canon opened the door and looked each man up and down as they entered. "There's coffee and donuts inside the office."

The men looked at each other before one of them asked, "When do we get paid?"

"As soon as we're done," Canon answered with annoyance in his voice.

"How about half now?" the same man asked.

"What's your name?" Canon roared.

"Who wants to know?" the man replied.

Canon pulled a pistol out of his pocket. "Smith and Wesson want to know."

The man smiled. "Okay. As soon as the job is finished."

"That's better." Canon wanted the last word. What he didn't notice was two of the men nodding at each other. Because he now had a total of fourteen men, he was starting to feel good about what was going on. *Once I get even with that chink, Min, I'll take care of Carlyle. And then this smart ass,* he thought.

"Grandfather, it is six o'clock." Sookie had turned on the light in Min's bedroom and stood by the bed with a cup of steaming hot tea. "Be careful so this does not burn your lip," she whispered as she laid it on the nightstand.

"Is Tuloc awake?" Min asked before his feet reached the floor.

"He is feeding baby Aaron, and awaiting your arrival to join you for breakfast."

"Tell him I will be there in ten minutes, and you can start breakfast now."

Soo Kim smiled. He knew that she hadn't made breakfast for them in over six months, but the old way of the daughter making the food was a hard thing for him to give up. Returning to the kitchen, she stopped to watch Tuloc try and put food in the baby's mouth. "I'll get the paper," she said, turning towards the front door.

"They live halfway down this block. Pull the Lincoln past the house with the brick steps and cut off their escaping that way." Paul was giving instructions from a white non-descript van parked behind a gray Chevrolet. "This car in front of me has two men drinking coffee. They're probably waiting for a third to go to work. When you guys get out of your car, we'll tell them to move on."

"Paul! Paul, can you hear me?"

"I can hear you, what do you want?"

"There's two guys in the blue Ford on the corner."

Paul turned and looked behind him. "What are they doing?"

"I think they're sleeping," came the reply.

"Don't wake them, but keep your eye on them. We don't need the police getting here before we're finished."

"Paul, this is Dennis. There's a lady coming out of Min's door. She's headed toward the paper."

"Let's go. With the door open, this will be easier than I thought." Paul gave the go ahead to his men.

"It's ten after six," Karen said as they sprinted into her driveway. "Pick up the paper."

Aaron bent over and took a deep breath. "It's old news. Why don't you just watch television."

"You can watch the television, I love to read what happened yesterday and get some idea of what's expected today."

"Why couldn't I get the paper?" Sookie asked as she carried little Aaron out of the kitchen.

"Get upstairs, and stay away from the windows," Tuloc answered with urgency in his tone.

"Mai Ling! Get upstairs with your sister and the other women. If anyone you do not know comes up the stairs, shoot them!" Min yelled as he looked out the window.

Mai Ling bristled at the thought of being relegated to watching the women rather than taking part in the battle, but knew better than to argue with her grandfather.

"Sorry to get you out of bed so early Lieutenant, but I think it's a good idea for you and I to talk to Min and Tuloc before things get worse than they are.

Cassius turned up the volume on the car radio. "Excuse me for a second, Captain. I want to get the scores of last night's games."

Captain Barry Sands shook his head. "All you young guys think about is sports." Looking at his watch, he continued, "You think they'll be up by six thirty?"

"I think they'll be waiting for us. When I called last night, Mai Ling told me we'd have breakfast with them if we got there by six thirty."

"We're going to be ten minutes early." Barry yawned as he pushed his hat over his eyes.

"We will have to hold them back for three or four minutes!" Min yelled over the noise of people moving around him and shots emanating from the street. "We've only got six men in the street, but the call has gone out for help."

"Shit!" Canon yelled. "Those guys in the cars are lookouts."

Paul emptied the clip of his automatic rifle into one of the cars occupied by two of the lookouts. "They won't bother us. Take care of those other two cars."

Two of his men had reached the front door. One of them was shot and fell across the threshold of the door, jamming it open. The other one stood with his back against the wall waiting instructions.

"Jesus Christ! What the hell is going on?" Barry yelled as Cassius skidded and turned the car sideways, blocking the street.

"It's Canon's men! They're attacking Min's home." Both men jumped out of the car pulling their weapons and opening fire.

"Follow me!" Paul screamed as he ran up the stairs. The man beside him fell from bullets that were now coming from the house. Pushing open the door and rolling on the ground as he entered Paul realized there was no one in that part of the house. He motioned for two of the five men that entered, with him to go upstairs. The others he waved to both sides. His mouth opened to shout a warning to the men climbing the stairs, but he was too late. A beautiful woman with jet-black hair appeared out of nowhere and fired three times. She was gone before the two men hit the floor, one of them lying where he dropped, and the other doing slow motion somersaults as he came to rest almost at the bottom.

"Let's get the hell out of here. This isn't going as planned," Canon said to the three men standing near him.

"What about the guys still in the building?"

"The hell with them. Get in the car before I leave you guys here."

The three men looked at each other. One of them, who had worked for Canon for the last two years, ran to the driver's side of the car. As he opened the door, he was hit twice—once in the leg and once in the side. Canon threw him aside and jumped into the car. The other two followed suit, one in the front the other in the back.

"The boss is leaving!" One of the men inside of the building shouted to Kiesler.

"That chicken hearted son of . . . let's get out. Head towards the van and stay low."

Kiesler waited until the three other men were underway before he moved out the door. With everyone's attention focused in their direction, he felt he had a chance of slipping away unnoticed. He had gone about twenty yards when he heard someone shout.

"This is the police! Stay where you are! Put down your weapon and raise your hands above your head."

Kiesler stopped and looked from side to side. He recognized both of the men standing behind a dark blue Ford. They were the police. The shooting almost stopped behind him, and he realized he only had one chance.

"I surrender!" he yelled back, holding his hands at his sides.

Cassius shouted, "Drop the weapon."

Barry yelled, "Cassius stay down!"

Kiesler fired twice, hitting Cassius before Barry was able to put four bullets into what was later described as Kiesler's shirt pocket.

The silence was eerie. The shooting had stopped and aside from the three or four men that were still moving, but lying on the ground, everyone had disappeared.

Barry bent over Cassius. "How bad is it?" he asked.

"Don't know." Cassius whispered.

"Stay still, help will be here soon." He could hear the police cars, and he hoped an ambulance.

Tuloc gazed out one of the windows while he spoke to the other people in the room. "The shooting has stopped. Our men that were able have left the area. It looks like Captain Sands has killed Paul Kiesler after he shot Lieutenant Sizemore."

"Cassius has been shot?" Mai ling cried out. She ran to the window and looked down the street. "He's hurt! I have to go to him," she said, turning toward the door.

"Mai Ling!" Min yelled. "Stay where you are. Do not go outside. We will let you know when it's safe. You know the rules."

She stood still. Turning, she looked at Soo Kim and then at Min. "The hell with your rules, Grandfather."

Chapter 64

"We want our money now!" said one of the men from the back seat.

"Will you take a check?" Canon sneered

"No, but I'll take it in blood."

Canon turned and found a pistol pointed at his nose.

"Are you crazy? Shoot me and you get nothing. I don't carry that kind of cash on me." The words spilled quickly out of his mouth.

"You owe us twenty thousand each. When did you plan on paying?"

"As soon as we get to my office. The money is there, but I got a better deal."

"Which is?"

"I'll give you twenty-five each plus another ten up front for another job."

The two men in the back glanced at each other and nodded.

"And how much on completion of this new job?"

"This is Karen."

"Karen, this is Barry. Do you know where Aaron is?"

"Right now, he's in the shower." She paused. "Is something wrong?"

"Maybe. Can you please get him?"

Aaron stood in the bedroom with a towel around his waist and the remote control in his hand as Karen entered.

"Finish the paper?" He asked.

"No, not yet. Barry's on the phone and he sounds ominous."

"Barry always sounds ominous." He reached for the phone as the television blared, "At least ten dead and another ten hurt." Watching the live picture, Aaron recognized Min's front steps.

"Barry! I just saw the start of the news. How bad is it?"

"Three of Min's men, eight of Canon's men including Kiesler are dead. Min has one man on the way to the hospital, Canon has four, and I have one."

"Who's yours?"

"Lieutenant Cassius Sizemore."

"What the hell was he doing there at six thirty in the morning?

"We were both here. We had a scheduled meeting with Min over breakfast, and this erupted two minutes before we pulled up. You better get over here. And bring Karen," he added. "I'll need some people to keep things calm. This isn't my jurisdiction; I just happened to be here and got involved. I think they're going to find my bullets in at least Kiesler, and maybe two or three others. I needed this aggravation like I need another piece of banana cream pie."

Aaron could picture him with his eyes never leaving anything unnoticed and an outward calm that was not what was going on inside.

"How is Cassius?"

"I don't know. Mai Ling went to the hospital in the ambulance with him, which I understand has caused a furor inside."

"What is Min saying?" Aaron was reaching for his shoes as he spoke.

"Absolutely nothing. That's another reason I need you here."

"I'm out of here in ten minutes. I'll probably need three hours at this time of the morning."

"See you then," Barry said as he looked at his Los Angeles counterpart trying to put everything together at the crime scene.

Karen came in fully dressed with an overnight bag that she was throwing clothes and makeup into. "I'll be ready in less than five minutes. I probably have enough clothes at your place—this is just in case."

"How'd you know?" Aaron asked.

"Between the television and listening to your half of the conversation, I figured we'd be leaving."

"Barry wants us to come to Min's. He figures he'll be there for at least three hours."

"It'll take us that long to get there, even with the way you drive."

"I've tried to call Pam and Troy and tell them what's happening, but they're not answering their phones," Aaron said as he started down the stairs.

"Young love is great," Karen responded as she followed him down.

"Old love isn't bad either," he replied.

When they reached the bottom of the stairs, there was a knock on the front door.

"Aaron?" Karen questioned quietly.

Aaron stopped and took a pistol out of his pocket.

"Who's there?' he asked.

"Mr. Carlyle, it's Troy and Pam."

"Don't forget me, Sergeant Hubbard."

Aaron opened the door and found himself staring straight at Colonel Ewing.

"I forgot to say I was here also." The colonel had a big smile on his face.

"To what do I owe this honor?" Aaron asked.

"I just wanted to meet Ms. Williams, renew old acquaintances, and repay the favor."

"What favor?" Aaron asked.

"Taking care of Troy."

"And you are going to repay it how?" Aaron smiled, but his eyes had turned cold.

"I have a helicopter standing by at Palomar. I thought you might be needing a quick ride to L.A."

"Your information is pretty good. Is the copter big enough to hold all of us?"

"Yes and yes. My information is good, again, and it will hold all of us."

There were two vans parked in front. Strikingly good-looking women drove each of the vehicles. Aaron was reminded of Pam's former job—women that drove for the banquet circuit.

"Why don't you get in the first one with me?" the colonel asked Aaron. "There are some things I think we should discuss before we arrive at your friend's home."

Turning to Sergeant Hubbard, Aaron said, "Sergeant! I'm entrusting you with my fiancée's well being."

The statement caught everyone off guard.

"What about me? Don't you trust me?" Troy demanded.

"I have found when it comes to blood, it's thicker than water."

"You have my word that nothing will happen to Ms. Williams," Troy stammered.

The colonel smiled. "You're very good, Aaron." Looking at Troy, he continued, "Of course Ms. Williams will be well taken care of."

"That's not what I asked the Sergeant to do." Aaron had stopped halfway down the driveway.

Karen, watching the verbal fencing, walked over next to Pam and put down her bag.

"Exciting, isn't it?" Karen asked without turning her head.

I'm not quite sure what's going on, but I don't think I'm going to like the ending," Pam replied.

Karen watched as the two women drivers get out of their vans and started to walk toward Aaron.

"It's time to choose whose side you're on," she again spoke to Pam without moving her head.

Anyone looking at Pam would swear that her features became hard. She stepped in front of Karen and put her hand inside of her jacket. She glanced at Troy who nodded his head as their eyes locked.

The smile left the colonel's face. He was an old hand at sizing up situations and he didn't like what he saw. Both Troy and Pam looked like they were aligning themselves with Carlyle.

"Hold on everyone!" he bellowed. "Let's not go crazy with the words we use. You have my word that Ms. Williams has nothing to worry about. I must speak to Aaron privately and this just looked like the best way."

"I'm glad that's settled," Aaron said to everyone. "Troy, I apologize. I am putting Karen's well being under your control. See you at the airport." Nodding at Karen, he entered the first van.

Chapter 65

"Now that we're all settled in, what did you want to talk to me about?" Aaron glanced out the back window, assuring himself that the car Karen was in was following right behind them.

"January, can you please raise the glass divider?" Waiting for it to fully close, the colonel started again, "This chapter is coming to a close. You're a bright man. By this time, you must have almost figured out the entire scenario. I just want to make sure when it's finally finished, I don't have an existing problem out here in California."

"Meaning what?" Aaron looked straight into his eyes.

"Do you remember the first time we met?" the colonel asked, averting his eyes.

"Singapore was the only time we met. I saw you at LAX three years ago, the day Karen and I went to Hawaii, but we didn't speak."

"I thought you had seen me, but I was never sure. But you're right. It was Singapore. I had it in my power back then to put you and your friends away in an Army jail for god knows how long. Ten, maybe twenty years. After the first ten, it wouldn't have mattered."

"Why didn't you?"

"You were the kind of people I fought wars for. You served your country with distinction. You were a modern day Don Quixote. You saw injustice and were prepared to do battle. You didn't care how big the opponent was if your cause was right. I liked that and decided to let you go. I wanted you to build a better life for both you and your lady fair. From time to time, I had to lend you a helping hand . . ."

"Bullshit! I never got any help from you. Whatever we accomplished, we did on our own. Scott, Tom, myself, and . . ." almost choking on her name, he finished, ". . . Marcia."

"Don't be naïve. This is America, not the Emerald City. You don't go off to see the wizard without some kind of help. Remember your first contract? The one that got the whole thing started. Do you think people just walk into a military sub-contractor and pick up million dollar contracts?"

"We worked our asses off to get that job," Aaron said, raising his voice.

"Calm down. We're just reminiscing." The colonel looked out the side window. "I know you worked hard, but companies that do work for the government are always trying to help out friends in high places. Do you remember when you went public? The stock came out at two dollars higher than you thought it would."

"The issue was oversold. People thought it was going to be a hot stock."

"I know that, but did you ever ask who purchased an extra fifty thousand shares the day Besafe came out? No of course not. It was a hot stock."

"I hope you made money on your investment," Aaron spat.

"That's one of the things I wanted to talk about. My function in life is to bring money into the government that can be used for other things."

"What other things?" Aaron asked.

"Buying of information that might save us American lives in some godforsaken jungle or desert."

When Aaron didn't reply, the colonel continued, "Congress doesn't like to know when we do some of these things and they watch the money they give us pretty closely. When I bring in an extra five hundred million or so, we know how to use it. The people I have to use are sometimes real low lives and I have to keep them on a short leash. Instructions have been given to every operation in California not to get involved with you or your friend Min."

"How come you included Min?" Aaron interrupted.

For the first time since they entered the car the colonel looked flustered. "I knew that if they got involved with Min, he would go to you for help." The colonel tapped the window between the front and rear of the car.

"How much further?" he asked as the glass came down.

"About ten minutes," January replied.

Aaron felt he was stalling, trying to get back on track. The question about Min unnerved him.

"Where was I?" The colonel mused. "Oh yes, the low lifes. What I would like to do is hire your firm to take care of the security of about sixteen to eighteen companies throughout California. It would require you opening in the Bay area and in San Diego, but you have over the years built an organization that has the talent to handle it."

"And what do you get out of this?"

"Number one, your company's stock will rise and my organization will make money, and number two . . ." he hesitated and Aaron felt this was the reason for the whole meeting. ". . . I want Troy to be part of your company." The words came out quickly as if they were asking rather than telling.

"You know I will have to discuss this with my friends."

"I knew you would."

"Just between us, why?" Aaron asked the question as a friend.

"Just between us, I came very close to becoming the white line on the asphalt highway system this week. I'm slowing down and being moved up to a desk job. It might become very hard to protect Troy in the future. With you he'll become part of a family. That's something I've never been able to give him."

"What about his mother?"

"She died about the same time your wife Marcia did, which brings up another question. Where the hell is Kebra Metcalf?"

"Kebra?"

"I've lost track off her and none of my sources have been able to locate her. This is personal, not business related."

Aaron smiled. "I think we can do business."

The limo pulled into the parking lot of Palomar Airport, followed by the one that had Karen, Troy, and Pam.

Chapter 66

"I've got millions tied up in this project. That Vietnamese guy whose house we were at is only part of the problem. There's another guy, Aaron Carlyle. He runs Besafe Security. He's a bigger part of the problem. If I can get him, that chink will cave."

The two men looked at Canon. "The Vietnamese guy was a handful. If this Carlyle is a bigger problem than him, it's going to cost."

"Did either of you guys ever see the movie *Shane*?"

"You mean where the dumb cowboy does all the work and doesn't get the girl?"

Canon looked at the two men and shook his head. "There's no honor any more," he muttered.

"What's that mean?" one of the men questioned.

"It means I give you your money for the job we just completed plus another ten up front for the new one."

"Who's the new one?"

"A kid and his girl. My contact told me to take care of him and he's still alive. I think because we messed that up, my contact hasn't called."

"This is certainly noisy," Karen yelled over the sound of the helicopter.

"And a little bumpy," Pam yelled back as it lifted off of the pad and headed towards the water.

"If you look down, you'll see the Marines training on the beach at Pendleton." The colonel didn't yell but his voice carried throughout the cabin.

Pam's fingernails were pressing into Troy's leg, but he was so nervous he didn't even feel them. "How long will this take?" he asked.

The sergeant shrugged and looked at January who was filing her nails as if she didn't have a care in the world. She looked up at him and said, "About an hour and five minutes."

"Captain, we just got a request for permission to land an Army helicopter in the middle of the street."

"From whom?"

"From someone who says they're friends of Captain Sands."

"When do they want to land?

"In about twenty minutes."

"Does this thing have a phone?" Aaron asked the colonel.

"It's up front with the pilot."

Aaron stood and after a few seconds, was able to walk to the cabin door.

"They got live television on that place we were at." One of the men said to Canon.

"Turn up the sound, let's see if we can learn something."

"Tom. Get Scott and find a place we can meet where we won't be disturbed later tonight. Bring any records on who our stockholders are and a list of all the customers we have under contract. Can't talk now, but if you keep your eyes on the television, you'll know when the meeting is. I'll call back later."

"Barry talk to me. What friend do you know who would want to land a helicopter in the parking lot?"

"Russ, you don't want to know. I'm in the middle of a break-in and murder investigation and all of a sudden I'm getting phone calls from some bird colonel in Washington. It's your investigation, but if it was me, I'd let him land."

Russ August had been a captain for more than six years and this was without a doubt the strangest thing he had ever been involved in.

"Barry, I've got almost a dozen dead, another six on the way to the hospital, including a police lieutenant. The shooters, whoever they were, are no where to be found, the people in the house are refusing to talk, and now we think a bird colonel's on his way here by helicopter. And all you can tell me is let him land? Can you at least tell me if this has anything to do with the shootout yesterday at this guy Min's warehouse?"

"Probably. It probably has to do with the shooting in my little piece of this planet also."

"Captain, they're less than fifteen minutes out. What should I do?" one of the policemen asked.

"Clear the street. Get the television cameras as far back as you can, and make sure our men are out of the way just in case there's not enough room."

"This is Judith Stample at the scene of this morning's apparent gang war shootout. Those words are mine, folks. The L.A.P.D. is refusing to use those words at this time, but we have learned that yesterday's shooting in Carson was at a warehouse occupied by the same men. We have also just been told that we must back away from the street because there is a helicopter preparing to land. The police are giving out no information in regard to who is in it or why it is landing here. Stay tuned for further . . . hold on folks. I have just been advised that we will stay live to bring you the news as it happens."

"A helicopter? What are they doing, bringing in the Army to help?"

Canon sat back with his feet on the desk. *This idiot,* he thought. *These must be the real players.*

"I won't be getting out. I'll call you later today to set up a time and place for us to meet." Looking out the window, the colonel continued, "Be careful. Canon is still out there and he is dangerous."

The door opened and Aaron exited without saying a thing to the colonel. He turned and held out his hand for Karen, who was followed by Troy and then Pam. Troy looked back at the open door and spoke to someone before the engine started again and the door closed.

"Ladies and gentlemen, you have just seen four people get off of the helicopter. Two men and two women, whose names we don't yet, but we will pass them on as soon as we identify them. They are now walking over to the police captain from Ventura County. They are obviously friends of some kind. The captain has shaken hands with the older of the two men and given a hug to one of the women."

"There are the two sons of a bitches we have to get. Canon's finger was pointing at the screen as his feet hit the floor. "The younger one first and the older one next, or if we can, both at the same time."

"Are they cops?"

"No. One's an executive from a security firm and the other's some snot nosed kid trying to learn the business."

"Aaron, let me introduce you to a friend of mine from the L.A.P.D., Captain Russ August."

Aaron shook the captain's hand. "Glad to make your acquaintance. Wish it could have been under other conditions." Turning to Barry, Aaron asked, "How is Cassius?"

"Haven't heard yet." Looking at the departing helicopter, he continued, "You certainly got here in a hurry. I assume it was the colonel."

Aaron turned to look at the helicopter as it disappeared from view. "Yeah, it was him. For some reason, he didn't want to get off. He's going to contact me later for another meeting."

"Anything I should know about?" Barry asked.

"If there is, don't worry. I'll let you know."

"I hate to break up this meeting you two are having, but I have a situation here that has to be resolved," Captain August interrupted.

"I'll go and talk to Min," Aaron replied. He took Karen by the arm and led her toward Min's house, followed by Troy and Pam.

"Hold it!" Captain August yelled. "No one is going anywhere until I get some answers."

"Captain, you can ask a thousand questions and we won't know the answers. Give us a half hour with Min and maybe we'll be able to help you."

The captain stared at Aaron. "At least tell me where you guys get the juice to commandeer an Army helicopter."

Aaron smiled. "It's my young friend here. His father's a bird colonel and happened to be in San Diego playing golf. It was no big deal."

"What's your father's name?" The captain asked Troy.

"I'm not allowed to tell. He could get in trouble," Troy replied.

"What's your name?"

"Troy Ewing. My friend's name is Pam Haviland."

"And that colonel is your dad and his name is . . . ?"

"I'm sorry, Sir. National security forbids my saying his name. By the way, Ewing is my mother's last name."

Aaron turned back to Troy. "Is that the truth?"

"Yes, sir. He's used that name as long as I can remember."

Aaron looked at Barry and shrugged. "Let's go see Min."

Chapter 67

Two policemen stood at the foot of the stairs leading to Min's front door. Barry flashed his badge and the five entered without so much as a sideward glance.

"Strange," Aaron said aloud. "Min would never allow anyone to enter this easily."

"Min is not here!" Tuloc responded loudly from the kitchen.

"Is he okay?" Karen asked, looking around.

Tuloc motioned for us to follow him out the back door into the garden. "There was a problem with Mai Ling. When Cassius was hurt, she disobeyed Min and left the house to go with the ambulance. Min became aggravated beyond belief."

"She's disregarded his wishes in the past. What made this such a big deal?" Aaron was reminded of the time she decided to move away from the family and live in San Francisco. "He knows she'll be back."

"I think it was the way it happened. He gave an order and she stood up and told him in front of everyone, 'The hell with your rule, Grandfather.' Then she left."

"Where is he?" Barry asked.

"He left through a private entrance at the end of the fence." Tuloc motioned toward the corner of the back yard. "He's got three men with him, and if I had to guess, I'd think he'd be somewhere near the hospital."

"Do the police know he's gone?" Karen asked and then

answered herself, "Of course they don't know. If they did, they would've told us outside."

Barry asked, "Tuloc, maybe you can fill us in on what happened?"

"We were having breakfast and awaiting your arrival when Soo Kim started outside to get the paper. The red light went on and . . ."

"What red light?" Barry interrupted.

"Oh!" Tuloc closed his eyes before continuing. "We have a signal when someone shows up at the front door unannounced, and we call it a red light."

"Who gives the signal?" Barry persisted with his questions.

"One of Min's relatives outside pushes a button. It is like a garage door opener. Anyway, the light went on and we could see men in the street with guns. Soo Kim was ordered back in the house and the next thing we knew, shots were being fired from everywhere. Mai Ling was stationed at the top of the stairs and she shot a few of them as they tried to go up."

"Was anyone inside the house hurt?" Karen asked.

"None of the immediate family. It looks like some of our cousins were not so lucky. The only thing that made Min more upset than Mai Ling leaving was Captain Barry shooting their leader."

"Do you think Kiesler was their leader?" Barry asked incredulously.

Tuloc looked the other way as he answered, "Who else could it have been?"

Barry looked at Aaron and then at Tuloc. "You're kidding, of course?"

Tuloc shook his head before he headed back into the house.

Barry turned to Aaron. "Something's wrong, Min has got to know that Canon is in charge. What's this bullshit about Kiesler all of a sudden?"

"Barry, come on over to my place. Tom and Scott are meeting me there. I think we have some things to discuss."

"What time?"

"Two hours from now. That'll give everyone a chance to do some thinking."

"Thinking about what?"

Aaron took Barry by the arm and walked him out the front door. Standing in the street with no one around, he started whispering, "Has it ever seemed strange to you that the colonel was always one step ahead of us? We know it couldn't have been Troy; he wasn't in on all of our conversations. It wasn't me, it wasn't Karen, it wasn't Scott or Tom. Was it you?"

"Are you crazy?"

"I didn't think it was, but that leaves only one other person."

"Min?" Barry answered.

"Think about it. I'll see you in two hours."

Chapter 68

"An attack on my family at home is inexcusable!" Min shouted to a man looking out a second story window. "In all of the years we have worked together, I was willing to take chances with my life, but not with the lives of my family. Someone is going to pay with their life for this insult."

Min stood there. The man looking out the window turned. "The problem was back in Washington, and I have taken care of it. We have shut down this operation and are in the process of cleaning up some loose ends."

"These are not loose ends!" Min continued shouting.

"Trust me, they are. That idiot is on the run. Most of his men are either dead or in the hospital. My people will have him found by tonight or tomorrow at the latest."

"And what will they do?" Min asked.

"Let me worry about what they will do."

The phone in Min's pocket started ringing. "I hate these things." Min punched at the buttons angrily. "This is Min!" After listening, he replied, "Tell our men to keep watching her, and I will be home in less than an hour."

"I must go. There is much to be done. Let me know when this little problem is cleaned up." He left without saying another word.

"Are you related to the lieutenant?" the nurse asked Mai Ling.

"We are planning our wedding," she replied as she looked over the nurse's shoulder at the closed door.

"I'm sorry. Only blood relatives and wives are allowed back here."

"Except when accompanied by someone from the police department." Both women turned at the sound of the voice.

"Captain Sands. Thank you for coming, they won't give me any information," Mai Ling spoke quickly.

"The nurse is only doing her job," Captain Sands replied assuringly. "How is my lieutenant, Nurse Pippin?" he asked, squinting as he looked at her nametag.

"The doctor has him listed as serious, but I've seen a lot worse pull through. If you want, you can go in and talk to him. He's awake."

"I'll stop in to say hello, then I have to leave. Mai Ling, why don't you stay with Cassius and let me know later how he's doing? My friend Captain August is leaving two men on duty. Tell them if you need anything. They're very interested in talking to your grandfather. He seems to have disappeared."

Mai Ling stared at the captain. "I have no idea where he is, and if I did . . ." She left the rest of the sentence unsaid.

Barry looked at Mai Ling. "I think I understand, but you know he can't hide from us forever."

"I do not believe my grandfather is hiding. He more than likely had something that needed doing."

"I believe that. Let's go say hello to Cassius."

As they entered the door to the emergency room, one of the orderlies put his broom against the wall and walked to the public phone at the end of the corridor.

"She is with the police captain called Sands. He has told her that they are looking for you and she has denied any knowledge of your whereabouts. Her exact comment was, 'That you more than likely had something that needed doing.'"

Min smiled. "I will arrive in less than ten minutes. If the captain starts to leave, ask him to wait for me." Breaking the connection, Min told the driver of the car, "Use the service entrance."

Chapter 69

"Captain!"

Barry turned to the sound of the voice. "Yes," he replied.

"I think you will find taking the service elevator to the basement a better choice at this time of day."

Barry stared at the Asian orderly. His shoes were shined and his hand that wrapped around the broom handle hadn't seen too many days of manual labor.

"Where's your hospital badge?" Barry asked.

"I left it home this morning," the orderly answered as he placed the broom against the wall.

"Where is the service elevator?"

"It is down the hall," the man replied. In the split second that it took him to motion in the direction of the service elevator, he came face to face with Barry's service revolver.

"Now tell me why you are being so nice to me, and why you addressed me as captain?"

The man's tongue ran across his lips. "I was told to ask you to meet my uncle downstairs."

"And your uncle is?"

The orderly became nervous. "If I told you my cousin was Tuloc, would that be enough?"

"Start walking toward the emergency room. Now!"

"All I am doing is delivering a message!" His voice rose to a higher pitch.

"And all I'm going to do is put a bullet into your kneecap if you don't start moving."

The two officers in front of the emergency door, noticing the confrontation, started walking toward the captain and the orderly.

"Stay where you are!" Barry shouted. "One of you go in and get Mai Ling out here."

A few seconds later, Mai Ling exited the room and walked cautiously toward the man who was now laying spread-eagled on the floor with Barry standing above him.

"Do you know this guy?" Barry asked as she got closer.

"What has he done?"

"A simple yes or no is all I want."

"Yes."

"Is he one of the men who works for your grandfather?"

"Why don't you ask me?" Min roared from behind.

Barry didn't even turn at the sound of Min's voice. "We've been looking for you."

"I am here. What is it you want?"

"First, is this man delivering a message for you?"

"What did he say?"

"He said . . . just answer my question. Is he with you?"

"Yes he is. You can let him off of the floor, please."

Barry nudged the man on the floor with his foot. "You can get up now." Motioning to Min he continued, "Follow me. We can talk inside."

Min followed Barry, passing Mai Ling like she was a piece of furniture.

"Grandfather! In case you're interested, Cassius will live."

Min stopped, but didn't turn around. When he spoke, it wasn't to Mai Ling. "Captain, I am extremely happy that you did not lose a brave officer." He then followed Barry into one of the rooms.

"I think our best course of action is to lay our hands on the kid and make that Carlyle guy come to us."

Shaking his head, Canon replied, "We'll do it my way. Kill the kid or Carlyle, whoever we find first, and then go get the other one. Maybe we'll get lucky and they'll be together."

"When do we get our money?"

"I'll give you half of it now and the balance when it's done."

"I don't want to tell you how to treat your family, but you could lighten up on your granddaughter." Barry stared at Min, waiting for some type of reply.

"My family business is not why I asked to meet with you."

"That's another thing. I don't like your invitations. You want to talk to me, call me. Don't send some goon with instructions. Next time I might not be so nice."

Min's lips tightened as Barry smiled. "The shooting at my house must be avenged."

"If you would have stayed home and talked to the police, they could have been halfway there already."

"I said avenged, not arrested and put in jail."

"You and I have had these type of conversations before. You know my feelings about your type of justice. Why don't you let the police handle it one time?"

With a contemptuous look on his face, Min replied, "I want to know where the colonel's son is. If I can find him, I can make this colonel do as I wish."

"You're sure the colonel is behind this craziness?"

"I am sure that if I had his son, he could stop it."

"Then you're smarter than I am. I go by the law, and as far as I can see, he may be a lot of things, but I don't see him behind this. Which brings up something else. Tuloc is spouting off that Kiesler was the boss. We all know it's higher than him—probably Canon. Why's he putting out incorrect information?"

"We believe there is a leak inside of Besafe. We don't know who it is yet, but we have a saying, better safe than sorry."

Barry stood there contemplating his next move when his phone went off. "Captain Sands!" After listening for a minute he replied, "It's funny you should ask. He's standing right here. I'll have him wait with your two men and you can ask him yourself."

"Who was that?" Min asked.

"That was my friend Captain August of the L.A.P.D. He will be here within ten minutes and he'd like you to wait for him."

"I have things to do. I cannot wait."

"I thought you might say that." Barry leaned into the hallway and motioned for the two police officers on duty in front of the room Cassius was in. "Please keep Mr. Min company until Captain August arrives. I would suggest that you also get his granddaughter to wait with him. She may have information that Captain August needs."

With a big grin on his face, Barry nodded and left the room.

Chapter 70

"I don't believe it!" Scott had just finished listening to Aaron's thoughts about Min working for, or with, the C.I.A.

"Think it through. I told you what he said to me." Aaron was pacing the room. "He could have had us put in jail when we screwed up the drug operation." He held up a second finger. "He agreed to let us keep the money, and according to him, our major contracts when we first got started were due to his leaning on our customers."

"I checked our stockholder list," interrupted Tom. "I can't find anything unusual in our stockholders except for that hundred thousand shares that shows up every year from overseas. We always thought it was Min."

"Aaron, you said that you think the colonel slipped when he told you about his operations. They were supposed to stay away from Besafe, you, and Min?"

"Actually, it was me and Min, but you're close enough. When I asked him why Min, he became flustered and said Min would go to us for help."

"You know it could answer a lot of questions," Scott re-entered the conversation. "The splitting of the two families, Min and Giac, the going into the building maintenance business and making sure our buildings weren't ripped off."

"Which is why Min was so upset about the break-in. His getting involved with Lan came after," Barry said.

"Min's people would have knowledge about what was happening at the plants they serviced and they could just pass it on, which brings up the big question, and why I've asked you all here."

Everyone stared at Aaron.

"Do we open two new offices, take on ten or fifteen new clients, and add Troy to our staff?

No one said a word.

Finally, Barry spoke up, "You don't need me to make those decisions. You three have to decide if it's worth the price. In fact, I don't know why you asked me here."

"Barry," Tom began, "as vice president of finance, I guess it's up to me to explain. You know we've offered Michael the job of heading up our new detective agency. We need someone we can trust to head up the security end. The three of us think you're the guy. The job pays double what you're making now, and if we decide to open up the two new places, you'll probably be vastly underpaid."

Barry, who had been standing against the wall, looked around and almost stumbled as he looked for somewhere to sit.

"You guys must be shitting me." He stared off into space, clearly nonplussed.

"You are treating me like one of those men who started the shooting. I am a private citizen who pays taxes and owns businesses. Why don't you find them and leave me alone."

Captain Russ August sat listening to Min rant with a bored expression on his face. When it became obvious that Min was finished, he continued, "Mr. Min, you left the scene of a crime. Your granddaughter shot at least three of the intruders, and five of your relatives were killed. The intruders left seven dead men behind, and I intend to find out who their leader was."

"My granddaughter is a licensed professional working for Besafe. The other people that were killed were neighbors, not relatives."

Before the captain could reply, one of the uniformed policemen entered the room. "Captain, the governor is on the phone, and I just got a call from headquarters. The mayor is on his way over."

"Tell the governor I'm busy and . . ."

"I don't think so, Sir. The commissioner's office called and told us you would take this call."

"Who from the commissioner's office?"

"The commissioner himself, Sir."

Shaking his head, he left the room. As the door closed, Mai Ling said, "Grandfather, I will accept your apology here and now."

"Pam, I don't have to apologize for my father. He's given his life for his country. I may not agree with all the things he has done, but he's done them believing they were the right thing to do."

"Troy, I don't want you to apologize for him. I just want to make sure you understand that if we get married, I expect you to give up working for the government. You don't need him to be successful. You have a job with Besafe. These are good people to be associated with." She stopped and looked at him. Leaning over, she kissed him on his chin whispering, "At least think it over. Don't turn it down without considering it, for me, please."

Chapter 71

"What did Barry say when you offered him the job?" Karen called from the kitchen where she was filling the dishwasher.

"He looked pleased, but said he would have to think it over," replied Aaron from the den, stretched out on the eight-foot-long sofa.

"How long did you give him?" Karen entered the room, drying her hands on a dishtowel.

"We told him we didn't need an answer today, but we did need his input. Why all the questions?" Aaron asked.

"This job will put him into a new tax bracket. I'll have to re-check his account."

"You're assuming he'll take the job."

"Of course he will. He likes you guys, and he's thinking of getting married," Karen replied.

"I hadn't heard that yet."

"You don't know everything," Karen said.

"How about us?"

"I've been thinking about it."

"And?" Aaron asked.

Before Karen could answer, there was a knock on the door.

"Saved by the knock," Aaron said as he stood up and walked toward the door.

"Aaron! Be careful."

"Who's there?" Aaron asked from his side of the door.

"Mr. Carlyle? It's Troy and Pam. We're alone."

"Hold on one second!" Aaron yelled then lowered his voice as he spoke into a miniature walkie-talkie, "Are they alone?"

"Yes they are." Came the reply.

"Keep your eyes open." Aaron put down the instrument and opened the door.

"What are you kids doing up and about?" Aaron smiled as he stepped aside.

Troy nodded at Karen before he started. "I wanted to talk about my future. Pam is willing to marry me . . ."

"I didn't say that. I said if we got married," Pam jumped into the conversation.

Troy sighed and then continued. "Pam said if we got married, I would have to leave working for the government. She thinks," he looked at her and then continued, "no, we both think, that I can do well working for Besafe, and I wanted to get your opinion before we go any further."

"What about your father?" Karen asked from the other side of the room.

"My father. That's funny. I haven't heard from him since he dropped us off at Mr. Min's. He does this all the time. He goes off and forgets about me on a regular basis, but expects me to listen to him when he shows up."

Aaron looked at Karen before he started. "What exactly are you looking for?"

"I think I'm asking for a job," Troy replied.

"You know how we operate at Besafe. We have to trust each other explicitly. Do you think we could learn trust you?"

"I hope so. You have my word, and if nothing else, my father taught me that giving your word is sacred."

"There are some things I would like to know about your father's operations."

"I'm sorry, but I can't give you any privileged information that I learned while working for his organization, but I can promise you that I will make sure I use what I know to make sure they don't bother us anymore."

"Have you given any thought to the division of Besafe where you want to work?"

"No. I just thought I would work here."

Everyone turned when there was another knock on the door.

Aaron hit the send button. "Who's out there?" There was no answer from his men outside. Aaron asked again, "Can you see who's knocking on the door?"

When there was still no answer, Aaron motioned for Karen, Pam, and Troy to move away from the door.

"Who's there?" he yelled as he backed further away from the door.

"Special delivery package for Mr. Carlyle."

"Just leave it. I'm a little busy right now."

After a moment's delay, the voice came back, "I have to have a signature."

"Bring it back tomorrow." Aaron now held a pistol in his hand.

"If you'll tell me your name, I'll just sign and I can be on my way."

"My name is Bond. Jim Bond," Aaron replied, smiling.

"Isn't Mr. Carlyle there?"

"That's the problem. I'm house sitting, and have no authorization to open the door. I don't have the codes." Aaron shrugged, looking at Karen.

There was no reply from outside.

"Are you still there?" Aaron yelled again.

"Aaron," Karen whispered urgently, "Look out back."

Aaron looked out the glass door to the patio. The lights that were controlled by motion detectors had gone on. Both Troy and Pam took pistols out of their coats as Aaron went to the phone to call for help, hoping he wasn't too late.

As he dialed, he kept looking out the glass doors. No one appeared, and the lights went out.

"This is Aaron!" Aaron spoke slowly, making sure each word was understood. "I've lost contact with our men outside my house and I need backup now!"

"Hold for a second, please. I have two cars within three minutes. Do you need more than that?"

"I don't know. I also don't know if I have three minutes."

"I'll pass it on, and I'll try the regulars to see if they have someone closer."

Pam had moved to the front windows. "There's a car pulling away, but I can't tell how many people are in it."

"Stay down!" Troy warned her. "I'll go out the back door and see what's happening."

"Troy! Don't open the door!" Aaron spoke quickly, "Wait for help to arrive."

"Hello! Hello!" The walkie-talkie on the floor started squawking. "Can anyone hear me?"

Aaron picked up the instrument and replied, "This is Aaron. Who is this?"

"This is Chris. We were jumped by at least two men. Mark is still unconscious. How are you?"

"We're fine. I've called in for help which should be arriving any second. Stay put. We'll be there in a minute."

Karen started toward the door.

"Hold it!" Aaron shouted. "We're not going anywhere."

"Your man Mark is hurt. He needs help," Karen replied.

"Troy's father taught me a lesson. Everything is not always what it seems.

Chapter 72

Less than two minutes later, with sirens blowing and red and blue lights flashing, the first Besafe patrol car pulled up in front of Aaron's home. It was followed quickly by a second, and then in drill-like precision, three patrol cars from the regular police.

"See if you can find our men!" Aaron shouted. "And be careful. They may still be in the area."

Lights started going on in the other homes in the cul-de-sac.

"Start checking the other houses. Make sure the people stay inside and keep their doors locked."

"I've found our men!" someone shouted from the side of Aaron's home.

"Are they okay?" Aaron asked.

"They're unconscious, but they seem okay."

Aaron started running toward the side of the house when Karen appeared at the front door. "Is everything all right?" she asked.

Looking around, Aaron stopped. "Get back inside!" he yelled. "There are too many men out here."

Karen stepped back inside the house as a series of shots erupted.

Aaron, facing where the voice originated, sensed a tug on his side as he felt himself falling to the ground. Karen, seeing him fall, ran across the lawn throwing her body on top of him.

After the first volley of shots, the silence became almost deafening. The police had taken refuge behind their vehicles. The

Besafe men had taken cover wherever they happened to be at the first sound of trouble.

Aaron rolled out from beneath Karen. “Stay put.”

“You’re bleeding!”

“It’s only a scratch. I’ll be right back.” Aaron started crawling as the motion detector lights came back on and two more shots rang out.

“Hold your fire!” Pam’s voice filled the night air. “We’re coming out. This one’s still alive. I only wounded him. Both of our men are okay.”

Pam came out with Troy supporting one of the men right behind her. The police searchlights created eerie shadows, which got worse as the beams jumped from one place to another.

“How many were there?” the first policeman to come out from behind a tree asked.

“There were two. The other one didn’t make it.”

The officer motioned for two of the other men to grab the man being supported by Troy. “Get an ambulance here in a hurry. I’m sure the captain is going to want to talk to this guy.”

Aaron walked over to the two Besafe men as they came out from the side of the house. “What happened?” he asked.

“They didn’t get here in a car. They must have come up the hill on foot. They probably arrived right before Troy and Pam and heard our conversation. It’s the only thing that makes sense.”

“Governor! It doesn’t make any sense.”

“Captain, listen to my words. You are not to harass Mr. Min. Period.”

“Governor, we have almost a dozen people dead, one police lieutenant in the hospital, and Mr. Min is in this up to his eyeballs.”

“Captain! A very high authority has told me that this is a matter of national security. Just do as I say and don’t mess it up. I think the mayor will be there momentarily to reinforce my position.”

Before he could say another word, the governor had hung up. The captain had emptied out the lounge to take the governor’s call, but he could still feel the eyes of the people looking in through the glass windows. Hanging up the phone, he found himself trying to formulate the words he would tell his men. After a few seconds, he realized that it didn't matter what he said, everyone would know what had just happened. Walking slowly to the door he said aloud, "Fuck it, I've already got my twenty in, and I don't work for the governor."

Putting a smile on his face, he walked out and said to his men, "Read him his rights and then arrest him."

"Captain, what are you doing?"

He didn't even have to turn. He knew the mayor's voice since the mayor was a lowly councilman.

"Good afternoon, Mr. Mayor. I heard you were on your way over here."

"Didn't you talk to the governor?" the mayor asked.

"I don't work for the governor. I work for the people of Los Angeles, and what I am doing is arresting a man who is a prime witness to what appears to be a gang related multiple killing."

The mayor took him by the arm and walked him back into the waiting room. "Russ, don't be an idiot. We've known each other for a long time. These calls are coming from damn near the president of the United States. Turn him loose and let us figure it out later. It's not worth it."

"Mr. Mayor, he has to give us something. For two days, we've had people getting shot on our streets. It's got to end."

Before the mayor could answer, there was a knock on the door and Min entered.

"You gentlemen are having a problem that I think I can solve. If I told you there would be no more shootings, and in two days, I will meet with you and give you all the information you need to close this episode, would that expedite my leaving?"

"How can you guarantee no more shootings?" the mayor asked.

"You will have to take my word, which has always been good."

The mayor held out his hand. "You have a deal." Turning toward the captain, he continued, "Captain, pick the time and place for the meeting."

"You're a great politician, Mr. Mayor. How about my office, forty-eight hours from now. That's five-forty-five on Thursday."

The mayor looked at Min, who nodded his head.

Chapter 73

"Grandfather, Tuloc wishes to talk to you." Soo Kim spoke as she served Min a cup of tea.

"Why doesn't he just come in and speak?"

"He wanted you to be comfortable before he entered."

With a scowl on his face, Min yelled, "Tuloc, come here!"

Tuloc entered and stood beside of Soo Kim. "Grandfather of my wife," he began, "it is with deep regret that I must tender my resignation from your company."

"You must what?"

"I must resign. You have been like a father to me and I hold you in the deepest of respect, but over the past week, I have been forced to do things that I cannot in good conscience continue to be part of."

"Like what?"

"The leaving of my friends at the scene of a shooting."

"The family comes first. It always has and always will." Min was almost shouting.

"I understand the words, but you consider family blood, and I am not of your blood. I have responsibilities elsewhere."

"Your responsibilities are to Soo Kim and little Aaron."

"What kind of father would I be if little Aaron ever found out that I let his namesake get hurt? What would Soo Kim think of me if I . . ." He stopped and looked at Sookie. ". . . if I forgot about my friends?"

"Soo Kim understands."

"Grandfather, I understand that I must do what my husband wants. I love you a great deal, but he is the father of my child, the father of your grandchild, and I love him very much."

"I would think you would try and talk him out of this foolishness."

"The same foolishness that drove Mai Ling out of our family?"

"She dishonored me."

"All she wanted was to go with the man she loves."

Min sat back. He understood he was losing the battle and maybe the war.

"Where will you go?" he asked Tuloc.

"There is a rumor that Aaron may be opening new offices in San Francisco and San Diego. I will ask him for a job."

"Aaron, this is Barry. I've talked it over with Carol. When do I start?"

"When can you get out of the job you have now?"

"I should give them two weeks notice, but I think a week's enough. Once I tell them I'm leaving, I'm history. Have you spoken to the colonel yet?"

"No, not yet. I'm going to call him tomorrow and set up the meeting. With you on board, I can sleep better, and that's what I'm going to do now, get some sleep."

Hanging up the phone, he heard the water from the shower stop. As he approached the bedroom, he saw Karen with a towel wrapped around her standing in the hall.

"Is it my imagination, or have you been too busy lately to spend any quality time with me?" she asked.

Aaron smiled. "It's not your imagination."

"January, I want to be out of here by Thursday at midnight. Arrange to have a plane standing by."

"Commercial or military?"

"Make it military just in case I get held up a bit. Has July had any luck finding Canon?"

"He hired two new men who tried to kill Carlyle and some kid.

If you can believe the story, the kid's girlfriend killed one of them and wounded the other."

"Anything happen to Carlyle or the kid?"

"Carlyle took a glancing shot through his side, which produced a lot of blood, but there was no real damage."

"Where is Carlyle now?"

"The last I heard, he was at home with his girlfriend. The kid and his girlfriend have disappeared."

"Disappeared?"

"We don't know where they are, but it's a funny thing. July thinks she knows the girlfriend from somewhere, she just hasn't put it together yet."

"I've got a good feeling about this." Troy was stretched out on the sofa in front of the television. "I think he's going to offer me a full time job. We'll be able to get married."

Pam, sitting on the bed, rose and started pacing. "I don't know about this getting married stuff. I don't think I'm ready."

"Pam, we've been through this before. You know how I feel about you. Why can't we get married?"

"Let's talk about it after they offer you the job."

"You're quitting?" Captain Russ August asked his friend Barry.

"They offered me a position with Besafe that I couldn't turn down."

"Let me be among the first to wish you the best of luck. I should apply for your job," he continued. "This guy Min has more clout than anyone I ever met before. The governor, the commissioner, and the mayor all contacted me about him. Is he one of Carlyle's friends?"

"They're more than friends, but I think Min is stretching the rubber band lately, and it might be getting a little thin."

"Well, whatever's happening will be finished by five forty-five on Thursday."

Chapter 74

"Who is this?"

"Who is this? It's Dennis Canon. I've been calling you for almost a week. I'm in trouble and need help. Where have you been?"

"You were given instructions and you disobeyed them. All contact between us is at an end."

"Wait a second! I did everything you asked of me. The only thing I screwed up on was the getting rid of the kid, and I would have pulled that off except for some girlfriend of his."

"You were told never to get involved with Aaron Carlyle, Min, or their companies. You disregarded that order. Don't call here again."

"I'm going to the cops for help. I'm a respected businessman and I'm not taking this lying down. I've got to get away." For the first time since the phone was answered, Canon believed he hit a nerve. The person on the other end didn't say a word, but he didn't hang up either.

"Are you there?" Canon asked.

"I'm here, and you're right. We owe you that much. As close as I can figure, you should have about two and a half million stashed away. Tomorrow at noon, I want you to go to Air Ways Travel on Sepulveda. It's about a half mile north of the airport. They will help you to transfer your funds to a numbered Swiss account. Keep twenty thousand hidden in your suitcase, and another ten in cash.

After you transfer the funds to an account that only you can access, they will give you tickets to Europe under a name other than your own."

"Why am I waiting until tomorrow?"

"Unless you already have a passport in another name, that's how long it will take to get one. Do you have any preferences?"

"I always wanted to go to France."

"Not countries—names. The country you're going to is Switzerland."

"Why there?"

"First, that's where your money will be, and second, they don't have extradition for any crime you may have committed."

"How will I contact you again if I need you?"

"You won't. When this call is over, so is any relationship we've had in the past."

Canon heard the click and quickly dialed the number again.

"The number you have reached is no longer in service. Please hang up and dial the number again. If you think you have received this message in error, please contact your operator."

"Aaron, in twenty minutes, meet me in the lobby of the Marriott at LAX."

"Not likely," Aaron replied when he recognized the voice of the colonel.

"What does that mean?" the colonel replied stiffly.

"I'm over an hour away from the Marriott. Try somewhere else."

"How about your office?"

"At Besafe?" Aaron couldn't believe his ears.

"Why not? You've got nothing to hide, have you?"

"I didn't think you'd want to go where I had home court advantage."

The colonel laughed. "Aaron, I trust you." After a slight hesitation, "If you can clean out the building, I'll see you in thirty minutes."

"I'll have Tom and Scott with me," Aaron said hurriedly.

"Is that necessary?"

"Only if you want to get something accomplished."

"You know I do. All right. Thirty minutes. Just the four of us."

Quickly dialing his two friends and partners, Aaron brought them both up to date. "We've been here before," he said. "Anyone want to do it differently? Now's the time to speak."

"I'm ready!" responded Tom.

"So am I," finished Scott.

As they hung up, Karen, who had been working on her computer, asked, "You will be all right, won't you?"

"I've trusted the guys in the past with my life. This is a piece of cake compared to some of the other things we've been through."

She stood and walked over to him, put her arms around his neck, and kissed him lightly on the lips. "I'll be waiting. Let me know how you make out."

As Aaron was leaving his home, Tom was on the phone to Michael at Besafe.

"Michael, it's time to go to alert status B. You have fifteen minutes from now."

Scott, who lived the closest to the office, arrived there as the lights started going out. As per Michael's instructions, all communications was transferred after the second ring to an office six miles away. Everyone in the building at night was given instructions where they were to report. In the fifteen minutes that Tom gave him, Michael was able to clear out the building of people, empty the parking lot, transfer all incoming calls, and set up the video cameras.

Scott entered the building and found Michael waiting in the lobby.

"The building is yours, Mr. Miller."

"Why so formal?" Scott asked.

"When I was part of the team, we used first names. You guys have left me out of the loop on this and I have to tell you I'm pissed. Don't you trust me?"

"Michael. This has nothing to do with not trusting. This goes back to Vietnam. We're going to put an end to something that started a dozen years ago. We can't take a chance on anyone besides ourselves getting hurt."

"Being part of the company means I take the same chance you or anyone else does. I'm forty-five years old. I'm not a kid."

"Aaron had a feeling you might be upset and asked me to give you this letter. It explains things that you're not aware of. He requests that you don't open it for three hours, at which time if we're not in contact, it won't matter."

Michael took the envelope. "It's not sealed."

"We wouldn't have it any other way."

Michael turned the envelope over two or three times and then nodded his head. "The building is yours." He turned his back on Scott and walked to the door. "Every door is sealed and alarmed. If they somehow get opened, the motion detector video will start. Even if you can't see who entered, you'll know they're coming."

Five minutes after Michael left, Tom arrived, followed closely by Aaron. Scott described all the precautions Michael had taken and the three friends sat down to await the arrival of the colonel.

"I guess he's not going to make it," Tom said, looking out of the window.

"He still has three minutes," replied Aaron as he looked at his watch.

"Here comes a car into the parking lot. It's a limo, driven by a woman, but no one is getting out," Tom told his friends as he peered through the blinds.

"That would be my ride home."

The three of them turned in surprise at the sound of the voice from behind them.

"How the hell did you get in here?" Scott sputtered.

"Through the front door. You were expecting me, weren't you?"

Aaron sat down at the conference room table. "Why don't you take the seat at the head of the table, Colonel, and let's get down to business."

Chapter 75

"I haven't much time, so let me tell you my thoughts." The colonel addressed the three men like school children.

"Suppose I tell you I don't give a shit about your thoughts. I thought we were going to discuss items of mutual concern." Tom stood as he spoke with his fists clenched tensely at his sides.

The colonel looked at his watch. "I thought this would be easy, but I can see that you need some convincing of the power I wield." He took out a cell phone and punched in a single number. "This is the colonel. Cut the electricity to this building for sixty seconds and then turn it back on."

"Sorry, can't do that colonel. If I turned off all the electricity, we'd have to reset all the clocks when this drill is over."

"Who is this?" roared the colonel.

"I's be da man in charge of security," the voice said comically, but his next words were spoken in a way that left no room as to their intent. "And by the way, your lovely driver is fine, but if anything goes wrong, you'll have a long walk home."

"You're that guy Michael. They told me you were a smart ass."

"Aaron has my cell phone number. Have him call me when your meeting is over."

The colonel snapped closed his phone without a comment.

"That wasn't a smart thing to do," he said to the men at the table.

"Neither was threatening to turn off the lights. Let's get down to business." Aaron looked around the table.

Scott said, "I'll start." He looked at Aaron who nodded. "I like the idea of our having Troy come to work at Besafe. Even if we don't land any new contracts, he'd be a welcome addition to our staff." The colonel nodded and Scott continued, "I'm not naive enough to ask you to promise not get involved, but I will insist on Troy's word that he not bring your relationship into the office."

The colonel shifted toward Tom who asked, "These companies that you think are in need of a security company, who's servicing them now?"

"They are being serviced by Interstate Security, who will be folding up shop in the very near future. Possibly even today." The colonel again looked at his watch.

"Might I make a suggestion?" Aaron asked. "Why doesn't Canon put the company up for sale and have us buy it? If the price is right, you could eliminate most of your headaches."

The colonel interlocked his fingers and closed his eyes as if deep in thought.

"We might be able to swing something like that, but I would have to split the company in half first. Many of its assets are tied into other companies, and of course you understand, Canon is no longer part of the equation."

"Where is Canon?" Aaron asked lightly.

"I don't know where he is right now, but I know where he will be tomorrow."

"Are you willing to share that information?"

The structure of the meeting had changed. Everyone realized that Troy had been taken care of, and the companies would sign on with Besafe. Now the real horse-trading between Aaron and the colonel would begin.

"I don't think so. That information would . . . or let me say could . . . jeopardize another operation."

"You know, of course, that he's wanted for murder."

"Aaron, you know that the words are 'in connection with a murder.' No one is sure he ever murdered anyone."

"Close enough. But I don't understand why you won't help us."

"Let me say I am helping in my own way."

"Another thing I would like is for you to sell your stock in Besafe."

"What difference does it make to you who owns stock in your company?"

"It doesn't make a difference. I just don't want you as a part of our business."

The colonel shook his head. "All right, I'll sell all that we own after the buy-out."

"One more thing," Aaron said. "If Min's company does not have the contract for janitorial services at any of these new locations we take over, would that create a problem?"

"You wouldn't give Min the contracts for cleaning services?" the colonel asked incredulously.

"I didn't say that. I just asked if it would make a difference."

"What you do with your company is your concern, not mine."

"The last question I have concerns you. When you walk out of here tonight, are you out of our lives forever?"

"You might see me at an airport, or at a wedding, but I don't envision ever having anything to do with you or Besafe in the future."

Aaron stared at him without saying a word. "I think I've heard that story before, but I guess I'll have to believe you."

"Now I have a question. Where is Kebra Metcalf?"

Aaron smiled. "This question is of a personal nature?"

The colonel stared straight ahead and didn't acknowledge Aaron's barb.

"She's in protective custody. Barry is prepared to let her go the minute we find Canon. If you can give me a number where she can reach you, I'll see that she gets it."

The colonel took out his cell phone and hit the single button. "This is the colonel, the meeting is over and I'm coming out. Please release my people."

"Let me talk to Aaron."

The colonel handed the phone to Aaron. "He wants to talk to you, and I will make sure you get a number for Kebra to call."

"Aaron, everything okay?"

"Everything is fine. I thought I told you to open the envelope in three hours."

"I wasn't sure my watch was working, so I figured it's better to be safe than sorry. See if you can find out how he got into the building. I thought I closed it down pretty good."

"I'll try. He's leaving the building now."

"If I was a betting man, I'd wager that he would like to know how I got into the building."

"You'd win. How did you do it?"

"When I called you, I was already here. I just walked into the ladies rest room and climbed into the ceiling and waited until they turned the lights out."

The colonel laughed as he walked out the front door and Tom practically ran to the ladies bathroom.

"It's a solid ceiling in there!" he said incredulously as he walked back into the lobby. "That son of a bitch lied."

"I wonder if that's the only lie we heard tonight."

Chapter 76

Canon stood across the street from Air Ways Travel, watching people enter and leave the office. He'd been there for over two hours and had counted fourteen people entering, and only twelve leaving. The first person to enter was a blonde dressed in a business suit. She needed keys to get the door open and Canon had decided she must have been the manager. That left one other person beside the manager in the store. At five minutes before the hour, Canon entered the store. There were airline posters all over the place.

"Can I help you?" The blonde that had opened the shop earlier sat behind a desk typing on a computer keyboard.

"I'm here to pick up some tickets," Canon said as he looked around the office for the other person.

"Your name is?" the blonde asked as she stood and went through a stack of envelopes on her desk.

"My name is Dennis Canon."

"Are you sure it's not Dennis Shane? I have a set of tickets for him leaving this afternoon for Switzerland."

"Right, my name is Shane. I believe you also have my passport." He looked away, more embarrassed than nervous.

"I have your passport, driver's license, credit cards, and blank checks. I understand you wish to transfer your funds to a Swiss account so that you will have access to it when you arrive in Bern."

"How do I know the money will be there?" Canon asked.

"I have the number of an account that has been opened under

the name of Shane. You will select a code number and no one except you will be able to take out funds."

"How do I enter the code?"

The blonde went back to the computer on her desk. "If you will sit here and hit the enter button, I will walk you through the process. Just follow the prompts and in five minutes, you'll be all set. I would suggest that you use a number that only has meaning for you, and is easy to remember."

Canon sat down and hit the enter key. Five minutes later, he was finished except for the transfer of cash. "I was thinking that maybe I should leave half my money where it is."

She frowned disapprovingly, but said, "You can do as you want, but in the event the government comes after you, that's the first thing they'll take."

Canon sighed out loud and then continued working on the computer. "It's done!" He announced satisfied, then added, "I forgot to ask. Am I going first class?"

"Yes, you are," replied a deep voice from behind him.

The other person, he thought. I'd forgotten about him.

"I'll leave you boys alone," the blonde said sweetly as she strutted out the door to a waiting limousine.

"Who the fuck are you?" Canon yelled as he turned to face the new arrival.

"You were told to leave some people alone, but took it upon yourself to try and kill them." The pleasant voice clashed with the silver handgun he held at his side.

"That was a mistake!" Canon yelled. "I'm leaving the country, don't do anything crazy." Shane left, wounded, but he left. Were his last thoughts.

"I won't," the man with the gun said calmly as he pulled the trigger four times.

Waiting a few seconds, he bent over the body, emptied the pockets of cash and other valuables, and then picked up the phone and speaking in Vietnamese, ordered a cleaning crew to come and clean up the store.

"I trust everything went as planned," the colonel asked January as they drove up the Pacific Coast Highway.

"The money was transferred, as per your instructions, to our account number. The secret code that he entered was changed as he punched it in so that we would have no problem accessing it."

"And the Vietnamese gentleman that was going to make sure he made the plane?"

"They were having a conversation as I left."

The colonel nodded. "The cleaning crew is putting the office back the way we found it?"

"I didn't call in the request, but it was part of the plan."

The colonel looked out at the ocean. "We may finish earlier than I originally thought. You have a plane standing by?"

"There are planes leaving for Washington every two hours until 11 P.M. After that, there is one every three hours. I have reserved room on every flight after five o'clock this afternoon."

"How long before we arrive at Troy's?"

"We should be there by two thirty."

The colonel pulled down the shade to block the sun. "Wake me ten minutes before we arrive.

Chapter 77

"Aaron, I would like to meet with you as soon as possible."

"Min, I expect to be a little busy today and tomorrow. How about Friday around nine thirty in the morning?"

"By as soon as possible, I meant today." When Aaron didn't answer, Min continued, "We have been friends for a long time. Surely you can spare some time for me."

"For a friend, I always have time. I thought you wanted to talk about business."

Min fully understood what Aaron had said. There was a saying in his country, "Friendship was worth more than all monies earned," and he had forgotten it.

"How about my place for dinner. Karen is still here and I'm sure she can put together something for us to eat."

"That would be fine. Can I ask one more favor?"

"What's that?" Aaron asked warily.

"Could you invite Tuloc and Mai Ling to join us?"

"Sure, if that's what you want."

"I don't want them to know I will be there. I am afraid if they know, they will not come."

"As long as I'm asking, is there anyone else you think should be there?"

"I think you might want Tom and Scott, more as a courtesy than anything else."

"Old friend, this does not sound like you. Is everything all right?"

"When the meeting is finished, it will be."

"You make it sound ominous."

"What does that word mean?"

"Gloomy or threatening." There was no reply from Min to Aaron's answer. "Min! Are you still there?"

"Yes, I am here. I look forward to seeing you at six o'clock."

"Colonel, we're about ten minutes from Troy."

Opening his eyes, he looked out the window at the ocean on his left.

"Don't you think it's time you took off the blonde wig?" he asked January.

"July and I were discussing how I looked. I might decide that blondes do have more fun. By the way, I finally remembered where I knew the girl that Troy's with."

"Oh?"

"She used to work for the company. I heard she left about three or four years ago to go to work for the San Francisco P.D."

"Interesting."

January glanced at the colonel in the back seat. *He knew,* she thought as July pulled up in front of one of the beach houses that dotted the landscape in Ventura.

"You can wait in the car. I shouldn't be longer than a half hour."

"Maybe Tuloc could drive you over. I've also asked him to join us," Aaron said.

Mai Ling was being difficult. "I really don't want to leave Cassius. He's sitting up in bed and I think it's good for him that I'm there."

"I wouldn't ask if I didn't think it was important. I'm sure Cassius would understand."

"What time do you think it will be over?" she asked.

"Dinner's at six o'clock, and we'll talk while we eat. You should be gone by eight o'clock at the latest."

"Mr. Carlyle, can't you give me an idea of what is so important that I must be there?"

"Not over the phone. I can tell you we've all had a lot of trouble recently, and I think we're about ready to bring it to an end."

Aaron could picture the seemingly hard-boiled Mai Ling sitting in the hospital trying to make up her mind.

"I'll call Tuloc and have him drive me over. See you at six o'clock. Is there anything you would like me to bring?"

"Just your appetite."

"Colonel!"

"Dad or Father will do. This is a personal call. Can I come in?"

"How did you find me? No one knew where we were."

"Have you forgotten everything that I taught you? Anything that is known by more than one person is no longer a secret."

"Pam?" Troy questioned.

Nodding, the colonel asked, "Do you have anything to eat here?"

Before Troy could answer, Pam replied from the kitchen, "We have tuna salad, American cheese, rye bread, and either diet or regular cola."

"Does Pam work for the agency?" Troy asked as he glanced into the other room.

"That would be on a need to know basis, and the last I heard, you weren't part of the group anymore." The colonel sat at the table and said loudly, "I'll have some American cheese on rye with a diet cola. If you have any mustard or mayo, that would be nice."

Troy tightened his lips together. "You said this was personal. How can I help you?"

Pam brought in the sandwiches and said, "I'll wait for you outside."

The colonel nodded as Troy shouted, "No! Please sit down with us and listen to what he has to say."

"Troy, this is between you and the colonel," Pam replied as she walked to the door.

"For Christ's sake. Didn't you hear him. This isn't the colonel. This is my dad."

Pam stopped and looked at the colonel.

He smiled. "You're growing up, but I think this conversation is better off just between the two of us."

"Father," Troy exaggerated the word, "what was it Rhett Butler said . . . 'Quite frankly I don't give a damn.' I've asked Pam to marry me."

"And?" the colonel replied.

"You two are talking like I'm not even here," Pam almost shouted. "I told Troy I didn't think I was ready, but now I'm not sure."

"What is that supposed to mean?" The colonel stared at Pam as he asked the question.

"It means I didn't think he was ready, but after watching him, I think maybe he is."

"Are you?" the colonel retorted.

"Don't answer him, Pam. After he leaves, you and I can discuss our future together."

"You little piss ant. That's what I'm here to talk about—your future. When I leave, you're going to be on your own." The white scar on the colonel's chin seemed to shine against his red face.

"I've been on my own forever." Troy's hands at his side closed into fists. "I'm not going through chapter and verse of all the times Mom and I sat and waited for you to come home, and all the times you never made it. You probably know them by heart. Why don't we just say that I've left the employ of the company and found a better job."

The colonel took a deep breath getting himself under control before he continued. "There are things I've got to tell you. If Pam is a part of your life she should probably hear them. If she's not, maybe she should wait outside."

The colonel and Troy both turned to face Pam.

"I don't know the answer to that question. I do know that I have decided to leave the company, so why don't I wait outside. If Troy and I go forward, I'll trust him to tell me what I need to know."

The colonel nodded and thought, *I hope she decides to stay with him; she's a bright lady.*

Troy smiled and said, "Don't go too far."

After Pam left, Troy said, "What is it that I need to know?"

"This is a little hard for me, so cut me some slack." He stared at Troy until he nodded his reply. "During the Vietnamese war, everything the company did was compartmentalized. I was responsible for the destroying of records and such, but the group I was with didn't know what the people in the next room were doing and vise versa. Aaron Carlyle was left behind because I didn't know how fast we were pulling out. Our government had made a deal with the North Vietnamese that let them take over, with a minimum amount of lost lives. The thought behind it was better them than the Viet Cong. The problem was that since the Cong were left out, so were most of us in the field.

"You got out!" Troy interrupted.

"No I didn't. When Saigon fell, I was up north helping some of our search and destroy pathfinders get out. We walked to the coast and were met by a submarine and taken to the Philippines. It was there that I heard the story of the men left behind. I flew to Singapore and ran into another group of company men with an agenda all their own. In a fit of anger, I gave Carlyle and his partners about two million in cash to get them started in civilian life."

"The government just let you do it?"

"I explained about their not saying anything and then told the brass my idea about raising cash. We could invest in different companies and use the money to help fund projects that we favored." The colonel took a long drink of his soda.

"Over the years, we literally raised billions. Our assets were the equal of almost any company in the United States. Over the past six to eight months, some funny things started happening. People started wanting a piece of our money. Some of our operations started falling apart." Pausing slightly before he continued, he finished the cola. "One of the rules I had instituted was that the money was never to be used for internal politics. Another was that we were never to come in contact with Carlyle, his company, or his friends."

"What made Carlyle a sacred cow?"

"Not a sacred cow, but someone to steer clear of. First off I'm sure he has written down the names and events of the operations in Vietnam. Second, he is a street fighter. He is the type of person that my type of operations should avoid if possible. He is honest, tough and usually above reproach. Anyway, these rules must have pissed someone off because I found myself having trouble internally. Fortunately, I also am a born street fighter. There was an attempt by some people to take over the running of Canon. The only way they could do that was to eliminate me. When they couldn't do that, they tried to get at me by getting rid of you. That's where Pam entered the picture. She was working for me up in the Bay Area. When I asked her to come down and keep an eye on you, it worked out fine."

"Did it ever occur to you that I didn't need someone to keep an eye on me?"

"No, it didn't. In fact, I had to promise her a big job if she'd do it, which is why I'm surprised she just didn't say good-bye to you."

"How big a job?"

"Let me put it this way. When I leave here, I'm being kicked upstairs. I'm going to report right into the White House, and I'm going to need a chief of staff."

"The president?" Troy's mouth stayed open.

"I said the White House. The president will always have deniability."

The colonel stopped talking. After a long pause, Troy asked, "What is it you want of me?"

"What I always wanted. Grow up, get married, and get me some grandchildren. Forget everything you know about the company and let's see if we can become a family."

Troy was amazed at what his father had said. In all the years, he never remembered his father saying anything this nice. He wished his mother was still alive.

"Dad, have you met any women since mom died?"

The colonel was stunned. He never expected this question. "I know a women. Her name is Kebra Metcalf. She worked for the company and was out here on assignment. If you can believe this, I lost track of her. Aaron knows how to find her and part of my deal with him is that he will give her my number, which is one more thing I need from you."

"What's that?"

"I will give you a one-time phone number that you can only give to her."

Troy's face broke into a saucer wide grin.

"What's so funny? The colonel asked.

'I'm going to be playing matchmaker."

For the first time that Troy could remember, his father's grin looked like a real smile.

The colonel rose and walked over to Troy. "Son, take care of yourself. You know where I'll be and you'll know how to reach me." He put his arms around Troy and gave him a hug. *I mustn't let him see my eyes,* he thought. He put on his sunglasses and walked out the door.

Pam was standing by the limo talking to January and July.

"Are you coming with us?" he asked.

Pam looked up the stairs at Troy. "Did he say anything that would make you change your mind?" she asked.

He shook his head.

"Then I'm staying, at least until I'm sure."

"You'll never be sure, but if it's any help, you're making the right decision."

He entered the car and never looked back. "There's a plane waiting. Put this thing in drive and let's get the show on the road."

Chapter 78

"Min didn't give you any idea why he wanted this meeting?" Karen asked as she moved around the dining room table putting down silverware.

"No, he didn't, and you're making this dinner very formal."

"You know how I love to cook, so I ordered seven chickens broiled, mashed potatoes, carrots, and three different kinds of pie for dessert. I'm going to put all the food on the kitchen table and have the people serve themselves. When they fill up their plate, they can bring it in here to eat. The only thing I'm making is coffee."

"If I remember correctly, you should have ordered the coffee also."

Karen laughed. "You'll pay for that wiseass remark."

Before he could reply, the bell rang. Aaron looked out the window and called back over his shoulder, "Scott, Tom, and the food have all arrived at the same time."

"Great. I can use the help."

Ten minutes later, Karen was ready. Aaron had given beers to his friends as they sat and waited.

At ten minutes until six, the phone rang.

"Aaron, its Barry. I've got some news, I think. About two hours ago, the Santa Monica Police found a dead body that was dumped along the beach south of Malibu. The body had a passport, driver's license, and some other stuff identifying him as a Dennis Shane. He had four bullets in him and about a buck's worth of change. It would have been listed as a robbery and murder, except the shoe had a tag that said Sunrise Gym. You know the kind where they have shoe care and after they shine them they put them in a locker."

Aaron remembered the day he spent at the gym, and knew this was exactly what they did.

"Well, they sent someone out with a picture of the body and they found the place is closing down. One of the instructors looked at the picture and said it looked like Canon, which is why they called me. It was Canon."

"Any ideas on who killed him?" Aaron asked.

"Ideas? Plenty. Proof? None. Just thought you might want to know. Talk to you tomorrow."

"Thanks for calling. I'll pass on the good news to Tom and Scot. By the way, I have a colonel that's looking to find what sounds like a lost love. I told him we would pass on a number for him to call after Canon was found. I guess this qualifies."

Aaron explained the call to his friends, finishing just as the bell rang.

"I hope you don't mind Sookie joining us," Tuloc said as he entered, followed by Soo Kim and Mai Ling.

"When Tuloc said that you told him it was important, I felt it was a wife's duty to be by her husband's side."

"I should have told him to invite you I wasn't thinking. We have plenty of food. Come on in."

Aaron walked over to Karen and whispered, "We do, don't we?"

"I'll cut one of the chickens in half, you're getting too fat anyway."

The bell ringing again stopped him from trying to think of some clever reply.

Mai Ling, who was standing closest to the door, opened it and came face to face with Min and Lan Burnett. Her eyes flashed, but her upbringing didn't allow for anything but a friendly greeting.

"Good evening, Grandfather. I didn't know you were coming to this dinner. Mrs. Burnett, how nice it is to see you again. Please come in."

Min, following Lan Burnett, stopped in front of Mai Ling. "Would you have come if you knew I was going to be here?"

"I was invited by Mr. Carlyle. I would not dishonor him by refusing."

Min nodded. "I understand Cassius is doing well."

Taken back by his obvious interest, Mai Ling answered, "He is doing much better. I hope to be able to bring him home very soon."

"That is excellent. He is a very good man."

Saying that, he entered the room to say hello to the others that were present.

"Karen, I told Min that this was an imposition. He should have called ahead and told you I was coming." Lan was apologizing to Karen as Aaron walked up.

"Lan, let me get you something to drink." As he led Lan towards the bar, he turned to Karen, "Guess who else is getting heavy?"

Twenty minutes later, they were all seated around the table trying to exchange small talk. Aaron glanced around the table. Directly across from him at the other end sat Min with Lan on his right. To Lan's right sat Scott with Mai Ling between Scott and himself. On Min's left sat Tom with Tuloc, Sookie, and then Karen, whose legs were rubbing against Aaron's in a way that was driving him crazy.

"Let me bring everyone up to date," Aaron started, silencing the table.

"Barry called and advised me that they found Canon's body about two hours ago. He said it looks like a professional job and he'd let me know later if anything develops. He also said that it looks like they are closing down Sunrise Gym."

"Mr. Carlyle, may I ask you a question?"

"Tuloc, in all the years we have known each other, you have never called me Aaron. Do you think for at least today you can give it a try?"

Tuloc glanced at his wife who nodded. He then began again. "Aaron, I would like to thank you for inviting me to your home, but for what reason are we here?"

"I was asked today by Min to have this meeting. He requested that I invite all of you in this room, except for Lan, whom he invited. That is all I know. Min, you have the floor."

Chapter 79

Min stumbled as he stood. Lan reached out to him, but he waved off her help.

"This is a very difficult thing that I am doing. I have rehearsed what I am going to say many times, but it doesn't come out the right way. If you will bear with me, maybe I can say it in the right order." Stopping, he looked around the room with his eyes coming to rest on Aaron. He smiled, and then continued. "It is always good to start at the beginning." Pushing his chair back, he walked to the window and looked up at the sky.

"Southern California in many ways is like Vietnam. The temperatures, the sky, and the clouds, are the same." He turned back to the group. "It was much like this three weeks before the end of the war. I was part of an American search and destroy team sent to meet up with a similar team that my friend, Tuloc's father, Giac was with. It was on this mission that I found out the Americans were going home. There was a major with our team that said we should go with him. He was meeting a submarine that was going to take him to the Philippines.

"Ewing!" exclaimed Tom.

"That was not the name he used back then, but it was the same man."

"Why didn't you go with him?" Scott asked.

"Both Giac and I had to find out about our families. We hoped they had gotten out, but in Saigon, we both had enemies that might have interfered. The major gave us a number to call when and if we got out of Vietnam. It was all that he could do.

By the time we arrived, most of our relatives had been taken care of. Mai Ling, my daughter and Soo Kim's mother, was unfortunately killed in an explosion."

Everyone watched as he walked behind Mai Ling. "Oldest granddaughter, I know that you believed I could have changed things if I hadn't been away on that mission. Your mother was headstrong. She believed in what she was doing. Even if I were in Saigon, she would have gone to the orphanage. Nothing would have changed."

Tears started down Mai Ling's cheeks. She neither turned around nor did she utter a sound. The tears just flowed.

Touching the back of her jet-black hair seemed to recharge him.

"There was much confusion. The structure of the city was gone. We used our rank to get inside of the compound, but once there, all we could do was wait. The ranking military person, as far as we could tell, was a young lieutenant on the roof. We had taken off our insignias after we entered and there was no way of our getting up the staircase to reach him. When we saw him come down from the roof with the other Americans, Giac suggested we follow them to where they were going. Once the enemy took over, it wouldn't take them long to find out who we were, which would mean instant death, if we were lucky."

Min walked over to Aaron and put his hand on his shoulder.

"Friend of many years, the next few weeks were some of the best of my life. The courage that you showed as we walked out of Vietnam was to me a learning experience beyond expectations. Not once did you flinch in the face of adversity. A lesser man would have bypassed the cesspool where they grew the illegal drugs. But you had your lady fair and two very good friends." Min nodded in the direction of first Tom and then Scott. "When we flew to Singapore and you were arrested, they separated us. You asked to see the consul or someone from the Army and you were refused, as was I, until I called the special number given to me by the major. He flew immediately from wherever he was to Singapore, where he, upon hearing my story, put your release in motion."

Min watched Karen take Aaron's hand as he continued.

"I wish I could tell you that they released you because they believed in your cause, but I can't. I made a pact with the devil. The major understood that in the years after the conflict, the country would back away from armed confrontation. He needed someone that could get information out of South East Asia, and he decided that Giac and I could do that. The deal we struck was simple. He made sure that you and your friends were given money, as were Giac and myself. When you started your business, he made sure you had clients. He convinced us that stocks and bonds were the wave of the future, and we had to get in on the bottom floor. When you took your company public, he made sure that the price of the stock went up. It did so nicely that he or his superiors decided to expand into more than just small amounts. He came and told me what part I was to play in the buying and selling of stocks, and how much of the profit I would be allowed to keep. What he didn't plan on was your getting involved in that accident. I didn't find out until later that the psychopath from Vietnam was his man. Part of my deal with him was that none of my family would ever be subjected to any harm. When that self styled general sent people to visit Karen and cut Soo Kim, they, as you say, crossed the line."

Here he stopped and stood by Karen. "You have to believe me. Had I known what was going to happen, I would have given my life to protect you."

She reached up and touched his face and nodded. "I understand."

"The past few years, the colonel's charter changed. The Central Intelligence Agency is not allowed by law to operate inside the United States. Someone decided they should take positions in companies that did business with the government. By doing this, they would have eyes and ears all over the globe. They knew what other countries were buying, or wanted to buy. Their representatives traveled the world negotiating with governments, and want-to-be governments. Your competitor, Interstate, got themselves inside of companies to find out what they were making and if it made sense to take it over. My company was required to give them information, except I had to uphold a promise made to you. No one would steal from a plant that you held the security contract with."

"It sounds like a sweet deal. What changed it?" Aaron asked.

"Providence!"

Everyone turned toward Lan.

"Do you mean, fate? Or Mrs. Burnett's company?" Tom asked.

"Maybe it was both," Min replied as he sat down.

Chapter 80

Min strolled around the table until he came to where Mrs. Burnett was seated. “You all know Lan Burnett. She was the adopted daughter of Mr. And Mrs. Lott. Most of you were present when she told us her biological parents were Viad and Serlyn Tran. What none of you knew was that Tran was my wife’s name. Her parents were killed in an explosion when the French ruled Indo-China, and she was sent to live with some relatives. I have been doing some checking and I found out that my wife had a sister who was adopted and left the country. My wife, your grandmother, never knew what happened to her sister. She probably thought she was dead.” He now looked straight at Mai Ling and Soo Kim. Lan Burnett is your great aunt.”

The entire table turned in unison from Min to Mrs. Burnett. Both sisters stood and bowed as a show of respect before approaching their newly found aunt.

“I never knew,” Lan exclaimed. “I believed my family perished in the explosion. When Min showed me the proof yesterday, I was astonished. I haven’t even told William yet. He is going to be very excited to find out he has cousins.”

“This is certainly good news. I’m glad you asked us all to be present to hear the news,” Aaron said as he walked over to shake Min’s hand.

“This was only part of the news,” Min replied, raising his voice to be heard over the sounds of everyone congratulating Mrs. Burnett. The room immediately became silent.

"When I found out Lan was family, I called the number I had for the colonel. A voice on the other end, one that I had not heard before, told me they were sorry, but events had moved too fast and could not be stopped. That was when the real trouble started. I told the voice that I would do whatever had to be done to protect my family. I spoke in anger before giving it real thought. Due to my carelessness, Dennis Canon was set free to do whatever he believed needed doing."

He looked at Tuloc, "It must be my advanced age because I then committed the worst crime imaginable." His made eye contact with Aaron, and could see the question in Aaron's eyes. *What could be worse than some of the things we have done?*

"I forgot who my friends were," he said the words simply, but with meaning. Everyone at the table realized how tough it was for him to make that statement out loud. "It was my people that left the door open at the stop before Active Components. I wanted to stop their arrival and give Canon's men time to get away. Because I wasn't strong enough to say no, I caused the death of one man and the wounding of another." He looked at the floor.

"I tried to impose rules on my family, that thank Buddha, they were strong enough and smart enough to ignore."

Sitting down, he continued, "I asked that my closest relatives and closest friends come together today so that I might say that I am sorry. To Mai Ling, I promise you the biggest and best wedding you ever could of imagined. I believe your man Cassius will make an excellent husband. To Tuloc, I say you are the heir apparent. Your father, my friend Giac, would be very proud of his son. Our family will grow and prosper with your guidance. To Lan, I am sorry that I did not find you sooner. I will try and make amends in the future."

He stood and raised a glass of water in Aaron's direction. "To my friend Aaron, I say this, you will never have to worry about my loyalty again. I have broken all ties with the colonel. I told him that my family was strong enough and that we no longer wanted anything to do with him. Any new business we did would be because of our own efforts and the business we already had we would keep because of our service." Taking a sip of water from the glass, he turned slightly toward Karen.

"I expect that in the very near future, I will be invited to your wedding."

Karen smiled and mouthed the words, "Of course."

Finale

"It's been two weeks since I passed on the number Troy gave us to Kebra Metcalf. I wonder if she and the colonel have gotten married? Barry said to Aaron and Scott as they sat in the conference room discussing their strategy for integrating the two security companies.

Tom entered with a big grin on his face. "Two more companies in the bay area have signed long term contracts with us. That makes a total of five up there and three in San Diego."

"Are we going to offer Min the contracts for maintenance?" asked Scott of his partners.

"You mean Tuloc, don't you?" Aaron chided him.

"What is Min doing with his time?" Barry asked.

"The last I heard, he was going to Denver to meet with some of the family," Aaron responded. His having to admit he was wrong was very tough on him."

"Are you sure they believed you?" the man with silver hair and thin scar on the side of his cheek asked.

"Of course they believed me. They have already started dealing with Tuloc about servicing their new contracts," the Asian man in a three-piece suit answered.

"This is the last time we can meet like this. We can't take a chance of someone seeing us. There's too much to lose." His fingers stroked his scar as he spoke.

"I have the emergency number, and you know how to contact me," the Asian man held out his hand. "We always seem to be saying good-bye—Vietnam, Singapore, Hawaii, and California. Someday we will both retire. Maybe then we can spend time together."

"For some reason, I don't see either of us retiring. Stay healthy and keep your eyes open. New opportunities are always presenting themselves."

Both men entered the terminal from the room they were in and walked in separate directions.

A woman met the man with the scar. "We may have a problem," she said as they walked toward the down escalator.

"What's that?" he asked.

"A fishing boat off the coast of California pulled up the body of a woman last night. There was no identification on the body, but they're trying to get a fingerprint match."

"That shouldn't create a problem for us. You know who to call."

"I've already made the call. Just wanted to make you aware of the situation."

"Are we flying commercial or military?"

Looking at her watch she replied, "Commercial. We have first class tickets. Denver to Chicago, Chicago to D.C. The plane leaves in thirty minutes."

"And what is our friend doing?"

The woman punched in a single number on her cell phone.

"It's me. What's he doing?"

After listening, she closed the phone. "He met four men and they stopped to get ice cream."

"What is he doing?" the Asian man asked as he licked his ice cream cone.

"He met the woman that we knew in California as Pam, and is walking through the terminal," replied one of the men who had a phone to his ear.

"Captain Sizemore, this is Captain Avery of the U.S. Coast Guard. I'm hoping you can help us with a little problem we have."

"I can try," Cassius replied from his brand new desk. This was his second day on the job as captain, replacing Barry Sands who had moved to a high-powered job at Besafe.

"We had a fishing boat bring up the body of a young woman in their nets yesterday. She has no identification and a quick search of the record bureau in Washington came up empty."

"How can I help?" Cassius asked.

"Well, she was wearing loafers and on the inside was a tag that said Sunrise Gym. When we checked, we found the gym had closed down a week ago. Since it was in your neck of the woods, I thought maybe if I sent you the picture you might know some of the people that worked there and they could I.D. the woman."

"Send it and I'll pass it around."

"I already did. It should be on your fax machine."

Cassius stood and started to the door. Smiling, he sat back down and yelled, "Sergeant, bring me the fax on the machine."

Picking up the phone he said, "Please hold on, Captain. It'll be right here."

The sergeant walked in and handed him the picture. The smile left Cassius's face.

"Captain, I'll have to get back to you. I think I know this woman."

Aaron, Tom, Scott, Barry, Michael, and Cassius sat around the conference room table.

"It's Kebra Metcalf," Cassius said.

"How long was she in the water?" Michael asked.

"Two, maybe three days," Cassius replied.

"What do you think happened?" Barry asked the group.

"I think they taught her a lesson and sent a message to the rest of their people."

"Do you think that's why Pam left Troy and went back to the company?" Scott asked.

"What I think," Aaron said, "is we'll never know the truth. What I know is that those people are in a world of their own. They don't care about life as we know it. Maybe someday things will change, but until then . . . " He shook his head. ". . . I don't know."